MW01330802

Bound By Flame

The Chronicle of Thyss

Dulkur
The Northern Jungles
King Chofir's Lands
Calumbu
The River Thss
Tajoru
Kaimpur
Berak'a
Port Dulkur
The Iron Mountains
The Iron Citadel

Upcoming Novels

Wolves of War – A John Hartman Novel (10/24)
Book 2 of The Dragonknight Trilogy (2025)
Spectres of the Black Sun – A John Hartman Novel
Advent of Judgement
The Horizon's Edge
Fractured Descent
The Dark World Novels:
- *Mirrored, Darkly*
- *A Reckoning of Ink and Blood*
- *Eternal Melody*

Other Novels and Works

The Oathbreaker's Daughter (The Dragonknight Trilogy Book 1)
*Blood and Steel (The Cor Chronicles Vol. I)**
*Fire and Steel (The Cor Chronicles Vol. II)**
*Darkness and Steel (The Cor Chronicles Vol. III)**
*Gods and Steel (The Cor Chronicles Vol. IV)**
*Blood Betrayal (The Cor Chronicles Vol. V)**
*Blood Loss (The Chronicle of Rael)**
Tendrils in the Dark – Eight Tales of Horror

*Denotes a novel of Rumedia.

Bound By Flame

The Chronicle of Thyss

By

Martin V. Parece II

ISBN: 9798326675286

Cover Art by Jan-Michael Barlow. www.janmichaelbarlow.com

To all the fans of The Cor Chronicles who kept asking, "When is Thyss going to get her own book?"

One thing – if you have not read The Cor Chronicles, you may find the Epilogue and my Afterword a little… spoilery.

PROLOGUE

The golden haired, bronze skinned girl wearing a dress of white flowing silk moved through the streets of the city at will. Like her unrestrained hair, it blew behind her in the warm lazy breeze, with only a simple rope clasped with gold about her waist. No one crossed her path. In fact, the people that crowded the city below her father's tiered temple-palace hastily avoided being in her way and not just for the burly, black-skinned bodyguards that followed behind her. The guards wore no armor, and in fact only loincloths and razor sharp scimitars adorned their bodies, allowing all to see the deadly definition of their muscles.

They all knew Thyssallia, the thirteen year old daughter of Mon'El on sight, and in the city of Kaimpur, her father's word was law second only to the gods. The people of Kaimpur worshipped her name, bowed and knelt as she passed, and they reveled long, ate until stuffed, drank and fucked on her birthday. Though, this day was not her birthday. It was a day like any other, but Thyssallia had longed to escape her father's gilded palace and walk amongst the people under the sun. She waited until late in the morning, until her father was well caught up in mundane affairs of state.

This usually did not take long, for the man had proven himself long ago to be the most powerful priest in this region of western Dulkur. With the vassalage of lesser priests, some of which bowed while others had to be conquered, Mon'El carved out a sizeable fief, four hundred miles east to west and double that north to south.

Unfortunately, such a large fiefdom required much administrative work. To accommodate this, the priest built a massive temple that also served as his palace on the great, wide River Thyss. Twenty levels and five hundred feet tall, each level was smaller than the last as it rose to meet the sky, a great stepped pyramid whose lapis lazuli veneered stone blocks glowed vibrant azure throughout the day. Silver and gold accents reflected the sunlight to give it that final, astounding aesthetic, and a stone channel ran from its lowest level east into the River Thyss.

It was on a lazy barge upon that river on the first warm day of spring that his daughter, Thyssallia, was conceived as the craft floated upon calm waters and the wind blew gently across the deck. Both of her parents' gods were present that day, both anxious to be known to the girl that would no doubt command much power.

Interestingly, Thyssallia found the city below the palace to be a place of wonder compared to the plush lifestyle within the palace's halls. Her sandals clopped on streets paved with smooth circular stones, and as per her father's edicts, the streets were clean of waste and debris unlike many other cities. Her brown eyes took in the people as they lived, as they toiled, breaking their backs under loads and whips. She watched overseers strike laborers for their weakness, and she watched whores ply their trade behind shops and in alleys. She smiled at it all, for such entertainment was not available to her within the palace.

The people around her varied so much in size and shape, though there were only three colors of skin of which to speak. Most plentiful were the brown skinned people native to this part of Dulkur and who made up most of the populace. They could be found in all of the castes from slave to laborer to merchant, excepting of course the priests who all shared the bronze skin of her race. And then there were those with skin so dark to be almost black, the strikingly gorgeous skin of ebony, against which the whites of their eyes and teeth were such a shock. There were few of these people here, as they come mostly from southern Dulkur, and most were employed in some form of protection or violence. They tended to have well-formed physiques, more common where the land was harsher and less tamed, and they were one of her mother's favorite appetites.

Thyssallia found herself in one of Kaimpur's many markets, a long and wide bazaar offering a wide variety of food and goods to those that milled about. Most of the merchants and vendors had makeshift stands constructed of wagons with canopies, upon which sheets of linen were draped to keep off the sun. A few had small storefronts that extended straight out from the buildings on the periphery of the market. Come nightfall, the former would pack their wagons and return to their homes, while the latter would pull their wares back inside the buildings, and all would return just before sunrise.

She wandered her way between the vendors as they hawked at passersby, though none propositioned her so. For that matter, here they did not bow or kneel, and at most, all she received was a respectful nod. As this continued, something boiled upward within her, and she fought it down with clenched fists and teeth. Her anger turned to joy when she passed a merchant with a wagonload of grapes, the perfectly sweet variety with pale green skin. Thyssallia carelessly swiped a bunch of these as she passed, smiling as the crisp fruits almost crunched between her teeth and the lovely juice covered her tongue. A few yards away she stopped to admire a merchant's silks, running a hand across them and imagining how they would feel against her skin. She looked up to see the merchant, a silk clad, brown skinned man with a full, foot long beard eyeing her, and as their eyes met, he bowed his head in deep respect.

Thyssallia released the silks and turned to wander elsewhere, and she realized with a start that one of her personal guards no longer stood alongside her. She looked back toward the wagon of grapes and saw her wayward bodyguard listening solemnly as a fat, brown woman blabbered on to him animatedly. Thyssallia's guards were considered as off limits as Thyssallia herself, so what reason could this old bitch have for delaying him?

Thyssallia stormed back to her bodyguard and, with sandaled feel set wide and crossed arms, demanded, "Woman, why do you assault my man with your words?"

The woman glanced over her shoulder for just an instant, and then stopped when she realized her mistake. She was ugly – a little over five feet tall and three times the woman she should have been to Thyssallia's eyes, lines of age showed on her face, and some of her curly black hair had begun to turn gray. She moved away from Thyssallia's bodyguard to take her place behind the wagon.

She bowed her head with closed eyes and said, "My apologies, Lady. I meant no disrespect."

"Answer my question," Thyssallia commanded.

"She is concerned about being paid for the grapes," the tall and well-muscled guard said.

"Paid?" Thyssallia asked, almost sounding confounded.

"W-Well," the merchantess stuttered, and the market grew ever quieter as more began to listen to the confrontation. "My Lady, it's only that your great father already receives our taxes, our tithes and whatever else his house and the gods require of us."

"Paid," Thyssallia repeated.

"I-I-I'm pleased to serve, but what is left must go far," she tried to reason.

"Paid!" shrieked Thyssallia. "Here is your pay!"

Thyssallia looked above the wagon, where plain white linen was draped over a wooden framework to keep the summer sun off the tender, juicy grapes. She stared at the linen for just a moment, willing her consciousness to ignore all else, as if nothing existed in the world except for the linen. It began to smolder, a wisp of black smoke rising upward from the focal point of her vision. Thyssallia took a deep breath, and the linen ignited outright into flame. Within moments, the fire spread across the linen, while the merchant screamed and called for help, but no one dared move. The cloth split from the flame and fell through the framework holding it up to land, burning, on the merchant's load of grapes. It continued to burn until there was no linen left, the fire shrinking the fruit and turning its skin black. Some of them split and burst forth, the juice sizzling as the wooden wagon began to burn too.

"You demand pay?!" Thyssallia screamed. "I'll leave you with nothing, you bitch!" As she said this, she pointed at the old, ugly fat woman, and a candle's worth of flame appeared in the woman's hair, almost as if the ends of her hair were a wick. The flame spread and grew, and within moments, the woman cried and screamed for mercy, for help.

"Stop this!" thundered a voice from the far side of the market, from where Thyssallia had originally come. Thyssallia nearly jumped out of her skin at the sound of her father's voice, booming unnaturally across the bazaar as it did when he used his powers of the air. She looked to see him storming across the market toward her, undisguised anger plain upon his face.

Her father, Mon'El, appeared as a giant to her, even though he barely stood six feet tall. Perhaps it was some kind of magical illusion that she did not understand, or maybe it was the fear of a child facing an angry parent. Mon'El always kept his face and scalp shaven, causing the sun to reflect off the bronze skin of his head ever so slightly, and today like most days he wore silk robes so pale and light blue to be almost white. His narrow face, sharp jawline and hawk-like nose often appeared imposing, but it was his eyes that truly showed his anger at his daughter's actions.

Thyssallia looked back at the havoc she had wreaked and saw both the merchant and her wagon blazing in baleful fires while the woman screamed. She tried to will the fire out, begging Hykan to give her the strength, but there was no answer. She called on Nykeema to aid her in extinguishing the flames. But the goddess of water required serene wisdom in all things, and Thyssallia shook with the emotion of it all. She heard her father sigh even over the fire's low roaring, and within moments an frigid wind came down from the sky to stamp out the flames.

"Tend to her," Mon'El commanded a priest in his entourage as he pointed to the merchant who lay moaning, "and take my daughter back to the palace. I will deal with her later."

Thyssallia leaned out her window, looking down the side of her father's palace and out over the river. The river was a one thousand foot wide, blue snake that ran west to the ocean some fifty miles away. Several large docks had been constructed on the River Thyss to accommodate both her father's barge and the numerous trading vessels that brought goods both up and down river.

She dreaded what was to come, for she had seen anger on her father's face before, but rarely directed at her. She didn't understand why her father was angry. Generally, she was allowed to do what she willed when she willed, as was proper of the bronze skinned rulers in Dulkur, but she was not yet a ruler. She wasn't sure she wanted to be if it meant she couldn't visit proper punishment on a mere peasant.

She waited for hours, as the sun passed its highest point, and her stomach began to growl with the realization that she hadn't eaten anything but the grapes. She grew sleepy and her limbs heavy, so she curled up into a ball on her bed not unlike a cat. When she awoke, the sun was halfway to the horizon, and still Mon'El had not come. She paced her large room like an anxious feline, looking for something to amuse her, and she found it in her two guards that watched her from just inside her door.

"Give me your sword," Thyssallia commanded one as she approached. It was a bronze handled weapon, long and curved, and her muscles protested momentarily as she felt the weight of it. The blade almost fell to the ground, though its hilt was firmly within her grip, but she recovered just in time. The guard to whom it belonged hid his dismay well. As she backed away, she looked to the other well-muscled guard and said, "Arm yourself."

Thyssallia was a slip of a girl, thin of frame, but she had taken to practicing with a sword at least twice a week. She of course was no match for her guards, professional fighters to be sure, but she smiled grimly at the sound of the steel whistling through the air. The first time one of her weak attacks had been parried, the impact vibrated through her hands and forearms, but she had done well. The man had to block the stroke lest he had been injured, whereas normally he avoided the sword altogether. After six months, Thyssallia had actually started to develop some small skill with the blade. Her foe had little trouble defending himself, and he only attacked gently with obvious blows that she could easily deflect. But still, she knew that one day…

"Must you do this?" her father's voice called over the ring of steel. It did not boom frighteningly as it had in the market before, but it still caught the combatants' attention.

Thyssallia reluctantly lowered the weapon and placed it in her man's outstretched hand. As he moved back to his place by the door, she said to her father, "I like it. One day, I will rend flesh with steel."

"Thyssallia -"

"I like Thyss."

"Thyssallia, it is unbecoming of a future priestess to use steel. When you are Chosen, you will have no need of such primitive devices. Also, it's at that time that you may change your name if you please," Mon'El admonished. "What you did today was unnecessary."

"That fat bitch dared -" Thyssallia started, her temper flaring, but her father cut her off.

"Do not argue with me! I said it was wrong, and my word is law here!" Mon'El shouted. He closed his eyes and took a deep breath to calm his ire, then he whispered, "Nykeema, grant me the strength to deal with such a child."

"Father," Thyssallia said, dropping her tone of defiance for something more reasonable, "you rule Kaimpur and the lands around, and I am your daughter. She had no right to demand payment for something so little as grapes. We take what we want."

"Yes, that is true," Mon'El agreed, "but I take when it is right. I take what we need to support us as befits our station, I take their girls when my body requires them, and I sacrifice those beneath us as the gods demand. But I take no more. What we leave them, they need to survive. Nay, they need to thrive. For if they all die out, we have no one left to support us."

"Then Father you are weak, for I will take the world by the throat, and it will give me all I desire."

Mon'El's face grew hard as stone, and his silver eyes almost seemed to turn blue with his next words. "That too is your decision to make once you are Chosen. Until then, I forbid you to ever leave these rooms again." He turned and strode away, but he stopped just before leaving to say, "Thyssallia, I find it interesting that you choose to shorten your name to that of the river below. Your temperament is not suited to the Water Mother."

Mon'El was true to his word in that Thyssallia was not allowed to leave her rooms the rest of the afternoon or that evening. Her evening meal was brought to her by servants, and her bodyguards, once her protection, were now her gaolers. She took to again practicing at swordplay, practicing until her hands grew raw and then numb, and she smiled every time the steel rung out in the hopes that the sound further aggravated her father.

When she lay down, she found herself unable to sleep despite the pleasant soreness and weakness in her limbs. She tossed and turned fitfully until the moon was high in the sky, and finally she rose from her bed, wondering if she might be able to sneak away from her new prison. Her eyes hurt from lack of sleep, and standing in the middle of her room, Thyssallia rubbed at them for just a moment.

When she opened her eyes, her room was gone, replaced by a landscape the likes of which she had never seen. In fact, landscape didn't describe it at all, for there wasn't one of which to speak. In fact, she could neither see nor feel ground beneath her feet at all, yet she stood. Fire provided the only light – a baleful blaze that ranged from white to red to orange and writhed with life uncommon to normal fire. To one side, a pool of serene water bordered the fire, and steam exploded constantly from where the two met. On the other side of the fire stood a small mountain of stone and earth which then mixed with the blaze smokily to create molten lava. A breeze took the smoke and steam away only to repeat the action when they returned.

"Thyssallia," whispered a man's voice in her ear or maybe her mind, "you are at odds with your father, but his mind is without bounds. Be mine and learn to be so."

"No," rumbled a voice not unlike the sound of a rockslide, "come to me and know the strength only the ground beneath your feet can offer. The mountain never bows to the wind."

Thyssallia cocked her head to her left and waived her hand dismissively. "No," she said, and the miniature mountain vanished. Also gone was the breeze, leaving the water and flame to spew steam frightfully.

The comforting yet powerful voice of Nykeema, Goddess of Water, implored, "You are strong, yet your strength requires wisdom. In my depths you shall find what will temper you to new strengths. You shall be my greatest priestess ever."

"Join me," Hykan hissed, the flames growing to frightful heights, "and you shall burn your foes away. No one shall ever deny you anything, and all shall be yours to claim!"

Thyssallia took one step toward the inferno, one step that could not have been more than a few inches in its direction, and the flame leapt from its place to engulf her fully. It should have burned, should have seared away her hair and scorched her flesh. It should have blackened her bones and melted her eyes in their sockets, and yet it did none of these things. It was a burning the likes of which only a small number of bronze skinned priests of Dulkur have experienced, but for Thyssallia, it was different from what even those before her knew. An ecstasy took hold of her as the blaze penetrated her very being, and she moaned and laughed with the feeling of it. Later, she would wonder if it was the same thing her mother felt when touched by her lovers. Her body absorbed the fire, merged it with her very being, and eventually there was no more to be seen. Thyssallia fell limply and slept on the ground which she could not see.

When she awoke, the sun shined warmly through the open windows into her room. With unexpected energy, she jumped to her feet and ran toward the light. Reaching one of her windows, she climbed up onto the stone sill, ignoring the danger of falling, and held her arms out to the hot, morning sun, laughing so that her voice echoed into the city below. She dropped from the window back into her room and crossed back to her bed. A once hot breakfast of fried bird eggs and fresh bread sat upon a silver tray on an ottoman nearby. Famished, Thyssallia considered it for a long moment, even poked it with a lone finger. Finding it unacceptable, she hurled the tray against a stone wall with a hiss. She felt strong, stronger than ever before as she padded toward the dark-skinned guard that stood inside her door.

"Give me your sword," she demanded.

"Mistress," he replied haltingly, his voice a deep bass, "I do not have another to spar with you."

"I said nothing about sparring! Give me your sword!"

Perhaps it was something about her voice, her newfound energy, or her eyes, but he did as he was told. He handed her the steel bladed weapon with something akin to regret, as if he feared that upon receiving it, she would skewer him or lop off his head. She did neither as she took the weapon, feeling its wire wrapped bronze handle against the callouses of her palm, and it did not threaten to fall to the floor as it had the day before. Her right arm held it firmly with neither a hint of weakness nor even soreness from the previous day's exercises. She strode out the door, and the guard did not stop her.

None stopped her as she nakedly climbed brown stone steps to the level immediately beneath the palace's apex, scimitar in hand. She found her father there, leaning luxuriously on a cushioned couch as three scribes and a vizier sat on the floor, likely recording matters of state, and they averted their eyes from the princess. Mon'El jumped to his feet at his daughter's unexpected, forbidden intrusion, preparing to make his fury known to all in Kaimpur.

"Thyssallia, how dare -?!" he thundered, and the palace shook for just an instant, but his words caught in his throat, as he looked into his daughter's eyes. Instead of the deep brown irises that he had seen for thirteen years, he beheld shining silver ringed black pupils that seemed to burn with inner fire.

"Henceforth, you shall call me Thyss."

1.
Eight Years Later...

"I do not understand. How have you yet to find her? I have paid you well. You are the best tracker in my lands, and yet you have no news?" the priest questioned angrily as he stared down at the man who stood before him.

Mon'El eagerly awaited news for weeks, and so had no qualms about interrupting breakfast with his wife, demanding his servants bring the tracker up to their suite atop the palace straight away. As King, High Priest and Chosen of Aeyu, He whom ruled the air and winds, Mon'El could have commanded the man to locate his daughter without any compensation at all. The priest felt extraordinarily generous in offering a sum of gold that would buy the tracker an estate on the river itself.

Much depended on Thyssallia's safe return. Thyss, he reminded himself.

The suite sat atop Mon'El's massive pyramid that stood in the center of his city and consisted of a large, central room with four open archways that led to others at each point of the compass. These all had grand balconies to allow Mon'El to look down on his people and to allow the currents of his god to pass freely through his abode. He and his wife maintained separate bedrooms to the north and the south, though they seldom slept alone, and the room to the east comprised Mon'El's private temple to Aeyu. His wife Ilia kept the room to the west, there indulging in whatever her heart desired.

Standing three or four inches taller than Mon'El, the ranger known as Guribda had smartly dropped to his knees upon being brought before the priest and king. It would have done him no good to physically overshadow a man who could send him to his death with a mere flip of a hand, but even kneeling, he felt himself shrink before Mon'El's ire even as the king seemed to grow and darken.

Guribda feebly replied, "Well, Highness, I have some news, and I will find her. I swear it."

"What news, then?" Mon'El demanded impatiently.

"Your daughter recently was seen in a village to the north, bordering on the great jungle there. I tracked her to the edge of it where at least six other people joined her before they entered the jungle," he explained, leaving out the part where he was sure Thyss had been accosted and taken prisoner.

"And what of the jungle?" Mon'El pressed, idly adjusting his robes. He had been told that Guribda returned to the city alone, so he opted for more blue in his robes than white, hoping that the calm wisdom of Nykeema would embrace him in the face of unwelcome news.

"I… I did not pursue them."

"What?!" Mon'El's voice smashed the interior walls, carried by a gust of wind as thunder cracked in a cloudless sky. Silk tapestries blew from the walls to the floor, and the plates of food on the table behind him rattled and moved about. One fell with a shattering on stone and caused his wife to sigh. He lowered his voice to a dangerous growl as he pressed on, "Explain carefully."

The tracker's eyes shot around the scene, lolling almost like that of a panicked animal as he assessed his chance of escape should he choose to run. There were four exceptionally large, heavily muscled men at each corner, excluding the one who had moved up to be but six feet behind him. All were armed with the best scimitars the city of Kaimpur could produce, and while the tracker was no stranger to swordplay, he doubted he could take out one before the others were upon him. And then he had the priest-god's magic to contend with. No, escape was not an option.

With hands open before him, almost in supplication, he responded meekly with a bowed head, "That jungle is well known to be cursed, Highness. There are monsters in that place that defy time, which predate the rise of men, and I admit to being a coward. Surely, you would have no fear with your immense power. You are blessed of the gods, but I am but a man. I beg your forgiveness.

"Highness, I have taken other steps, however. The jungle borders the sea to the north, and a vast, lifeless desert stretches from its southern edge all the way to your lands. If she does not return to the village, she has little choice but to travel to King Chofir's city on the other side. I have paid for eyes in both places. She will not escape me."

Mon'El's anger seemed to abate as the tracker spoke, for the priest did remind himself that most men were in fact weak and powerless. So few of Dulkur's people wielded the power of the gods, and Mon'El was one of those Chosen few, arguably the greatest of them all. The tracker's words placated him enough, and he nodded at the mention of Chofir. He knew the king well, and a smile touched the corners of his mouth at the thought that the fat merchant-king might try to impose his will on Thyss.

"Very well," Mon'El replied calmly after a moment. "See to it that she does not. She has been gone too long, this time, and I demand her presence. She must be at my side in one month or much may be lost. Go."

The tracker turned to leave, and the guard returned to his post in the corner. As Guribda made his way down the steps that would lead him down the outer wall of the pyramid shaped palace, Mon'El heard the tracker issue a relieved sigh. Mon'El clenched his fists, anger brewing again, but not aimed toward the man who had just left. No. Yet again, his daughter tested his patience and his will, as she had for the last ten years or more, and he was beyond allowing it. What was soon to happen would have repercussions throughout all of Dulkur, and she was the integral piece on the gameboard.

"Must you scheme so?" Ilia, called from behind him as he began to pace.

He turned back toward her and approached their breakfast table, calm having once again reclaimed his demeanor, but he did not sit. The table was laden with citrus fruits and fried pork, and a scantily clad, light skinned servant girl placed a new plate covered with dates and figs to replace the one that lay shattered on the floor. This she carefully scooped up to avoid cutting herself before making her way out. Mon'El's eyes lingered on her retreating backside for a long moment, and then his attention cut to his wife, finding her doing the same.

"For nearly a year," she admonished, "you have allowed yourself none of the pleasures we deserve. I will call the girl back and let us take the time to enjoy her together."

"No," Mon'El replied with a sigh and a slight shake of his head. "Enjoy her if you wish, but I have too much to prepare. In a month, I will have either doubled my kingdom or will be fighting for it."

"Why does it matter so?" Ilia asked with a slight frown. "We have all we desire – servants, whatever foods suit our tastes, gold, delights of the flesh – we have no need for anything else. Let us enjoy ourselves."

Mon'El shook his head briefly, but he leveled a loving smile at her as his voice was filled with false admonishment, "My wife, lover of life's pleasures. I wish I could see things as you do, but the world has so much more. We deserve all it has to offer, and Aeyu grants me the power to make it so. There is no greater evil in the world than to squander one's gifts."

He fell silent as he again considered his daughter, purposefully lost somewhere in the northern jungles or perhaps even striding into Chofir's domain at that very moment. While he chafed at her having been Chosen by Hykan, God of Fire, over the far more intellectual Aeyu or even Nykeema, he silently admitted that it made sense. Both willfully acted on the demands of their egos, ignoring, or even outright challenging the established order of the world. For Aeyu's sake, the girl carried and even fought with a sword when she could incinerate a foe with little more than a thought!

"You're thinking about her again, aren't you?" Ilia asked.

Mon'El hadn't realized that he was staring off past his wife. Her question returned his attention to her face, that bronze face with its almond shaped eyes that enslaved him years ago, and he replied, "You always know what I'm thinking."

"Not always," she replied with a shrug, pushing a plate of half-eaten food away from her, "but when it involves our daughter, you always begin to frown. And you squint a bit as well. It is most unbecoming, creates small lines around your mouth and eyes."

"I am sorry, my dear. I know how important my continued beauty is to you." Mon'El sighed heavily before adding, "I must meditate, allow Aeyu to guide me."

Ilia returned the sigh and pushed her chair backward, the wood legs scraping harshly on the stone tile floor of their chambers. Without pushing it back toward the table, she harumphed in annoyance toward her personal sleeping chamber, her naked feet slapping on the cool stone in another sign of her aggravation. Ilia never bothered to hide her emotions or thoughts, another trait she passed on to their stubborn daughter. As a dark curtain fell across the archway obscuring his view of her nude, delicious form, Mon'El thought he would make it up to her later in one sensual way or another.

Sensuality was all Ilia understood or cared about. At least that quality in their daughter was tempered by Mon'El's ambition.

He padded into his personal shrine and knelt in the center, surrounded by idols and graven images of the god of the air, the god of the winds and sky, Aeyu. Reliefs carved of ivory, sculptures of worked gold, and tapestries of silk all displaying various artful incarnations of Mon'El's god stood silent as he closed his eyes. Breathing deeply of the cool breeze that entered the shrine from his balcony, he lifted his arms out to either side, hands lifted upward in supplication. The God-King of Kaimpur cleared his mind and sought communion with the deity that literally ruled above all others, begging for the patience and wisdom he would need in the coming days.

2.

A lone figure trudged across fiery sand dunes under a blazing hot yellow sun. The desert started as a flat plain of dried, cracked ground at the edge of a jungle before turning to white sand as fine as that on any beach in the world. The amount of sand increased, leading to fifteen or twenty foot tall dunes that towered over the gulleys between them. Small clouds of dust blown back and forth from one shifting hill to the next. From a great distance, the wanderer looked as nothing more than an unclear form, blotted and made indistinct by waves of heat. Upon closer inspection, the form was a frightening creature of unknown origin with an hateful snout and a skin that hung loosely upon its bones, as if its skeleton and musculature were too small to support the creature's full size. However, one walking with the desert traveler would have found a bronze skinned, golden haired woman with an angular, almost feline face and eyes that shined silver in the overbearing desert sun. The skin of a terrifying reptilian beast draped over her head and shoulders, shielding her from the brilliant orb and keeping most of the heat off of her skin.

Today marked the fifth day of her journey across the northern desert, a trek she was sure she could manage. The skin she wore once had the added power of camouflage, seeming to shift and vary its appearance with the surrounding sands, but that wore off two days ago as it turned into a fetid, rotting hulk. She left the jungle hauling a sled of cooked meat behind her, which she abandoned yesterday when her water supplies ran dry. She called on Nykeema, Goddess of Water, to refill her water skins or for even a few pitiful drops of rain to ease the searing heat and wet cracked lips, but her prayers went unanswered. Hykan, at least, never abandoned her, though she had to concentrate almost constantly on the powers He granted her to remain resistant to the arid death that threatened to consume her. As the sun rose directly overhead, she could walk no more. She barely had time to lay out her bedroll so her flesh didn't scorch on the burning sand before she passed out.

The woman struggled back to consciousness, the sun having passed overhead to set off into the west. The shadows of the dunes spread across the area between the ridges and hills, allowing the air to cool just enough. She licked at her dried, cracked lips and found that she didn't even have spit enough to moisten them. She reached for her water skins and realized that they were gone – she had dropped them at some point earlier in the day without even realizing it. She rose from the bedroll, an act of pure will contesting aching muscles and joints and left that behind as well as she continued south.

The dunes began to level off as she trudged the miles, the hills of sand decreasing in height and frequency. They gave way to flatlands, cracked and barren, but at least here or there were signs of life – a tiny sprig of a green plant growing from a crack in the hardened ground, an anthill, or a tiny black lizard that slipped away as soon as she stepped toward it. She thought the desert must end soon. Where any green grew at all, there must be water, even far below the ground, and if she could just continue southward, she would surely find more vegetation as she left the sand dunes further behind.

The sun hung low in the sky, almost to the horizon, when she tripped over her own sandaled feet and fell hard to the ground, barely lifting her hands in time and skinning her palms in the process. She lay there, panting hard, her short exhales blowing small puffs of dust and dirt away from her face as her once flowing, golden hair lay in filthy disarray. She had no strength to go further, and her mind couldn't find the wherewithal to consider the possibility. A tiny black scorpion scuttled by her, and she opened one eye just enough to look at it.

And then she saw what helped her find deeper reserves of strength. As the scorpion left her peripheral vision, her eye focused on a plant growing in the distance. It was no more than three feet tall, had two large finlike protuberances that grew from a squat central stalk and was arrayed with two inch long spines that pointed in all directions, a way for the succulent to protect itself from things that might eat it for the water it contained. She pushed up onto her hands and knees and, with all her remaining strength scrambled toward the cactus. As she came close, she closed her hand around the hilt of her scimitar, breathing a sigh of relief that she hadn't left the weapon somewhere in the desert along with all her other belongings.

The weapon's cool, leather wrapped hilt helped her focus her mind and energies as she drew it and lashed out at the plant with one frantic motion. The cactus fell to the side as she reached into the stalk and brought a handful of cool liquid to her lips. More flowed languidly from the decapitated bulk, and she tore a piece of fabric from her sullen tunic to soak up as much of it as possible. There was little water to be had, and the taste of it tanged bizarrely in her mouth and burned in her throat. But it eased her thirst just enough, and she stretched the soaked fabric across her head and face as she lay back to enjoy the new, wonderful sense of coolness. Her strength returned, and the woman rang the last few drops out of the fabric into her mouth.

Grit mingled with it, but she ignored this as she looked about for more of the cacti.

She almost jumped to her feet at a sight to the southeast – civilization! A grand city stood perhaps only a few miles away. Golden spires rose into the sky, and huge marble and feldspar ziggurats, even to rival her own father's, dominated a skyline of smaller granite buildings between those towers. She had crossed the desert, and with renewed strength, she sheathed the scimitar and ran with abandon toward salvation.

She tore across the landscape heading for the city, but somehow, it grew no closer as she pushed onward and onward. She puffed almost breathlessly, a pain growing in her side as she couldn't find air. Her lungs seized and refused to function, but still she hurried. Darkness crept in around her peripheral vision as rings of purple and red invaded the center, but still she charged. Her gait became uneven, and the colored rings began to turn to darkness, leaving just pinpricks of light in the center of her sight. Then this too failed, and Thyss collapsed to the ground to die.

3.

As she lay in her dehydrated stupor, some part of Thyss, some tiny animal instinct in the back of her brain shouted at her she was dying, and yet she was powerless to stop it. Depleted, her body could go no further, and her mind had grown weak from constant exposure. In her torporous state, the sorceress could do nothing to save herself. She would not regain consciousness again, and so she dreamed as she laid prone near death.

At first, she found herself amongst the glorious city in the distance, the city whose boundaries she never gained, and she marveled at the construction of the place. What she thought to be a tower of gold in fact appeared to be made of glass and steel, reflecting golden yellows and oranges in the sunlight. Other smaller buildings abounded, wrought of stone the likes of which she'd never seen, as it all seemed to be one continuous block with no seams or mortar. The ziggurat she saw at a distance turned out to be a gleaming beacon of white with steps leading to a dais and a massive portico with columned façade, over which loomed a huge white dome with spire.

No persons of any kind or race walked these city streets, and Thyss pondered what could cause a people to abandon such a place.

Before the alien, domed structure stood a marble fountain of sorts, still bubbling with cool, clear water despite the city's apparent lack of occupation. This she sat upon the edge of and dipped her hands into the coolness to press it about her still burning face, and she reveled in the glory of such a feeling. Thyss brought her mouth down to the water and began to drink deeply, washing away the grit and dust of the desert from the inside of and around her mouth, but the water suddenly flowed upward to meet her, overflowing her mouth. It pushed into the back of her throat and went down the wrong way. Thyss panicked as she coughed and choked, and then she fell backward against the marble fountain, her vision again blacked out with unconsciousness.

She had no way to gauge the passage of time when she came to, but she levitated above the ground, lifted into the air by some unseen force. She cracked her eyes open, such a simple thing that took all of her energy to accomplish, but her blurry sight refused to clear. Thyss sensed that she flew at an infuriatingly slow pace, just a few feet above the droughted desert ground. The paved city streets, wondrous buildings, and marble fountain had vanished. She wondered at how she tended to move so slowly in such dreams. She willed her flight faster to no effect, and the angle of her view never changed. Between boredom and further exhaustion, she fell deeper into sleep.

Another dream pulled her closer to consciousness. This time she swam, perhaps in the river that was her namesake, and cool water washed over her, gloriously cooling her aching and burned skin. She floated limply, her hair ridding itself of the grime and grit of the desert sands. A fleeting thought passed, a consideration if she should be worried about the crocodiles and hippopotami that dwelt in such places, but as it was only a dream, she pushed such concerns away. She turned her face and opened her mouth, but Thyss began to choke as soon as she began to gulp the salty water.

Rough hands lifted her out of the refreshing respite, and an accented voice said, “No, you mustn’t drink it.”

Next she knew, she reclined on a plush bed, soft fur brushing against her palms and fingertips. Muffled light seeped into a round room from around the edges of a simple black curtain that hung in a doorway. An ebony face of the darkest skin she'd ever seen hovered above her, and it flashed a terrifying smile, bright white teeth in sharp contrast to the skin around them as she grew certain of their intent to consume her. Thyss tried to speak, but her lips refused to move as did the rest of her body. She felt hands massaging her naked flesh while a pungent though not unpleasant aroma filled the air, and she tried to lift her own to fend off the assault. Her arms would not move, and exhausted by a such minimal effort, the panic ebbed away. Thyss dozed into oblivion again.

Thyss awoke with a start, sitting upright in one gasping motion and working to catch her breath as her heart pounded. After a few moments, she calmed down and began to pull great breaths of air through her nose, causing her pulse to slow as she let the breaths out through her mouth. She gazed around, finding the round room that she dreamt of was a hut of the sort of mud bricks used by Dulkur's lower peoples. She sat upon a soft bed of arranged furs and skins, and her eyes narrowed at the plain, clean linen shift she wore that was so thin that she may as well have been naked. Her clothes sat folded on a stool to one side, but her scimitar was nowhere to be seen.

"Welcome back to the living," a woman's voice said, thick with the Low accent.

Thyss had completely overlooked the dark skinned woman that leaned against one wall of the hut, her mind having dismissed or ignored her as a servant or even less. The woman smiled warmly, her teeth as well as the orbs of her eyes matching the striking contrast to her skin that

Thyss saw during her languid dreaming. Her coarse, naturally curling hair had been shorn off recently near her scalp, and she wore a curious set of silken tunic and leggings, pure black but for the curious sparkle of silver amongst the threads. If she weren't obviously of the servant caste, Thyss would almost think her beautiful.

"We were afraid it was too late," the woman said as she climbed to her feet. She walked almost silently across the hut's floor which was covered in thick linen not too dissimilar from the long, loose chemise Thyss wore, and she held out an earthen jar. "But when your fever broke yesterday, I knew you to be strong. Please, drink."

Thyss took the jar and looked down into the vessel before taking a shallow sip. Assured that it was in fact water, or perhaps uncaring as hungered thirst took hold, she tipped the jar back and gulped as the water overran her mouth and down the sides of her face.

"Careful, not too much," the woman said, taking the jar from Thyss hands, and Thyss repaid her with a baleful stare. "You'll make yourself sick."

"More," Thyss commanded, her imperious nature returning.

"More you shall have, Highness, but you must drink small amounts at a time. The desert almost claimed you."

"Where am I?" Thyss demanded.

"The kingdom of Calumbu."

"Calumbu," Thyss repeated, trying to recall where she'd heard it before, and then she blurted laughter. "Calumbu? Kingdom? A tiny little fiefdom of Low people!"

"Careful what you say, Highness," the woman warned, though not in an unfriendly way. "King Harpalo himself is the one who saved you. He may expect more gratitude and less insults."

“I’m sure I know what gratitude your king will expect, and I can tell you of the gratitude he can expect from me!”

“Easy, Highness, King Harpalo is not like many such men you may have met.”

“Why do you keep calling me ‘highness’?” Thyss asked in a huff, and then she added, “and where is my sword?”

“Are you not a Highborn?” she asked in return. “You have the bearing of one, and one cannot miss the silver eyes bespeaking one Chosen by the gods. I assumed you come from one of the kingdoms elsewhere in Dulkur. If you do not wish to be called Highness, what shall we call you?”

“My name is Thyss. Where is my sword?” Thyss repeated.

“It will be returned to you when you are well enough. You drank deeply of the *palua* cactus, the water of which is thick with fermentation. You would have died if King Harpalo and his party hadn’t seen you from afar.”

“I am well enough now,” Thyss determined, and she stood to her feet.

If it hadn’t been for the quick reactions of her attendant, or perhaps the woman was ready for such a thing to happen, Thyss would have likely cracked her head against the mud brick wall or the floor of the hut. The moment she stood, the hut rocked crazily from side to side and spun, as if it were a ship in a storm or caught in a maelstrom. She felt strong but gentle arms catch her quickly from behind, looped under her own arms as she fell.

“I am sorry, Lady Thyss, but I think not. Your skin is terribly sunburned, and the blisters are just beginning to form. You still need to drink much water, but never more than a mouthful at a time," the ebony woman explained, motioning to the jar after she settled Thyss back into bed.

"What is your name?" Thyss asked with a sigh, the hut returning to its normal, unmoving state.

"Nekala."

"I… thank you, Nekala."

Nekala tilted her head slightly, and a wide smile returned to her face, just cracking her lips to reveal the gleam of her teeth. "There is no need for thanks, Lady Thyss. You were in need, and Calumbu can provide. Rest now, and drink if you are thirsty. Remember, no more than a mouthful at a time. I will inform the king that you've awakened."

Nekala gave Thyss' left hand a gentle, almost motherly squeeze before she stood from her bedside and crossed the ten foot wide hut. She pulled aside the dark curtain that served as a door, allowing bright streaming sunlight into the darkened interior, and Thyss grumbled a bit as she turned her head and shut her eyes tightly against it. With a woosh of the drape returning to its place, both the sunlight and Nekala vanished from the hut, and Thyss was left to wonder what sort of man King Harpalo of Calumbu was and what demands he would have of her. Or worse – what demands he would have of her father once he realized whose daughter she was.

It seemed hours passed by the time King Harpalo arrived, a calculus Thyss could only arrive at based on the angle at which the sunlight broke into the hut around the thick drapery that hung in the doorway. The curtain was pushed aside, and a huge man ducked his way into the hut, followed by Nekala. He stood over six and a half feet tall and had a frame that seemed almost as wide. Magnificent iron thews bulged across his arms and upper body, both of which were decorated with a necklace, bracelets, and other ornaments of gold. Scars from both beasts and manmade weapons crisscrossed his body and even his face, and he looked down upon Thyss with intense and thoughtful eyes. He wore a simple gold circlet about his forehead, and long, braided locks topped his head.

"Welcome to Calumbu," he boomed, "I am King Harpalo. Nekala tells me your name is Thyss."

Thyss thought to stand, but as she pushed herself upward, a wave of nausea overcame her. She had been drinking regularly from the water jar. Children she assumed to be servants checked on her every so often and replenished it, but now she considered that the jar didn't contain only water after all. Perhaps these people mixed something into it to keep her weak, and she again tried to rise, determined to show her strength.

"Please, remain comfortable," Harpalo said with an upraised open palm. He went on, misinterpreting the reason for her struggle to rise, "You are my guest, and I do not demand tribute every time I walk into a room."

"You brought me here?" Thyss asked, searching the huge man's face.

"I did," he answered with a nod. "I was out with a hunting party, and we saw you emerging from the desert. You ran as if a devil pursued you."

"I… I saw a great city of gold and marble, spires, and columns. I thought it my savior."

"An illusion brought on by so much time in the heat and sun, combined with the *palua* water. We harvest it sometimes. In small amounts, it can be pleasant to enjoy, but you consumed much. And with the heat, well, you are lucky we found you. I still was not sure you would survive."

"And what of me now? Will I survive being your prisoner?"

Harpalo's laughter thundered throughout the tiny hut, seeming to shake the very walls. He turned to Nekala, who shrugged, before he explained, "You are no prisoner here."

"You saved me just to let me go on my way."

"If that is what you wish, when you are well of course," Harpalo nodded as he spoke.

"And what will you desire of me? Men are not in the habit of giving aid without expectation of payment."

The king pursed his lips for a moment and then sighed as he said, "I desire whatever you are willing to give. We need no payment from you, Thyss. I helped you because you needed help. You bronze skinned people think us savages, and maybe some of us are. Here in Calumbu, we treat each other well. You may leave as soon as you desire but stay awhile and grow well."

"My king," Nekala said from behind, "I should attend to Lady Thyss' burns and blisters again."

"Of course," Harpalo agreed, and before he ducked his massive bulk through the doorway to leave, he added, "Lady Thyss, no doubt you have your beliefs about us, but know one thing. If I had ill intentions toward you, rest assured they would already be in motion. After all, I know who your father is."

He was gone before she considered a reply, and she eyed Nekala suspiciously as the woman approached her with a bowl and a clean, white linen cloth. Thyss asked, "What are you doing?"

"Let me help you up and out of your gown," Nekala replied, receiving a defiant look from her charge. "You have terrible burns from the sun and the rocks. They blister. This paste will help soothe and heal them."

Thyss relented, though it injured her pride to lie sprawled so and naked, barely able to move a limb as exhaustion spread throughout her body. As the woman applied the medicine, Thyss gasped as sharp momentary pains shot through her skin, but as they cooled, a pleasant tingling sensation replaced the white hot lances. By the time it was done, she had no desire to move again, settling into languid comfort and falling into a deep sleep. Rather than try to force the bronze skinned woman back into her shift, Nekala instead pulled a linen sheet up over Thyss' shoulders to protect her dignity from any who may look in on her. She then added a thin animal skin to that as proof against the cooler air that would soon be approaching with the sunset before she made a stealthy exit.

4.

"How much longer am I to be held here?" Thyss demanded a few days later, sitting with her back leaning up against the wall of the hut.

Nekala's brow furrowed in confusion, and she replied, "I have told you – you are not a prisoner here. If you wish to leave, there is the exit," and as she said this, she motioned toward the curtain that served as the hut's door.

"You've said as much, and yet I still do not have my sword at hand."

"Then, I shall go retrieve it for you at once, but there is no need for it here. You are safe and amongst friends," Nekala replied, and the woman stood to make for the curtain.

"I would feel safe with it at my side, and if I am amongst friends, then I will have no need of it," Thyss reasoned, though she felt as if her arguments fell on deaf or otherwise uncaring ears.

Nekala just stared back at her for a moment with pursed lips and a lack of comprehension before she shrugged, pushed aside the curtain to allow bright sunlight to spill into the room, and left. As the curtain sagged shut behind her, Thyss caught just a glimpse of other dark skinned individuals moving about, accompanied by the chattering and other sounds of a village or town. Her father had been clear during her childhood as to the ways of Low Dulkur, and their physical prowess made these people ideal laborers, warriors in his armies, and personal guards. She refused to believe that these people in this place called Calumbu had no ill intentions toward her or that they were civilized at all.

Assuming she had at least a few minutes, Thyss lifted her latest linen robe over her head, and she struggled with the act of pulling it completely from her body. Whatever salves Nekala concocted for use on her terribly sunburnt skin had been tremendously effective, she grudgingly admitted, and the blisters had all but disappeared from where she'd been exposed to the desert sun. As they disappeared, however, the skin on her arms tightened substantially, causing a degree of sudden pain when she stretched them too far. It almost felt as if her flesh wanted to split. Nekala told her that it would continue to heal and return to normal, as would her normally bronze skin tone that had darkened noticeably on her arms, feet, face, and neck. Thyss tossed the shift aside and reached for her plain, woolen clothes, and she was busy tightening the straps of her sandals about her feet and ankles when Nekala returned, Harpalo entering just behind her.

"Nekala says you have asked again for your sword," the huge man stated flatly.

Thyss stood only a few feet from him, her stance wide and arms crossed, and yet he looked no less a giant than when she had been bedridden looking up at him. She had no doubt Harpalo could wrestle a jungle boar, or some other great beast, able to break its neck with his bare hands. She wondered how many of the scars on his body were caused by such a feat. Impressive though he was, Thyss worried little for her own safety, for Hykan would give her the strength to burn him where he stood if necessary.

"Yes," she answered, and her eyes lingered on the scimitar that the king had attached to his own belt.

"Then you will have it," he replied as he drew it, and Thyss' eyes narrowed for just a moment at the thought that he may attempt to strike her down with her own sword. Instead, he held it between the two of them, neither offering it to her nor keeping it in his possession as he said, "With one simple condition. While you are in Calumbu, you shall not draw this weapon or use any of your magicks against my people. I care not what infraction or slight you perceive someone to have caused you, my law rules here. Swear this to me, and your sword is yours."

"I'll swear no such thing," Thyss shot back defiantly, and she felt the burning of her very being. "I swear no oath to any ruler. Return my sword."

"So much venom when all we have showed you is kindness."

"To Hykan's fires with your kindness."

Harpalo sighed deeply and closed his eyes for a few heartbeats, and Thyss knew she'd won the test of their wills. When he opened his eyes again, he turned to the comparatively diminutive form of Nekala who looked as small next to him as a small child next to Thyss' own father. Nekala simply shook her head sadly, looked to Thyss, and then glared at the floor. Harpalo handed the sword over to the woman, who took it grudgingly and brought her eyes back up to Thyss' own.

"Very well," Harpalo said, his voice distant. "Nekala will go with you to the border of Calumbu, whichever border you prefer. Once there, she will give you your sword, and may you journey safely to wherever it is you choose to go."

The corners of Thyss' mouth lifted with her victory, and Harpalo turned and bolted from the hut in apparent disgust at his defeat. Nekala turned to follow him and stopped on the other side of the doorway, holding the curtain back with her free hand. The sounds of civilization came to Thyss' ears as the bright sunlight again filled the single room. She swaggered through the doorway and out into the sweltering day.

She stood in a wide avenue, a well-trodden dirt street that separated rows of clay and mud brick buildings that varied little from the one she had just left, except that some of them were bigger and likely contained multiple rooms. People moved about this village – that's what it seemed to her, rather than a proper city – heading from one task to another, and very few paid her any attention at all, something that to one who was both the daughter of a king and Chosen of a god felt very strange. It seemed almost as if those facts meant nothing to these people. Children laughed and ran amongst the huts and adults, bringing about annoyed scolding from some and joyous smiles from others. As she looked left and right, up and down the village's main path, she saw that more narrow roads intersected it every so often, these also unpaved, and there appeared to be quite the bustle several hundred yards or more to the left.

Nekala waited for Thyss to get her bearings, but after a few moments asked impatiently, "Which way, my lady, do you wish to go?"

"This is Calumbu?"

"Calumbu is the name of Harpalo's kingdom but also of this village where it started. This is the… capital, I think is the word you would use, but there are nine other villages and towns," Nekala explained patiently.

"What's down that way?" Thyss imperiously questioned with an outstretched finger to her left, uninterested in Nekala's explanation of Calumbu as a kingdom.

"Calumbu's largest market is that way, as well as King Harpalo's palace."

"I'd like to see them," Thyss replied, and arrogantly stormed that way.

"Lady Thyss. Lady Thyss," Nekala called after her and, receiving nothing close to a response or a sign that Thyss had even heard, she sighed. Nekala rushed after her, weaving her agile form between people hauling clay pots of water, baskets of vegetables, and other burdens, before catching up to the woman and in fact passing by Thyss to stop in front of her. "Lady Thyss, the king asked that I take you from Calumbu. When I asked you which way you want to go, I meant which way from Calumbu."

Thyss moved to push past the woman, but Nekala stepped sideways to block her, resolute in stopping her from continuing to the market. Thyss fumed, "If I am to leave Calumbu, I need provisions. Or did you save me just to doom me again?"

"Fair enough," Nekala agreed with a slight nod, and then she turned away to lead Thyss. "This way."

The press of people thickened as they moved further into the village, and Thyss wondered if she needed to reconsider Calumbu's size. A cacophony of sounds filled the air from the squeals of children to the ringing peals of smiths hammering metal. As she passed through intersections, other avenues led away, revealing dozens upon dozens of huts, little more than mud brick piles, some so tiny as clearly meant for a lone occupant like the one in which she had been recovering. Others were quite large, easily the size of eight or ten of the smallest, and she assumed whole families lived in these. All stood less than twelve feet tall, comprised of a single level as fitting their station. To build to the sky was reserved for people like her… and her father.

She heard hawkers offering wares – a common thing to be sure in cities – but was astounded when a dark skinned old woman simply handed a plucked and headless chicken to another, younger woman without any form of payment. The exchange would have made sense to Thyss had one been of obvious higher station than the other, but both had the dark, almost ebony skin common to Dulkur's peasants. The two women smiled at each other, exchanged a few words Thyss couldn't hear over the mass of undulating voices around her, and parted ways.

Feeling eyes upon her, the old woman then looked directly at Thyss and raised her voice to ask, "Are you new here? Do you have need of something?"

To call the woman old felt incomplete or inadequate. She stood less than five feet tall, her spine having shrunk and bent her back as the decades passed. A shock of almost pure white hair adorned her head, a sharp and striking contrast to her dark skin. Thyss had seen the same type of contradistinction in Nekala's smile, her shining teeth against the darkness of her lips and face, but this woman had only a few teeth left that could be seen as she spoke. Ancient, wrinkled, and sagging, her skin almost hung from a withered skeleton, and Thyss marveled that such an elderly woman still lived, still was allowed to live despite her usefulness having long swept by her.

Thyss turned her gaze elsewhere and continued up the body clogged village street. Once the mass of people closed back around her and Nekala, shielding them from the view of the oldster, she turned to Nekala and asked, "How old is that woman?"

"I don't know," Nekala shrugged. "Zyata had children when my own grandmother was born. Why?"

"Why do you keep her alive?" Thyss questioned, receiving several glances from those around them. "She is of no use. She is a drain on your people."

Nekala stopped and placed a light hand on Thyss' arm. There was little pressure or force in the touch, and yet it was enough to stop the sorceress and cause her to turn abruptly. An imperious anger burned in Thyss' eyes, but she neither said anything, nor reacted at the contact, though back home in Kaimpur she would have threatened any common peasant who dared to lay a finger on her. Nekala not only dared, but even urged Thyss to a stop in the touch, and it was only the woman's caring ministrations that kept Thyss from lighting the woman's clothing on fire.

Thyss also attempted to ignore that the world had begun to spin along with her movement to face Nekala.

"We do not discard our elders here," Nekala replied reproachfully, "nor do we place value on people by what 'use' they are. Calumbu's people act as one. We serve each other to provide for the needs of all."

"Ridiculous," Thyss spat, nearly hissing as she did so.

"If you say so, Princess," Nekala returned, sneering the title as she said it, and then she motioned a hand forward. "Shall we continue so that you may leave?"

Without another word, Thyss turned to continue their journey up the street – nay, the dirt track that separated lines of poorly built, almost savage homes, but as she did so, the world careened the other direction. Thyss' stomach turned, and her knees buckled, causing her to fall into the dirt and the dust. She knelt there, fighting to keep her gorge down as the people of Calumbu gently parted and flowed around her. Within moments, Nekala knelt beside her and placed the back of her hand on Thyss' brow which was now damp with sweat.

"Your head is burning. Do you feel sick?"

Thyss hazarded a glance at Nekala, unable to summon ire at being touched or spoken to in such a familiar tone and gone was the anger or indignation that had been there just moments before, replaced with nothing but wide eyed concern. Thyss dared not speak, lest she vomit on the spot, and she had no intention of shaming herself here, not in front of these people. She nodded briefly.

Nekala nodded and said, "Let's get you back. You need rest and, maybe later, another cool bath in the river."

Tightening her throat and jaw to keep the contents of her stomach where they were, Thyss allowed herself to be gathered to her feet and led back to the pitiable mud brick hut.

5.

The next day, Thyss enjoyed the luxury of staying bedridden within the tiny hut, the curtain of dark cloth the only thing separating her from the village and all of its life. Her brief expedition into its streets showed Calumbu to be larger than she expected, not a village of dozens but maybe a city of hundreds or even more despite the nearby savage jungle and uncivilized building materials. Regardless, she stayed indoors, slept most of the day, and greedily consumed cool water when Nekala called on her throughout the day with fresh clothes, clean wrappings, and salves for her still healing skin.

Unlike the previous few days she spent resting, intruders disturbed her repose several times. The first was two small boys who pushed into the hut chasing one another. Thyss barely had time to shout at them before they were gone, the curtain that hung in the doorway briefly swaying in the breeze before it settled again. She mumbled something about childish urchins and rolled away to face the wall, drifting back into sleep.

Nekala brought her a midday meal of light pieces of bread and some unidentifiable vegetables. Thyss ate this in quiet disgust, controlling her desire to refuse the food and demand something else, and Nekala joined her, the two women sitting in uncomfortable silence. A spear of light pierced the gloom of the hut, causing Nekala to turn toward the doorway. Thyss looked up and spied several sets of eyes, none of them more than three feet from the ground as they looked in on Nekala and the woman with the strange bronze skin. Thyss' caretaker shooed them away.

But the children came back. More than once, Thyss awoke to the sounds of soft voices or even giggles as small forms crouched outside her hut, peering in past the curtain pulled to one side. She would shout at them, they would run away, and she would return to sleep. Once, a slight pressure, a pulling on her hair caused her eyelids to snap open to find a small boy running his hand across her straight, silky hair that had spilled out on her makeshift pillow, his dark skin a sharp contrast to her hair's golden hues. The boy froze, caught in her glare for a long, static moment before her face screwed up in anger. She screamed obscenities, fumbled for her scimitar, and chased the boy into the street outside her hut, children scattering in several directions into the crowds of villagers as the latter looked on in shocked surprise that turned to indignation or angry glances at Thyss. But the children did not bother her again.

Thyss expected Harpalo to show his face, for surely the man wanted to gloat over her continued inability to leave his… kingdom? Thyss found it difficult to think of Calumbu as a kingdom, for that would put Harpalo on the same level as her father, and that was laughable. But despite its poor and savage appearances, Calumbu was far more than a simple village. Her one venture into the streets showed her throngs of people living and working together no differently than in a large city such as her home Kaimpur. Her mind refused to make sense of this place, its people, and their supposedly idyllic lives, but more importantly, the mountain of a man named Harpalo did not visit her that day.

The following morning, she dressed in her own clothes, discarding the fresh linen shift Nekala provided her, and paced the tiny hut incessantly. She felt no sudden onsets of weakness or nausea, and the blisters on her sunburned flesh had fully disappeared. Her scimitar leaned against the hut's wall, and Thyss longed to feel its weight in her hand, to hear its blade cut through the air, but the hut was too small to accommodate it. She impatiently awaited Nekala, who would arrive any moment based on the morning sunlight threatening to overwhelm the curtain that hid her from the view of the other villagers. It felt like hours, and finally Thyss hefted her sword, secured it in a leather thong at her belt, and strode to the curtain beyond which she heard all the morning sounds of the village waking up. She flung it aside, and Nekala's dark form stood framed by the early morning sun just on the other side with a hand lifted as if to part the curtain herself.

Nekala lowered her hand and smiled as she so often did, saying, "You look well, Princess! Are you quite ready to leave, then?"

Thyss looked at the bundle in Nekala's arms – another set of airy, pale linen clothing and wrappings that stood out in sharp relief from her own black silken clothing as well as a jar of slimy, greenish salve that she'd used many times on Thyss' sunburns. She replied in a commanding tone, "I am well enough. I may stay another day or so as it pleases me."

"Of course," Nekala agreed softly with a slight nod, though the smile had run from her face. "What do you need, then?"

"I would," Thyss lingered on the word for a moment, "like to see Harpalo's palace, and then find someplace I can stretch my muscles."

Nekala nodded again as she saw Thyss' hand come to rest on the hilt of her scimitar and said, "Easily done. Shall we?"

Calumbu already bustled with its people as they set about their daily lives, and whatever that entailed, Thyss hardly cared. Such mundane existences meant nothing to her, nor would they ever. Within minutes, she grew restless at the seemingly endless throngs of people that surrounded her and Nekala. They were everywhere, almost marching with frustrating sluggishness toward their destinations, and even though she attributed the slow pace to the sheer mass of people around her, she still grunted and harumphed her displeasure. Her golden skin and silvery eyes would have parted the sea of people almost anywhere else in Dulkur, but here they paid her no mind, as if somehow in their eyes she were no more important than anyone else.

They arrived at an enormous square, well over a hundred feet in either direction with multiple alleys and narrow streets leading into it, and Thyss recognized a market when she saw one. Stands, most of them little more than lean-tos with canvas coverings to protect the vendor and goods from the sun, lined the perimeter, and dozens more abutted each other in the center to fill the square with the sounds of city life. Vendors called to potential customers and to each other, proffering goods and services to one another, but as before, Thyss saw no money exchanging hands. Occasionally, eggs would be swapped for a jar of some inscrutable substance, meat she assumed to be pork for an armload of fruit, but usually the vendors provided their goods for no payment of any kind.

She shook her head at the idiocy of it all.

"You wanted to see the palace?" Nekala asked as she led Thyss through a narrow lane between vendors' shacks that Thyss was almost certain could be disassembled and hidden away with minimal effort. "You can see it more easily on the other side."

The sea of villagers and their traded or freely given and received wares parted on the far side of the square revealing a squat structure. It was almost as wide as the market square itself, and unlike the mudbrick homes and other buildings around Calumbu, cut and quarried stone blocks comprised solid walls that had no openings or windows save one. A large door, shaped and crafted from planks of dark wood banded together in bronze appeared to be the only entrance. Dark, ensconced torches stood to either side of the door, and others protruded from the stone walls every twenty feet or so in either direction. Standing perhaps twelve feet tall, Thyss calculated the palace to be smaller than most of the levels in her own father's.

"This is the palace?" she asked wryly. "This is where your king lives and rules?"

"Not really," Nekala replied with a brief shake of her head. "This is merely for show, for official purposes. King Harpalo lives over there."

Thyss followed Nekala's finger, lifting her head left and then right to see where the woman pointed, endeavoring to get a view beyond the heads and burdens of those around her. For a moment, the crowd cleared, and Thyss beheld a hovel built of mud bricks, very little different from all the others in Calumbu, thatched roof and all. It was bigger than most, likely consisting of two rooms, one of which had a second level stacked upon it, but it was no place for a king.

"He lives in that shithole?" Thyss scoffed, turning away from the edifice that so affronted her.

Nekala's face became like granite, and her eyes stared back hard, cold, and dead as she replied, "He lives as his people. He says he is above none of us."

"And yet you call him King," Thyss returned. She again laid a hand on her scimitar, her fingers touching the cool metal of its guard. "Where can I go away from this? I wish to train."

"This way," Nekala replied, and she turned abruptly, striding away and forcing Thyss to hurry to keep up.

The whole village looked the same, and Thyss wondered how anyone in Calumbu even knew where they were. They walked east through the narrow lanes, sometimes cutting in between haphazardly placed brick hovels and always weaving between throngs of its dark skinned inhabitants. Thyss began to count the faces she saw, some smiling and friendly while others looked warily with suspicion, and she eventually gave up on the task. Despite the shoddy workmanship of its edifices and a complete lack of apparent planning in its layout, Calumbu appeared more city and less village.

They walked a mile or more by Thyss' reckoning, entering another small square bordered on two sides by thirty foot buildings made of stone much like the palace. Despite the apparent lack of sophistication, she recognized a barracks and mustering yard when she saw one. A few pairs of warriors sparred with a variety of weapons, their blows and parries slow and soft, easy to block or evade. Two racks of weapons stood in a corner where the two buildings came together, and one side of the square laid open with the jungle only a few dozen yards beyond. Several tables also lined the perimeter, and some of these had other warriors taking meals, conversing, or even betting on the sparring partners.

"Will this do?" Nekala asked succinctly, coldly without turning to face Thyss.

Within moments, Thyss' eyes passed over everything and everyone in the square, choosing not to let her eyes linger on any one of Calumbu's warriors for more than a heartbeat lest they mistake her gaze for some sort of interest. She stepped past her guide a few yards into the square, ignoring the questioning stares, and drew her scimitar. The steel shined brightly in the sun, a blinding pinpoint of light traversing up its edge as she tested its weight against muscles that hadn't wielded a sword in a week or more, to say nothing of her being bedridden while her body healed from the hateful caresses of the intense desert sun and arid air. She cut the air with a few light strokes and then turned back to Nekala.

"Yes."

"I have things to do," Nekala said, an uncaring edge plain in her voice. "Can the princess find her way back or does she have further demands on my time?"

Thyss smoldered, flames dancing in her eyes as she beheld the impudent hussy that would dare speak to her so. A sharp retort and a threat of fiery death came to her lips, but she stopped herself just before loosing the words as she considered navigating the city with its near identical mudbrick buildings. She held her tongue for a moment, then offered a calmer reply, "If you would return in an hour to guide me, I would appreciate it."

Nekala nodded curtly before turning to leave, and Thyss could neither see the smile that spread across the woman's face, nor would she have understood the meaning of it. She likely wouldn't have cared.

Thyss turned back to face the yard, the muster area, and its some dozen warriors that stood, trained, or sat around it, and she gripped her scimitar with both hands to hold the blade vertically before her. She continued to ignore the stares, whether they were interested or bored, and moved her blade through a variety of guard positions. Some required both hands while others only one, reflecting different stances and holds on the weapon depending on the type of adversary she faced. She cycled through eight such poses, holding them for ten seconds or so each, and she enjoyed the burning test of stamina they brought to her muscles as she repeated them ten times in turn. The final stance held the scimitar over her head, the edge facing the sky as its point aimed along the same axis as her free left hand at an unseen enemy before her. Her right hand was held high in the air behind her head, and her triceps flared with the delicious trial of their will over a long ten seconds.

And then she struck, bringing the sword down and to the left, its deadly blade whistling as it sliced the air diagonally. Thyss became a whirlwind of steely death, a dervish of lethality as her razor sharp weapon cut down imagined foes all about her. Sweat ran freely off her brow, down the muscles of her arms, and soaked the back of her tunic. Her sinews complained with the stress under which she placed them, but still she forced them onward. Her skin, newly healed and tight from the horrific sunburns Nekala treated so expertly, almost threatened to split with the movement and flexing of thews, and yet she continued to swing her blade in a glorious ballet of ruination.

Thyss brought herself around again, the scimitar cutting a wide arc before her, and it clanged with jarring impact against a similar blade of bronze. The bronze scimitar sparked and bent with the collision, a large part of its edge hacked away, and its wielder tossed it to the side in disgust. A woman stood before Thyss, her match in height just below six feet, and she wore a brown leather jerkin, some sort of buckskin trousers, and soft leather boots. Her skin, nearly black as night, covered rippling muscles in her arms and abdomen, and she spoke with a flash of white teeth.

"I would duel you," she said, and voices around the yard called and shouted their agreement and appreciation.

"Leave me," Thyss replied angrily, her knuckles aching from the blocking of her blade.

"Duel, or are you afraid?"

"I fear nothing."

"Then duel," the woman repeated in Thyss' own Highborn language.

Thyss' eyes narrowed with the understanding that this intrusive woman was more than a native jungle villager, and she warned with a dangerous tone, “Duel me and risk death. I do not use training weapons.”

“No matter,” the woman shrugged.

“N’tuli!” a deep voice called, and a heavily muscled man dressed in nothing but a loincloth tossed a bronze scimitar toward the woman. It arced through the air almost lazily at the warrioress, and the blade began to rotate and spin downward dangerously. At the last moment, she stepped backward and to the side, and with a hand as quick as a striking viper, she caught the flying sword by the hilt in midair.

The woman named N’tuli took another step backward and adopted a defensive stance, the sword held in both hands behind her lead shoulder and said, “I am ready, Highborn one.”

Thyss smiled viciously and took a step backward, her own blade held high in the air with both hands in a stance known as the *hahkbar*. Particularly aggressive, it used the weight of the steel to increase the power of its strokes, and it put N’tuli’s own *pehrleth* stance at a disadvantage on the first strike. Thyss’ opponent would struggle to bring her sword up in time to parry the opening attack, and she found the lack of such thought so typical of mere village warriors.

The two circled in the hot sun for several seconds, each woman stepping to the left, watching, and waiting for the other to attack first. Of course, this fell to Thyss, and she launched her assault without warning, with neither a grunt from the effort nor a battle cry, and to her surprise, N’tuli made no attempt to parry for block the attack. Instead, the muscled fighter showed phenomenal grace by leaping to the side not just once but twice as Thyss followed through the attack. She struck nothing, and Thyss would not underestimate the woman’s agility again.

What followed was a dazzling display of swordswomanship, strength, and dexterity as the two women engaged and disengaged. They sidestepped each other's attacks, parried quick strikes meant to inflict small but draining wounds, and steel and bronze clanged as they blocked massive blows. The assembly around them grew as more warriors came from inside the barracks buildings to watch, as nearby villagers found the spectacle of these two warrior women more interesting than any daily burden. It was as much a clash of culture as it was bronze against steel. All recognized the royal nature of Thyss' bronze skin, golden hair, and the silvery sheen of her eyes that marked her Chosen by a god, but they all shouted their support for their dark skinned sister who fought with lithe grace in the style of one who was self-taught.

Despite the status of her birth, it was Thyss who fought with savagery becoming a lioness. She sneered and spat every time the woman named N'tuli evaded or parried a blow, and her lips curled violently whenever the bronze blade nearly caught her. She screamed her fury that she could not break the defense of her opponent, and inwardly she howled at herself for her own weakness. Thyss' arms grew tired, her guard dropping inch by inch as the duel raged on, and her quick movements slowed and grew cumbersome, while her opponent didn't break a sweat. She knew she could not carry on for much longer, and Thyss was certain her enemy was well aware of the fact.

The moment that ended it came in a two handed blow that Thyss brought straight down at N'tuli, and the latter avoided it by stepping to her left. Unable to stop the momentum, Thyss nearly buried her scimitar's blade into the sandy dirt of the yard, and N'tuli stamped a foot down on the inside edge of the weapon while bringing her own around at a strike on Thyss' hands. Thyss had no choice but to release her hilt and dance backward.

N'tuli closed in slowly to the jeering, supportive shouts of her fellows, and with a relishing grin, she commanded, "Yield, lady."

Thyss had no choice left to her. She lifted her arms from her sides, hands before her and turned upward almost in supplication, and her opponent's mouth opened even further in a triumphant smile. Calling on Hykan, Thyss bent forward suddenly and blew into her open palm. To the casual onlooker, she may have been blowing a kiss to a lover, but as her breath left her hand, a huge gout of flame shot forth directly at N'tuli's head. Wide eyed and shocked, the warrioress barely ducked away in time, and the stench of singed hair wafted in the stifling air. Seeing her chance, Thyss launched herself forward, pounding her shoulder into N'tuli's ill defended form, and the two women went down in a heap. Thyss rolled as they fell, landing hard on her opponent's midsection, and a gale of exhalation blew from N'tuli's lungs. Before N'tuli could regain her breath, Thyss already stood on her feet with both scimitars in her hands, the blades crossed over each other a mere inch from N'tuli's neck. Pulling the blades away from each other would remove the woman's head from her shoulders.

"Yield," Thyss said, and the fires dancing in her pupils showed everyone there that something inside her burned with the hope that N'tuli would not.

"Magic! You cheated," N'tuli gasped.

"And you lost," Thyss replied, and she dropped the bronze scimitar in the dust, turned, and strode from the muster yard, heedless of the wordless stares that followed her.

6.

"I am gratified that you have decided to stay with us despite being well enough to leave," Harpalo boomed gregariously as they walked about the market in one of the village's many squares. "Perhaps our way of life is rubbing off on you?"

A cool wind blew across Calumbu from the west, dispelling the damp heat that had risen with the sun. Dark clouds rolled in with the wind, covering the sun and casting gray light across all of Harpalo's kingdom. They announced the coming rain for all to see. The people put out barrels, basins, bowls, or anything that could collect fresh water to replenish their supplies.

"Not so much," Thyss replied flatly, bored while Harpalo tapped the side of a melon.

"Wonderful, thank you," Harpalo said to the dark skinned woman behind the stand as he took his selection, and they continued their walk. He carefully slit the melon down the middle with his curved dagger. "I hoped that in time you would come to realize the world can be this way."

"It's been but a week," she said, accepting half of the melon. Its reddish orange flesh contrasted starkly with a tough, pitted, pale ring, and it had a refreshing sweetness with just a hint of a sour aftertaste.

"Perfect," Harpalo noted as he took a slurping bite from its innards. "You see, we must pick them at the right time. Too soon, and they are nothing but sour. But within days of total ripening, not only do the sour notes disappear, but the entire melon begins to rot from the inside out."

Thyss yawned, making no effort to stifle or cover it, and Harpalo frowned.

"Do I bore you?"

"Yes," she stated bluntly. "This entire existence bores me. It is so… idyllic and perfect. What is life without strife, without contest, without the struggle against death?"

"Stay here long enough, you might find that you'll learn to live for other things."

"Bah," she spat to one side. "I have no interest in this. I intended to take my leave this afternoon, but perhaps I'll wait until tomorrow. I do hate the rain."

"And yet the rain helps give us life. Look around you," the towering hulk of a man motioned in a full circle around them. "Our river is death to drink. While I have never seen an ocean, I am told the river contains more salt than the oceans around Dulkur, and that certainly has its uses. We are fortunate that it rains often here, but we miss no chance to collect the water. The rain feeds our orchards, our crops, our livestock, as well as us. It's part of us.

"I know you to be Chosen of Hykan, but you surely know of the other gods. I don't pretend to understand the relationship you Highborns have with them, but have you ever felt the presence of the others? Were there any you felt as keenly as Hykan?" he asked.

Thyss sighed and placed her hands on her hips, her stance defiant as she replied, "Nykeema. Where are you going with this?"

"While the other villages are not as reliant on the rain as Calumbu, you would bring so much to our kingdom and way of life. Nykeema holds dominion over water, does she not? With one such as you amongst us, the people would never fret over water again."

Thyss blurted a guffaw in response as she looked around at the villagers engaged in their daily tasks, the same tasks they carried out at the same time every single day of their lives, and she pitied them. Returning her eyes to the towering Harpalo, she searched his hopeful face for just a moment and wanted to vomit as she came to a realization. She then broke out into haughty laughter, gasping out, “You are serious?”

His expression turned grim, almost sorrowful, as he nodded and waited for her to finish her mocking of him, his people, and their way of life. He nearly whispered, “I had hoped…”

“Hoped what?” Thyss queried, as she reined in her laughter. As she considered his words, a fire formed in her chest, shown in her eyes as she repeated, “Hoped what? Hoped that I, Thyss and Chosen of Hykan, would find your quaint, pathetic kingdom beautiful? Hoped that I could find joy in such a monotonous, tedious life? Hoped what? Hoped that perhaps I would stay, become your queen? Help you rule your tiny plot of land with a weak, open hand?”

“If that is what you wished,” Harpalo breathed almost inaudibly.

“What makes you think I could wish such a thing? I would as soon throw myself into a volcano or drown in the salt river. Look at yourself! You are strong and powerful. You could be a conqueror, truly rule a huge kingdom if you but put the land to the sword. But you would rather talk of peace, friendship, and some ‘way of life’ that runs counter to the laws of nature.”

Harpalo’s face hardened so that anyone idly glancing at the man might have mistaken him for a statue, an amazing work of art sculpted by the greatest of masters. When he spoke, his voice was no less made of granite. “Understand, Lady Thyss, I have no designs on you. I was wrong in thinking one such as you, Highborns,” he spoke the word with a venom that made Thyss' eyes narrow, "could accept what we've built here. In Calumbu, we are free. We live together, we help one another, and we are content. I realize now that you can never be more than what you are, and I apologize for thinking otherwise."

As he bowed his head slightly, Thyss accepted his words, quenching the fire burning in her soul before it consumed her, all though she still felt the hint of insult in them. Harpalo showed her proper deference befitting her place in the world as compared to his; after all, he was little more than a village chieftain of Lowborn peoples, and yet, some part of her felt as a child, apologized to by a parent who couldn't make their daughter understand some important lesson.

"Lady Thyss," Harpalo said formally after a moment of silence, the familiar tone having dissipated, "as you now intend to leave tomorrow, perhaps, you would attend my palace tonight?"

"Why?" Thyss asked, her voice low and suspicious.

"You have perhaps heard that I have guests arriving within the next few hours?"

"I have not."

"Very well," he said softly, "Paddo, a chieftain of a large village some fifty miles to our west will be here soon. He is… aggressive and offers war to anyone who comes near his lands. I invited him here to see the way we live, hoping he will join us."

"You expect a war chief to give up his sword and spear to live under your rule?" Thyss nearly giggled as she said it, the thought so absurd.

"Not under, with," Harpalo corrected. "Paddo is an intelligent man, and I believe he'll see the wisdom in this. That together, we can bring more into our way of life."

"Until your way of life grows beyond its means. Eventually, you will be crushed and enslaved by those who wield power you cannot combat."

"People like you?" Harpalo appealed with a raised brow, but his eyes held no challenge.

"People like my father and his rivals," Thyss explained. "I have no need for that way of life, either. Just boredom in another form."

This woman exasperated Harpalo to no end. She found contentment in nothing. He sighed again before continuing, "We ready the palace to make room for Paddo and fifty of his warriors –"

"Fifty!?" Thyss spouted. "Are you mad or just stupid? You invite this Paddo to your palace with fifty warriors?"

"In such politics, it is important that he feels safe and secure. It also shows our strength; it shows him that we're not afraid of him. Let him bring a hundred warriors, all of his warriors, and we will receive him with grace."

"By the gods, men are so stupid. You are always blinded by either your ideals or your wants," Thyss rasped, and she desired nothing more than to rattle off the stream of swears running through her head.

"Are you any different? Acting on whatever whim or desire burns within you at the moment?" Harpalo countered.

The flame returned, and Thyss felt it burning in her eyes as she looked on this man who dared to challenge her at the core of her being. That desire to burn rose up through her gut and into her chest, and she could almost hear the urgent, needing words of Hykan as they whispered, *"Do it! Burn him!"* into her mind. After a moment, she began to smile as she realized that, despite everything about Harpalo, his people and their lives not only disinterested her but in fact seemed to be an afront to the very nature of the world, he still had layers she had yet to peel back.

"I suppose I do owe you my life," Thyss said, ignoring the king's almost self-deprecatory shrug. "I will leave tomorrow, but tonight I will attend your court, King Harpalo, if only to be sure this Paddo does not cut you down in your own stupidity."

The squadron of warriors made for an impressive display, even Thyss had to admit. Their dark skin, so common to the peoples of Dulkur who oft endured blazing heat and brilliant sunlight, ran slick with rain as it blanketed the procession. Each wore a helm of bronze anointed with a trophy of some kind, usually the preserved head of some great animal that she easily recognized – crocodile or hippo – or the carapace of a giant insect. They marched in perfect step, mostly men but some women, fit muscles in arms and legs flexing with each step. They carried bronze tipped spears about seven foot in length in their right hands and a large oval shield in their left made of a black chitinous material that gleamed in the rain. On their left hip where it could be quickly drawn once the spear had been thrown or abandoned, each carried a bronze sword, not as strong as Thyss' own steel scimitar, but no less deadly. Bronze hauberks and loincloths of a black silk much like Nekala's own clothing completed their ensemble, and Thyss knew she looked upon a professional and well trained fighting force as they marched in unison, their bare feet slapping water and mud to the beat of two drummers behind the formation.

She wondered how many more like these the man at the head of the column had back in his home villages. He stood shorter than King Harpalo, under six feet tall and close to Thyss' own height, but he cut perhaps an even more imposing figure than his host. He marched nearly naked in front of his warriors, wearing only a loincloth, as if to challenge the gods and their elements themselves or to show how he cared not for the weapons of his enemies. The rippling iron thews of his arms led to massive shoulders that bulged larger than even those of her father's guards. The muscles of his chest, each as large as the melon she'd shared with Harpalo earlier in the day, overlooked two vertical rows of well-defined muscles on his abdomen, and the muscles and tendons of his thighs and calves undulated with each step. No one would mistake his warrior bearing with the hilts of two swords, one scimitar and one straight, western style longsword hanging from the leather belt about his hips, as well as the handle of a massive, double bladed labrys held onto his back by a thin brown strap.

Throngs of Calumbu's people gathered at the edges of the main avenue, some of whom had travelled from the other nearby villages to observe the moment, this meeting between kings such as they knew. Harpalo, perhaps ever the optimist, broke into a wide, friendly smile as the column of warriors came to a halt some ten feet away from the king as he stood in the main square. Thyss noted, however, that Harpalo's foolishness only extended so far, as she waited with the ten or so individuals of his own warriors he selected for this reception, and he had more stationed throughout the crowd. Paddo's sharp eyes missed none of them.

"Well met, Paddo!" Harpalo called as he approached with an open arm. "I am sorry the gods have chosen rain for this momentous occasion, but we shall ignore the portent and make the best of our time."

Paddo's face remained impassive as he watched the approach of the king, guarding his thoughts and intentions well. After a moment, he too stepped forward and smiled, but something in that leer reminded Thyss of the vicious grin of a lioness just before she took down her prey. Thyss tensed, ready for battle, as Paddo's arm lifted. Then he took Harpalo's arm in a firm grasp that appeared more a battle of wills than a greeting.

"We from Jiddal care nothing for the rain, Harpalo, or for any weather. We brave either rain or burning sands with bare feet and chests."

"Be that as it may," Harpalo responded, releasing the other's arm, "let us enter the palace to enjoy the dry, food, and drink while we discuss what the future holds for our two kingdoms? I am afraid that only five of your warriors will fit within."

"You expect me to enter your palace with only five of my warriors to protect me?" laughed Paddo, but his voice betrayed no humor. "You are more fool than I was led to believe."

"I am no fool, Paddo. I invited you here with only good intentions. I will join you with none of my warriors present, but a few of my servants, and one special guest. Bring five of your warriors and leave the rest here to see how my people live."

Paddo's eyes gleamed at the opportunity, the realization that he would have a great advantage, and he nodded, "Very well, Harpalo, but I will brook no deceit."

"There is none here," Harpalo replied with open hands. "Come, please."

The taller man turned, another show of trust at which Thyss mentally shook her head, and his warriors split into two rows to open a path to the palace's open doors. Harpalo, willfully ignoring any danger or concern, strode right between his warriors as Paddo warily followed, his eyes darting back and forth between the faces, hands, and weapons of Calumbu's people. Ten rows of five warriors each comprised his own column, and the first rank broke away to follow their leader. Thyss quietly filed in behind them.

The hall had been emptied of nearly everything, including Harpalo's own throne at his command so as not to appear aggressively dominant over the visitors. Several torches burned smokily on the walls to provide light that shifted and flared to show two rich furs had been laid out toward the center of the hall, separated by ten feet of empty floor, and Harpalo took his place sitting cross legged on that which was furthest from the door. Paddo took his place as his five warriors sat upon waiting skins arrayed in a semicircle behind their chieftain. Thyss meandered toward Harpalo's side of the hall and leaned casually against the wall.

"Who is the stranger, Harpalo," Paddo asked with a jutted chin.

"Lady Thyss, daughter of Mon'El."

"King Mon'El," Paddo gasped in recognition, but he quickly controlled his surprise. His eyes closed slightly, and his brow furrowed in suspicion. "And is her purpose here to show strength? That you have the backing of the god-king?"

"Lady Thyss is here only as my guest. She, too, does not understand the ways of Calumbu, and I hope our words together today will go further than just our kingdoms."

Paddo's eyes glanced back to Thyss in consideration of this, and upon seeing her yawn, he responded, "Very well. What do you have to say?"

Harpalo spoke long and easily, clearly much of it rehearsed over and over or even written down, as some of the villagers came and left through the hall's rear, bringing food and drink. They brought fish from the river, joints and haunches of game animals from the nearby jungle and plains, and refreshing melons. They brought the warriors cool water in earthenware jars to wash down the meat, and lesser amounts of liquor from the *palua* cactus to ease nerves.

The aroma of cooked flesh filled the room as the villagers came and went, and Thyss' stomach began to grumble against the backdrop of the tiresome droning of the host king. He spoke of how Calumbu spread from being one large village to a kingdom of nine all through his belief that people can work together to build rather than fight to destroy. He spoke of respect and fairness and freedom and various other high minded ideals that Thyss had seen firsthand but still she wasn't sure had any real value. He continued ceaselessly for an indeterminate amount of time that Thyss thought had to be days, but eventually Paddo's head began to nod in agreement.

"And Paddo, you are a man of great strength and greater will. Your people are strong and proud, and they have earned that. If you join Calumbu, we will all be stronger for it. We can forge bonds that others will admire, and they too will want to join us. We can all be free, and eventually, our way of life will spread throughout Dulkur, even freeing those under the god-kings, as you called them. Imagine, my friend, what the world can be!" Harpalo concluded.

Paddo ceased his nodding at Harpalo's words, and the two men held each other's gazes for a long moment. Paddo took a long draught of water from a jar and set it back on the floor before him before asking, "And… I would serve under you, King Harpalo?"

"I am King by the will of my people, Paddo. No one serves me. We all work for each other, and I am no exception. I believe you, as the greatest among all of our warriors, would lead them, to be used purely in defense of our people of course."

"Of course," Paddo agreed, but he said nothing else for a few moments. He raised his voice when he spoke again, "You're a man of high ideals, Harpalo, and a foolish one at that. Do you honestly believe that others will allow this great, free kingdom of yours? Even if I were to join you, how many others would do so? Either they would believe they can conquer us, or eventually we would grow too large and attract the attention of others. Kings like her father," Paddo said with a nod toward Thyss, "would crush and enslave us the moment our borders reached his. It is better to go unnoticed."

"Our people would never accept such," Harpalo argued. "It would cost him too much to keep us enslaved. Our people have tasted true freedom, cooperation, and love. No one can weed that out once it has taken root."

"The Highborns," Paddo almost spat as he said the word, and he turned his face fully toward Thyss, "have the powers of the gods. We have but witches and alchemists. Which God are you Chosen of?"

"The gods did not choose me. I chose Hykan," Thyss answered, an edge to her voice.

"And there you see the pride and arrogance of her people," Paddo said with a pointed look at Harpalo, causing Thyss to bristle. She wasn't offended, but she felt as if she should be as Paddo looked back to her and asked, "And with the powers of the fire god, could you not burn Harpalo's entire kingdom to the ground without the aid of warriors, soldiers, and horsemen?"

The question hung in the air for what seemed like minutes as Thyss mulled it over. She had no interest in letting these men her know her true power, or her limitations for that matter, but the voice of Hykan whispered in her brain. The few villagers in the hall stopped where they were, and all the assembled faces, even Harpalo's, turned to behold Thyss and await her answer.

The fire took hold, as did her steely will, and those present could almost see the conflagration burning in her black pupils wrapped by silvery irises.

"With Hykan's power, I can burn down the world," she almost whispered as a shiver of errant pleasure ran up her spine. Paddo's warriors murmured to each other, and a shudder went through more than one of Calumbu's villagers as they returned to their serving duties or left the hall to fetch more food or drink.

"Magnificent," Paddo leered with a wicked smile, his own eyes burning with admiration and lust instead of godly strength, "and yet Harpalo believes he can tame you, as he believes he can tame me."

"No man tames me," Thyss pushed away from the wall to stand defiantly with widespread feet.

"Nor should they," Paddo replied with a bowed head, and then he returned his attention to Harpalo, "but it still proves you to be a fool, King Harpalo. Even now as we eat and speak as civilized men, two hundred of my spearmen and women march into your west-most villages, killing your men and taking your women and children. Your pitiable fighters will stand no chance against mine. As we are hardened by war, you are softened by peace."

"Is it true?" Harpalo breathed, and again, time seemed to stop as he searched Paddo's face. The tension built with the silence, and Harpalo roared, "Betrayer!"

Paddo leapt to his feet in an instant with his sword in hand, as did his warriors. One of these shot out the door into the square beyond to give the signal to those awaiting outside. Of the other four, one grabbed a comely villager by the hair and dragged her screaming toward the door, while another chose to slaughter instead of enslaving, cutting through two of the servers with lightning speed, slashing blood across the floor and walls.

Thyss, having no intention to let a battle be joined without her, decided almost instantly on whose side she fought, because after all, Harpalo saved her life and showed kindness. While she still failed to understand the man, she showed her gratitude by lunging with her scimitar at the closest of Paddo's warriors – an ebon skinned beauty with iron cast thews so defined she could have been a magnificent work of art. The two women clashed, curved scimitars meeting and sliding down each other's edges to sprinkle sparks on the floor. The woman struck with strength beyond Thyss', and she had the raw speed of a great jungle cat. Thyss could hold the warrior off only so long.

Paddo reared back for a great strike meant to cleave the immense Harpalo right in two at the midsection, but he underestimated the impressive speed of the giant. Before he could bring the blade around, Harpalo closed the distance with two huge steps and placed one massive hand on the other's sword arm, the other around his neck. Paddo strained his sword arm but couldn't move against the larger man's iron hold. His thick neck resisting the crushing hand, he brought his free hand up in a wrecking blow to Harpalo's chin, whose head snapped backward as he released his grip. Paddo, seeing his opening, brought his own sword around in a wide arc, and the giant Harpalo only partially evaded its whistling blade.

The woman pushed Thyss back against the wall that she only moments ago leaned against casually, and the sorceress decided that a fair duel was not in her best interests. The woman closed in with a vicious white smile, preparing a fullisade of strikes that would likely end her Highborn opponent. Thyss took her eyes off her enemy for just a moment to focus, and the warrior stopped, scenting a wisp of smoke. She began to shout and scream as her loincloth burst into flame, and she dropped her sword to beat open palms on tender parts of her anatomy that were doubtless scorching under Thyss' horrific gaze. The woman realized too late that Thyss' blade cut through the air, cleaving through where her neck met her shoulder and all the way to her breastbone. Thyss' opponent gargled in shock, the light fading from her eyes, and Thyss kicked the lifeless body off her curved blade.

Harpalo grunted and grimaced as Paddo's scimitar sliced cleanly through his right side, under his ribcage. As blood poured freely from the wound, he could only hope the wound could be healed and none of his innards were permanently damaged. Paddo, in his haste, overextended his swiping attack, and Harpalo landed a massive fist against the side of the man's head. The fighting paused for just a moment when the cracking of bone accompanied that clubbing blow. Paddo went down, still conscious, but the man babbled incoherently and couldn't regain enough control over his limbs to stand back up.

Harpalo fell back a few steps, clutching at his wound, while two of Paddo's warriors lunged forward to retrieve their fallen chieftain, pulling him back toward the exit. The third and last remaining of those vicious fighters closed on Harpalo's retreating form, no doubt intent on taking the king's head as a trophy for his own advancement. Harpalo grew weak and stumbled backward to fall on his ass while trying to staunch his bleeding flank; he saw the attack coming, but he could do nothing to defend himself. As the warrior stood over him, relishing the moment of victory, a wall of flame suddenly burst from the now disheveled furs Harpalo had earlier knelt on, placed right between the king and his would be killer. Before the man could divine what happened, Thyss' scimitar took his left arm above the elbow, followed by a return stroke that cleaved his head from his neck. The head tumbled forward and bounced into the flames as the body fell backward to the floor and poured its blood in a great pool from the stump of its neck.

Thyss dismissed the flames and took a quick scan of the hall. Blood and the dead littered the room, but there were no more enemies to kill. Paddo's people fled as their leader fell. She turned toward Harpalo to find the man lying in a spreading pool of his own dark vitae, but already several villagers attended him, pressing linens and anything thing could find to his garish wound.

"Nekala! Go find Nekala!" one shrieked at another, a young girl of no more than twelve, and the girl nodded wordlessly before running from the hall.

Thyss rushed to Harpalo's side and said, "You are bleeding to death. You will be dead before Nekala arrives. I can stop it."

Harpalo caught Thyss' silver eyes and held the gaze while he hastily weighed his options, and he had seen enough terrible traumas in his life to know she was correct. Paddo meant his blade to cut the king completely in half, and only the king's quickness prevented that from happening. Even still, the bronze sword cut deeply, and he knew he had but moments to live. He nodded gravely.

"This will hurt," she warned, and then she looked to the girl holding blood soaked linens against the king's wound, "Find something he can bite down on. Quickly."

The girl was gone mere seconds before returning with a leather sword belt from the last man Thyss felled, and the sorceress nodded her approval as the girl shoved it into the king's mouth. Harpalo bit down hard and nodded his readiness as Thyss bent to her work. She was no surgeon to be sure, but she knew enough about the body from her various melees. Gently, she separated the cut flesh away from itself, the huge man squirming and grunting in pain as her hands grew slick with his blood. She found no cleaved entrails or other organs, but copious amounts of blood poured from the wound. She focused her attention as far into the gash as she could see, Harpalo groaning, and then the stench of burnt flesh accompanied wisps of smoke as Thyss called upon Hykan, God of Fire, to cauterize rent flesh. Harpalo, to his credit, bore the pain well, letting out no screams or shouts despite being in great agony.

"Bind him," she commanded the girl. "It's the best I can offer, but he should have time now."

Harpalo yanked the leather belt from his mouth, his eyes still locked on Thyss, and growled, "See to the people."

Thyss jumped to her feet and headed for the hall's main door without question or hesitation; curious that. Throughout her entire life, even as a young child, she often defied commands or expectations with her initial reaction. Sometimes she gave in after she thought better of it, but often she continued to resist anyone who would put their will above hers. As daughter of a great king, she got away with such behavior, except when it challenged the king himself.

As she reached the door, it burst inward and the girl sent in search of Nekala shouted, "Nekala is gone! They took her!"

"What?" Harpalo queried, the weakness in his voice spreading throughout his body.

"They took her!" the girl repeated. "Along with ten or twelve others!"

"Who is there to help him?" Thyss asked, pointing at the prone king.

"Déré is on the way."

"Déré is here," boomed a deep, gravelly voice as a tall, gaunt man in leather leggings entered behind her. "I will see to the king."

"See to the people," Harpalo again called to Thyss, and she nodded before heading into the village square.

7.

Paddo's force killed twenty seven of Calumbu's people, including fifteen warriors and twelve others, some of whom tried to flee. They struck before the defenders could free themselves from the crowds and fought and killed with cold precision. Amongst those killed was a ten year old boy who showed enough bravery to pick up a fallen spear and attempt to fight back. When Paddo fled the palace, held up by two of his men, he called for his people to take what they could quickly grab and make their way out of the village. They were last seen heading west into the jungle, having taken eleven of Calumbu's women and children kicking and screaming with them, including the healer Nekala. Calumbu managed to fell but seven of Paddo's warriors, including the two Thyss herself killed. All this Thyss told Harpalo less than an hour after the battle as he looked on gravely, flinching and grimacing in pain under the ministrations of the healer Déré.

A handful of his own warriors stood arrayed about King Harpalo, and he looked to one as he spoke slowly, slightly drugged, "We must go after them, get our people back. Prepare my weapons and armor."

"You're going nowhere, sir," Déré murmured as he attended the wound. "Had Lady Thyss not acted quickly, you would already be dead."

"Then it is up to you," Harpalo slurred at his fighters. "You must catch Paddo before he reunites with his army."

"We will need all of Calumbu's warriors, and it will take too long to assemble them from all the villages," argued one.

"We have but twenty here," agreed another.

"Then we wait, and it is war with Paddo, then," Harpalo groaned. "I did not want this."

"No," Thyss shook her head, "We go now while we can. Twenty can move faster than forty, especially forty with some wounded and who fight with or carry unwilling captives along the way."

"Who will lead?" Harpalo asked.

Thyss responded without hesitation, headstrong and sure, "I will."

The warriors thundered over each other in disbelief and dismay with shouted questions and exclamations such as, "We cannot trust her! She is an outsider! I'll not follow her!"

Harpalo locked eyes with Thyss, summoning every ounce of his strength to remain conscious, and then roared over the indignant fighters, "Enough! Silence!"

"Damn it, my king," Déré whispered as he rocked back from his stitching, "you've opened the wound again."

Ignoring him, the mountain of a man questioned Thyss quietly, "Why would you do this?"

"They took Nekala, and she looked after me, helped me get well again. I will not see her be a breeding slave to one of Paddo's dogs," she replied, spitting to the side. "We can move much faster than they, perhaps even catch up to them within an hour."

"He needs rest," Déré told the assembly as he restitched the king's wound.

"Go quickly, then. If they left by way of the western jungle, they will not have gone more than a few miles. Go with her, and follow her commands as you would mine," Harpalo said to his people, his eyelids growing heavy with the sustained effort, and then his head slumped backward as sleep overtook him.

"The king has spoken," said one female warrior, looking around at the misgivings plain on the others faces.

"Come," Thyss ordered, and she turned to leave the hall not bothering to see if the warriors followed her.

Outside, the rain fell without remorse, seeming to bite into flesh with tiny pellets of water propelled at terrific speed. Blood still mingled with the muddy water throughout the village square, having not yet washed away by the storm that threatened overhead with additional thunder. A score of Harpalo's warriors, far less impressive than the fighting force Paddo brought into Calumbu, waited in a semicircle outside of the palace, perhaps expecting their king to emerge and command them. The other villagers had retreated to their homes, some to dress minor wounds and others to mourn.

Thyss glanced around, noticed that she had been followed outside and raised her voice to be heard over the storm, "We are going after them. We must move swiftly, so bring nothing to weigh you down. No armor, no food, a small skin of water, your sword, and one javelin. Our only chance is to catch up to them quickly and strike from behind."

"We have a chance some six miles out," said a voice behind her. Thyss turned around to find the warrioress she had dueled with several days before. She matched Thyss in height, a few inches under six feet, and she had the deep ebony skin and dark eyes of most of Calumbu's inhabitants. Thyss' eyes flared in recognition, first in anger but then in the understanding that she could count on this woman.

"I fought you. I do not remember your name."

"N'tuli."

"And what is this chance you speak of?"

"The river," N'tuli explained, all eyes having turned to her, "bends to the south some six miles out. It is a barren patch of ground, very open, as the salt in the river allows nothing to grow there. Paddo will have to ford it to continue westward."

"Difficult with wounded and slaves in tow," Thyss nodded, and a plan started to form in her mind. "Very good. Do we have any liquid that burns? Oil perhaps?"

"We have precious little oil," a well-muscled man to the left answered, "but *palua* water burns easy enough."

She turned to him, "You look strong, but does your endurance match?"

"What did you have in mind?" the large man asked with raised eyebrows and an insinuating smile, and his cohorts either guffawed loudly or rolled their eyes, each reaction defined largely by the gender of the individual.

"Can you carry a cask or barrel of the *palua* water for several miles without tiring?" Thyss asked, pointedly ignoring the implication toward inuendo.

"Easily," he nodded, dispelling his good humor.

"Then fetch it quickly," she demanded, and without even being sure he obeyed, she turned and asked the rest, "Who is both the fastest and stealthiest among us?"

"I," responded N'tuli.

"You can track?" asked Thyss, receiving a solemn nod. "Then go now and follow them. Go as fast as you can but be quiet about it. We will be coming behind you in but a few moments. If you see sign that they have changed direction, come back to me, and do not approach if you happen to catch up to them. Am I clear?"

"Yes, lady. At once," N'tuli half bowed with a hand on her short scimitar, turned, and sprinted down the western avenue, her feet splashing in the rain and mud.

The huge warrior strode up one of the alleys toward the square with several heavy waterskins slung about him.

He called, "I could only find these, but each is two stones worth. Will that do?"

"It will do," Thyss replied.

"But how will you light it?" he asked as he returned to the semicircle of waiting warriors, one hand held aloft toward the rain.

"You needn't worry about that."

"Ah, yes," he mused, "Highborn magic."

The image of this man tossing a scimitar to N'tuli flashed through Thyss' mind, and she turned to address them all again, "Remember – your sword, a javelin, some water, and that is all. We move quickly!"

The eyes of Calumbu's people tracked the tiny contingent as they made their way out, following the light tracks of N'tuli and the hard beaten path created by Paddo and his warriors. Within minutes, they entered the western jungle, a rolling expanse of green inferno as far as the eyes could see. At least the canopy protected them from the falling rain, and the storm thundered overhead as loudly as it would have under any roof. The air hung thick and hard to breathe with steamy moisture. Moments after entering, Thyss felt as if a thousand ants crawled along her back, an anxiety driven by that most primal instinct of the hunted being watched by the hunter, but she dismissed it to focus on the task at hand. Her recent experience in the great, northern jungle seemed to have inflicted scars invisible to the eye but there, nonetheless.

As expected, the squad moved with ease through the jungle growth without heavy armor and provisions to weigh them down. Their front spread five warriors wide with four or five feet between each, and Thyss stayed in the middle of the front row. For the first mile, even Thyss easily tracked the path of Paddo's troops, as the ground level foliage and ferns crowded the jungle thickly, but the enemies crushed a wide swathe of them underfoot in their retreat from Calumbu. Then smaller plants thinned out to leave nothing but grass and moss, a few vines, and scant ferns, and they slowed their pace, having to carefully look for a snapped twig here, a displaced log there, or perhaps a ruffled patch of fallen leaves.

Thyss mentally tallied that they traversed four miles in the first hour, and only a few minutes after that they saw N'tuli's fit form emerge from behind a scorched tree that had fallen some time recently, its trunk and root system wrenching a giant, round clod of dirt and clay to make a crater in the ground. The young woman approached with cool confidence, almost a swagger in her step that Thyss appreciated, and the fire sorceress called for a halt.

"I was correct, Lady," N'tuli stated flatly. "Paddo and his men await on the riverbank. I crept as close as I dared, but it sounds like he expects his host to be here within a few hours. He plans to wait until they arrive. We have little time."

"Indeed. How far?"

"Just about a mile. They seem to have stopped for," N'tuli paused as if she searched for the applicable word, but she finally settled on, "recreation."

"I'll cleave every one of them myself," grumbled the giantish warrior, whom Thyss learned to be named Da'irda.

"Peace," said another.

Thyss herself shared his outrage, and for just a moment, all of those gathered around her felt a wave of heat wash over them, and what few raindrops made it through the canopy to the ground below, sizzled and burned away when they touched her. After a few seconds, she regained control of her emotions, and she agreed, "It does us no good to rush in there. They outnumber us two to one. Did they post guards?"

N'tuli nodded as she knelt to the forest floor and began to draw lines and other marks in the dirt with her fingers, dislodging ants and other tiny vermin. "Yes, this is the river, and it's about thirty feet from the water to the edge of the jungle. They've taken an area almost fifty feet across on the riverbank and posted sentries here, here, and here. But," she added softly, "the guards have already lost interest in watching the jungle."

Thyss nodded, "Perfect. N'tuli, take the *palua* water from Da'irda. Go ahead of us again and apply as much of it as thickly as you can at the edge of the jungle near their camp in a line as long. Is that clear? Then wait in the brush at the southern end of your work while we approach.

"Da'irda," Thyss stood from her kneeling position next to N'tuli, "how is your throwing arm?"

"Strong. And accurate."

"Good, take the nine best hurlers and all the javelins. That should give you two each. You will wait at the northern edge of N'tuli's line."

"Wait for wait?" he grumbled.

"For the fire," Thyss' entire face broke into a wicked smile.

He repeated his question from some time ago with a tilt of his head, "You can light the fire in the rain?"

"Hykan gives me strength. I can light it easily enough, but I cannot maintain such a lengthy blaze for long."

"The *palua*," N'tuli nodded in understanding.

"If our foes are properly… distracted," Thyss hissed venomously, "they will not notice the fire right away. When the alarm goes out, my group on the southern edge will come out onto the riverbank. A small force, they will come at us immediately and with abandon. I can protect us for a few moments. That is when you, Da'irda, and your group emerge from the jungle behind them and throw your javelins. Paddo will have no choice but to turn about and engage you. N'tuli, when you see this, signal me. I will then lead my group into their rear. We will crush Paddo from both sides."

"A fine plan," N'tuli agreed. "Let's to it."

"We could kill our own people with the javelins," worried Da'irda.

"Then do not miss," N'tuli shot at him, but the lopsided smile she carried took any sting from the words.

The tiny host split into their two groups, and then followed the vanished form of N'tuli deeper into the jungle. Before long they heard the rush of water, somewhat muffled by the distance, foliage, or both, and Thyss knew they approached the river. They slowed their advance somewhat, worried that every slight footfall or crack of a twig underfoot would alert their quarry. Thyss spied N'tuli lying on the ground up ahead and to the left, so she motioned for the groups to split and go their separate ways, keeping low and silent with N'tuli motioning to Da'irda to indicate where to stop his group of javelin throwers.

From the look and sound of things, stealth was unnecessary, however. Thyss saw no sentries, as they had clearly joined in the revelry, and grunts and moans of pleasure mingled with the whimpers and cries of pain and sorrow. A bonfire burned in the middle of the warriors as they fucked one another, raped and tortured their newfound slaves, and laughed raucously at their idea of merriment. Even Paddo's female warriors seemed to take delight in all of this, and Thyss felt her stomach churn with disgust. Try as she might, she could not lay eyes on Nekala amidst the debauchery.

Thyss waited until N'tuli nodded in the affirmative that Da'irda and his retinue were in position before she sought out the trail of *palua* water. Despite the rainfall of the stormy day, she picked out the wetness of the *palua*, as it differed in shine from ordinary water, and the two did not mingle. N'tuli had done her work well – the line Thyss had asked for was over a foot in width, and she even managed to pour it down the trunks of several of the jungle's trees. It would make a glorious display. Thyss stared at the band of *palua* wetted foliage, but in her mind, she focused as she envisioned the entire strip. Concentrating, a slight snap and hiss sounded in the air as small flames, undulating in height from one to two inches, erupted from thin air. The almost pure alcohol of the *palua* ignited, and the flames hissed and smoked as they encountered wetness from the storm. But powered by her god's favor, Thyss' flames overcame the dampness and began to grow and smoke. It grew quickly, fire raged down the edge of the jungle with flames two or even three feet high, clouds of gray and black smoke lifting into the air before the first shouts of, "Ho, there!" and, "Fire!" carried from the riverbank.

Thyss drew her scimitar from her belt, and as her small contingent of warriors did the same, she lifted her head slowly, breathed a brief prayer to Hykan, and said, "Now."

She and her nine warriors emerged from the jungle on the southern flank of Paddo's encampment, shouting challenges and insults to their befuddled enemies. Confusion reigned in the small camp as men and women disengaged from merriment and torture and awaited orders regarding the fire. The sudden appearance of Thyss and her fighters caused many to draw steel or reach for their sword belts, though many had been discarded in the revelry. Paddo materialized from the center of the buzzing encampment, a great bruise forming on the side of his face where Harpalo punched him (a blow that would have killed many lesser men).

He shouted, "Kill them! Except the bitch Highborn! She's mine!"

Their leader's voice brought order to the chaos, and they formed neatly into ranks, some of them still stark naked from various activities. They charged Thyss' position some twenty feet or so away from the bonfire. The onslaught came with terrible alacrity, and Thyss dared not wait. She placed her attention on the ground only a few feet in front of her, lowered her sword arm and seemed to proffer her free hand to her enemies, palm up and fingers extended. They felt the heat just before the yellow flames burst from the barren ground of the riverbank in a wall of fiery death.

Though Thyss couldn't see it through the conflagration, Paddo and his troops skidded to a halt in the salt ridden black dirt but not quickly enough. One tried to stop in time but failed, and another, knowing her momentum would carry her too far forward, propelled herself bodily with a powerful jump. The first came through screaming and engulfed, while the second landed in a somersault, hair singed and eyelashes gone but no worse for wear. Thyss' warriors stood still in shock and awe at the power they witnessed, but they shook it off to slaughter these two.

And then cries of anger and disorientation rang through the air as Da'irda, at N'tuli's called signal, charged from the jungle with his crew and loosed their first volley of missiles. Though the flames blocked Thyss' view, and even if they hadn't she couldn't take her attention away from maintaining them, she heard death screams and the telltale sound of weapons piercing flesh.

All heard Paddo bellow, "Turnabout! Behind us!" as he rallied his fighters the opposite way despite the second round of javelins that rained into their midst.

Thyss weakened. Creating flames, even massive infernos, for just an instant was one thing, but maintaining such a large continuous fire sapped her strength. She whispered, "Hykan, I beg you, just a moment longer," beseeching her patron god for whatever strength He would lend His death dealing fire priestess. Sweat from the effort poured off her brow, soaking her woolen tunic more than the climate ever could, and her limbs shook from the effort.

"Tis time, Lady Thyss!" called N'tuli, and Thyss went slack as she expelled a massive held breath. She dropped her hand, and the giant wall of flame dispelled with it. Her hands fell to her knees, and she gasped for breath as her followers charged headlong at the rear of their enemy. They screamed terrific war cries as bronze scimitars flashed in the guttering light of the bonfire. Men and women screamed in pain and fright, suddenly beset on both sides by enemies after losing no less than a dozen to the javelins. Even N'tuli herself joined the charge, tired of being scout and tracker, ready for her sword to drink the blood of those who assaulted her home and king.

The battle ended in minutes, just as Thyss regained a modicum of strength and sauntered toward the battle. The constant misdirection and assault weakened the defenders in both morale and fighting ability, and without their armor, they fell quickly to Calumbu's warriors. The last four alive threw down their weapons, refusing to keep fighting, and Da'irda unceremoniously slew one of them anyway. Thyss passed Paddo on the ground, still alive, but a javelin pierced through the thick muscles around his midsection, a fatal wound to be sure if left untreated. She kicked dirt in his face as she passed.

Thyss glanced over her warriors, finding she'd lost but four, but she had more interest in searching the faces of those they'd recovered. After all, warriors died in combat; it was the way of such things, but this pursuit and battle had been about revenge and retrieving those Paddo had taken. As she gazed round, she saw the tear streaked faces and naked, beaten bodies of women and children, but she did not see Nekala.

And then she stopped in her tracks, her eyes alighting on a still form, laying naked and face down in the dirt near the fire with a pile of black, silken garments at her side. She hesitantly stepped toward the body, knowing what she would find but beseeching Hykan for it not to be so. She knelt on the riverbank, her knees sinking down into sodden black dirt as she gently pulled the naked woman over by the shoulder. Nekala's face serenely shone back at her, eyes and mouth closed in peace. A wicked slash ran across her throat from ear to ear.

"She was the bravest of us," called a sobbing woman from behind Thyss. "As one of them took her, she pretended to… then she gouged out his eyes with her thumbs."

Thyss ran her hand over Nekala's shorn hair, almost lovingly. She had no explanation for why she did it, except this woman, as had Harpalo, shown her care and kindness when so many others would have given terror and pain. As thunder continued to rumble overhead and rain fell to mix with the blood of the battlefield and rinse it into the river, Thyss realized that maybe Nekala was to her what people called a friend. It was something she'd never had or understood.

A tortured laugh from somewhere behind her broke her from these thoughts, and she was back on her feet in an instant. She turned to see Paddo lying twenty feet away, and despite being in obvious pain with his hands wrapped around the shaft penetrating his gut, he chuckled. She stormed toward him, the fires of Hell burning in her eyes, every nerve alight with intense hatred for this man and desire for what needed to be done.

Paddo coughed, blood flecking his lips, as he taunted, "She was brave, but bravery is stupid if it gets you killed. She died like a slaughtered pig."

Thyss towered over him, listening to his gargling mirth, and without any warning, she reached out and grasped the end of the javelin's shaft, pushing it down toward the ground. Paddo screamed in furious agony as his body writhed and wriggled like a worm subjected to flame, but she was not to be satisfied with just that. She pushed forward on the javelin, forcing the shaft toward an upright position, and then she grasped it with both hands and pulled downward against it with all her weight. The chieftain could do nothing but issue tortured wailings as the javelin's point, buried in his abdomen, severed tendons, and mixed torn entrails. She continued at this for several seconds, filling the jungle with Paddo's cries before a soft hand pulled on her shoulder gently. Thyss wheeled, sword high, to find N'tuli standing there with tears running down her cheeks.

"It is enough, Lady Thyss. You will not bring Nekala back with this," N'tuli intoned.

"No," Thyss agreed, "but she may rest easier."

With that, Thyss turned faster than a flash of lightning, bringing her scimitar down in the rain, and cleaved Paddo's head in twain from its crown to his neck. She ripped the weapon free, ignoring the blood and bits of brain and skull, and returned it to her belt as she herself returned to the body of Nekala. Thyss squatted down and struggled to scoop the woman, her equal in size if not weight, into her arms. She then groaned and strained to stand, the body lovingly cradled in her arms.

Da'irda strode toward Thyss, the firelight playing over his grim features and hard muscles, and he reached his arms forward under Nekala's limp form. "Let me."

"No!" Thyss shouted as she stepped and turned away. She then brushed past him, still carrying Nekala as she headed up the sloping riverbank for the smoking jungle. The fire had burned itself out against all the wet rain and plants, especially with no more alcohol from the *palua* cactus to fuel it. The people of Calumbu watched as she merged into the scorched greenery.

"Collect our dead," said N'tuli as she rejoined Da'irda, still watching the retreating form of the Highborn sorceress. She reached down to retrieve Nekala's discarded silken clothing from their pile and added, "and salvage any weapons and armor we can carry. Leave their dead to rot."

8.

"You still don't understand, do you?" questioned an exhausted Harpalo from his bed of furs and linens, his side a great mass of bandages that needed to be changed every few hours. "Even if I could lead, we do not conquer others."

"But now is your opportunity," Thyss argued. "Paddo's people are scattered and disorganized. They do not know what to do next. How long before someone strong takes control and chooses revenge instead of peace?"

Harpalo did not move as he considered this with closed eyes, sprawled as comfortably as he could make himself. When Thyss and her company returned, the king slept soundly and was not expected to wake for a long while due to the wound, the loss of blood, and the drugging ministrations of Déré. Truly, the man only regained consciousness about two hours after sunrise the next morning, and Thyss relayed everything that happened at the battle, including the losses. He bore those gravely.

Opening his eyes, he replied, "We do not make war on others. It is against our way. I will send emissaries offering peace and cooperation."

Thyss snorted and rolled her eyes. "They'll be killed, their heads sent back to you in sacks."

"I pray not."

"And to what gods do you pray, Harpalo?" Thyss asked more viciously than she intended. "Our gods here in Dulkur are elemental. They are forces of nature, and such things do as they will. My will reflects that of Hykan, and I *am* his avatar in this land. We have no gods that favor weakness and peace."

"You think highly of yourself, Lady," Harpalo responded, receiving a withering, blazing glare in response. "What of Nykeema? Is she not wise and calm? Is peace not aligned with both?"

"Perhaps, until she summons a tsunami a hundred feet tall to destroy the coastal city that blasphemes against her."

Harpalo sighed, "There is no point discussing such things with you. So young, yet so set. Unable to see beyond your own will and desires."

"Caution, King Harpalo."

Harpalo paused as he closed his eyes and took a deep, cleansing breath. At the inhalation's peak, a twinge of pain shot through his side, and he coughed as he released it. He took several shallow breaths as he regained control of his body, adjusting his torso to put less pressure on the garish wound that had begun, again, to seep blood through the linen bandaging. Thyss' eyes narrowed on the sluggishly expanding red stain and wondered.

"Worry not," Harpalo waived her gaze away, "I will recover, but it will be slow. For now, Déré tells me that I mustn't move and to drink as much water as possible."

He switched topics away from his health, "I apologize for offending you. You are whom the gods made you, whom you made yourself. I ask, do you intend to stay any longer?"

"I will, for a short time. I wish to pay my respects to the dead at the pyres tonight," Thyss explained, holding back the name of the one person amongst the dead she knew, and Harpalo's eyes showed their understanding. "Also, it would not do to leave Calumbu when its king is ill equipped to help defend it. A couple of weeks, perhaps, as you regain your health?"

"You have my thanks for that," Harpalo breathed softly, his strength ebbing again as his eyelids grew heavy, "and my thanks for saving my life and rescuing my people. There is one other thing – a parcel for you. There."

As the colossal man finished his words, he had the energy to lift but a single finger to point where he indicated. The finger dropped, and soft snores emanated from him as his chest rose and fell with his gentle breathing. Thyss' eyes rested on a rectangle of white linen folded about something dark with twine tied around it to keep the parcel together. She worked the knots open and pulled the twine away, reservation building in her fingers as she considered what could be inside. She unfolded the linen tentatively, first to the left, then to the right, as a black fabric shone through the thin white linen.

Her hands trembled as she lifted a black silk garment, shining in the flickering torchlight of Harpalo's hall with veins of silvery steel weaved throughout. It would fit her, somewhat form fittingly perhaps, she thought as she held the tunic before her. Another article still lay amongst the linen which Thyss knew to be a set of leggings. She gathered them into her arms, almost lovingly, as she shot the sleeping figure one last, long look before leaving the hall.

Thyss wished she had a large mirror as she stalked her way to the large square outside the palace, but she doubted one existed within the entirety of Calumbu. She wore Nekala's silken tunic and leggings to honor the woman, though they didn't fit quite right. The silk hugged her torso and chest, accentuating both the attributes that men's gazes tended to linger on as well as her fit form. On

Nekala, the material had come over the shoulders and covered her arms just a bit, but Thyss' upper arms stayed completely bare. She thought she liked the effect. The leggings, so tight and yet so pliable, felt almost like a second skin and due to Thyss' larger height stopped just at the end of her calf muscles. She laced her sandals around her ankles and lower leg to complete the ensemble, and eyes followed her throughout Calumbu. Though Thyss usually ignored the stares and scrutiny of lessers, she now bathed in them as the sun sank its way into the west.

She arrived at the main square, finding it empty of the usual stalls, shacks, and tents that populated the area. A crowd had formed already, at least several hundred people, and she knew that soon the area would be so packed with onlookers and mourners that none of them would be able to breathe without inhaling the stench of humanity. A huge wooden pallet, really just a collection of dried sticks consumed most of the square's center, and upon it lay the bodies of thirty of Calumbu's people, all cut down by Paddo and his warriors. Green leaves over a foot long swaddled the dead in their repost, weaved together to bind them tightly, and each corpse lay on a layer of the same. The scent of *palua* filled the air.

As she began to move around the perimeter of the pyre, Thyss spied Harpalo on the far side near the entrance to the palace, and two burly fighters, Da'irda and another she didn't know, flanked him to either side as he sat upon a high backed wooden chair. She strode purposefully toward him, and as she drew close, Thyss nearly gasped at the sight of him. A mountain of a man when on his own two feet, Harpalo's massive thews looked almost sagging and deflated. Unable to sit upright, he slumped in the chair with his legs stretched out before him, rolled woolen blankets supporting the angle of his back. His countenance was drawn, his pallor ashen, and great purple rings under his eyes stood out from the darkness of his skin. Even with all of that, he smiled as she approached.

"I would stand, Lady Thyss, if I could," he wheezed, and even these few words consumed most of his strength.

"It is nothing, King Harpalo," she shrugged, waiving away his words with one hand.

"Is that a modicum of respect for us I hear?' Harpalo queried with a weak smile. His eyes roamed up and down, from her head to her toes and back again, and with continued effort he said, "Nekala's attire suits you well."

"Attend to your lecherous eyes before I pluck them from your skull," Thyss retorted with the slightest of smiles, and there was no threat of violence in either her eyes or tone.

"My apologies, Lady," he said, returning the smile, and with a sigh, he settled his head back against the chair to watch his people arrive.

She gently laid a hand on his thick forearm, leaving it there for a long moment before patting it once, and Thyss moved past him, receiving a respectful nod from Da'irda. N'tuli emerged from the assembling crowd and joined Thyss to stand silently facing the soon to be funeral pyre. The woman had covered her jerkin and skins with a black tar or dye and had used the same to paint her eyelids black as night. Two trails of the dye traversed her cheeks downward in a semblance of tears that Thyss could barely make out against her dark skin in the failing sunlight. Once the horizon consumed the sun to bring night, only the whites of N'tuli's eyes would be visible. She would be a ghost in the darkness.

"You honor Nekala," N'tuli said, her voice almost a whisper, and she stared unblinking across the pyre and the dead.

“She was,” Thyss paused as she searched for a word she so rarely used, “kind to me.”

“We all loved her. You would have come to as well.”

“What are the leaves?” Thyss asked with a slight nod at the pyre.

“We gather them in the jungle. When burned, their smoke smells sweet.”

“It covers the stench,” Thyss nodded in understanding.

“We wish the trip to the afterlife to be as pleasant as possible, not amidst the horrors of burning flesh.”

N’tuli sounded as if she had nothing else to say, and Thyss fell respectfully silent. Her eyes roamed over the wrapped bodies of the dead, and she finally settled on the one she knew to be Nekala. Emotions swirled in her heart like a maelstrom. First came furious anger and the fire of hatred that always accompanied it, and Thyss fought to control it. After all, she had already defeated the men who had done this. She’d killed their leader himself, causing him great pain before splitting his skull, and that brought a tingling warmth. Satisfaction flowed through her limbs, but as she stood looking at the still form of Nekala, a sickness entered her gut. Her heart almost seemed to ache, and Thyss couldn’t understand what it meant. Even if she wanted to turn to N’tuli to explain it, she doubted that she could make any sense of it.

The mudbrick buildings of Calumbu cast long shadows across the square, as the sun died in the west, its final rays touching the sky. Torches around the square were lit, their flames catching and flickering smokily in the breeze. The people of Calumbu choked the square and all the streets and narrow alleys around it, and they had even climbed atop all the nearby homes or workshops for a better view. The silence was almost deafening in and of itself, but for the occasional cries or mourning wails of a mother for her son, brothers and sisters for their fallen siblings.

Harpalo softly cleared his throat. He wanted to speak, his eyes deep wells of sorrow for his people, dead and living alike, but he lacked the strength to speak. Thyss wanted to go to him then, somehow lend him the strength he needed, a thought she'd never had about anyone, but she let the moment linger. Finally, Harpalo nodded to Da'irda, and the warrior who stood naked but for a loincloth took a torch from its sconce and approached the pyre. He held it down to light the edge of the pyre, treated as it no doubt was with *palua* before he tossed it toward the middle of the pyre.

Thyss glanced around the square and found others did the same, and within minutes, a warm, blazing inferno filled the square, flames engulfing the still silhouettes of the dead within it. A musty sweetness permeated the air, a gentle and innocent scent that somehow evoked a further sense of sadness when Thyss inhaled it, and under the scent of the burning leaves was something sicklier akin to the cooking of meat but wrong. Thyss lowered her head in a silent prayer, begging Hykan and Aeyu to ease the suffering of the dead and help their souls find peace as a lone tear hotly streaked its way down her cheek.

9.

The city of Kaimpur lay nestled in a curved bend of the River Thyss as its calm waters flowed gently from the northeast to the southwest through plains made fertile by its bounty. Late afternoon sunlight gazed lazily from the west, and the entire city glowed with a saffron light as it struck the stone common to the eastern quarries. Farms once lined the riverbank, but these had vanished long ago, replaced by docks, markets, and massive warehouses that serviced the river galleys and triremes that brought trade from other cities. Wide avenues crisscrossed the city between thousands of stone buildings that served as the homes and businesses for its denizens, and a dozen pyramids of the priests that once vied for power rose above these, dominating the section of the city they once controlled. One marvelous structure stood out from and dwarfed them all, the great stepped pyramid of the kingpriest known as Mon'El, the one who united (or destroyed as they preferred) the priests of Kaimpur and now ruled for a hundred miles in every direction. The yellow stone had been sheathed entirely in lapis lazuli, gold, and silver, a testament to the unprecedented prosperity he brought to the city, and it stood as a beacon to all those he ruled. Some said it could be seen from across the entire continent of Dulkur.

A procession of some twenty persons marched gloriously into the city of Kaimpur on the western road, the bright afternoon sun illuminating them from behind. The sunlight gleamed off vast amounts of cloth of gold and matching adornments, making it obvious to the Lowborn citizenry that a king walked among them. Of course, the entire city knew about the coming of King Kerim and his son, the prince Kerim'El, and they received him with prostrated forms as he passed and cheers after he had gone by. All of Kaimpur knew the importance of his visit, having whispered about the coming nuptials for weeks.

The king and his son each sat upon a thronelike chair crafted from acacia, carved into the likeness of a giant, almost humanoid serpent with smaller snakes for appendages. Gold leaf adorned each throne, and four hulking servants (bodyguards by the curved swords on their belts) carried each the king and his son. Were he stripped of his wealth, most onlookers would be unimpressed by King Kerim. He stood under six feet, and a once narrow but thin frame now carried much excess weight from years of good living, which was obvious to all who watched for he went bare chested. He wore gold plated metal legguards and armguards, impressive to look upon but ill-suited to combat, and most knew the king had won his impressive lands through political maneuvers and well timed investments of wealth. A heavy crown of gold encrusted with numerous jewels of incalculable wealth sat upon his head.

His son, Kerim'El, on the other hand boasted of youthful vigor. Strong and fit, his body bespoke of one who had physically trained his entire life. He picked up the sword at only four and learned to hurl spears as young as seven. The bow, the lance, and the horse all made his repertoire, and it was known that he often chose to compete in the brutal horse sports of the Kujari desert nomads. As his men carried him through Kaimpur, he stared straight ahead, not deigning to look upon any of those below him.

While King Kerim and his son both carried the bronze skin common to the rulers of Dulkur, it was widely whispered that neither had been Chosen by the gods, and that rumor was evidenced by the deep brown eyes that had never changed to silver. They ruled through a different kind of power than Mon'El of Kaimpur.

The eight hulking bearers carried the king and his son steadily down Kaimpur's main avenue, the Road of the Kingpriest, toward Mon'El's enormous palace pyramid, and their faces barely registered any discomfort at all as their iron thews bulged with the effort. Just like their king, they wore gold plated guards on their legs and arms, but no one doubted their proficiency with the steel scimitars at their waists. Twelve persons kept pace behind the warriors, their heads slightly bowed in silent submission to their liege despite the celebration of their arrival. The first two men wore the robes and tall hats of advisors or viziers. Ten young men and women dressed in cloth of gold or scantily clad in silks trailed them, clearly pages and servants to King Kerim and his son.

Kerim shifted restlessly as the column continued its deliberate, steady pace across three miles of Kaimpur to Mon'El's palace. He appreciated the turnout of the city's people, and he wondered at how much the crowd cost their king. Regardless, he quickly grew tired of the procession and the endless cheers of Kaimpur's citizenry, and he even considered if he should have the bodyguards lower him so that he may finish the march on his own two feet. Well, he considered it for only a moment; it seemed like much effort. From the moment they entered the city, the great pyramid built in worship to Mon'El and his patron Aeyu the air god, always remained in view, and yet they never seemed to draw closer to it. Kerim yawned.

"Look," his son called with a pointed finger, the muscles of his outstretched arm ridged and defined beneath his skin.

King Kerim smiled and relaxed in satisfaction, even as he heard the gasps of his own procession. The crowds ahead seemed to part and reveal the lower levels of King Mon'El's palace, and he struggled to contain his own dazzlement at the sight. He endeavored not to marvel at the structure that rose five hundred feet into the air, daring to reach up to Aeyu Himself. The intense blue of the lapis lazuli glowed vibrantly in the sunlight, and the silver and gold accents almost seemed to turn the sun's rays against itself, reflecting them back brilliantly. Though Kerim paid no attention or homage to the gods himself, he reflected silently on Mon'El and his wife's choices in erecting this monstrous edifice. Mon'El was Chosen of Aeyu, Ilia of Nykeema the goddess of water, but it seemed to King Kerim that their palace directly challenged the other gods. They imprisoned the stone of the earth god in aesthetics both loved by their own patrons and hated by Hykan, God of Fire.

And yet their daughter was Chosen by Hykan. Even King Kerim, who prayed to no god, questioned the wisdom of such arrogance, but he said nothing of it. Instead, his smile widened as he considered that he found one of King Mon'El's weaknesses, and knowing your opponents' weaknesses in battle, be it a war of swords or wits, was paramount to all other things except knowing your own. He had built a kingdom on that belief.

His smile faded somewhat as his eyes alit on the one who awaited their procession, and he said nothing as they came to a halt some ten yards away. The voluptuous form of Queen Ilia stood in their path, wrapped in the deepest blue silks Kerim had ever seen, and he felt a stirring in his loins as he viewed her through the sheer material. A dozen servants flanked either side of the golden haired queen as they knelt in the dusty street just behind her with downcast eyes. Kerim reflected that they were well fed and appeared healthy, unlike the servants of many other kings he'd seen throughout the years, and his keen eyes did not fail to miss the spear and sword armed guards that were both behind the servants and surreptitiously placed in the crowds.

"Welcome King Kerim and Price Kerim'El to Kaimpur," announced Ilia as she raised her arms, affording him an even closer look at her body beneath the flimsy silk. "Praise be to Nykeema that your journey was so undemanding. The city celebrates your arrival and the bond that will soon tie our kingdoms together!"

At a motion, the bearers began to lower their king and prince to the ground, and once it was done, Kerim and his son stood from their serpentine thrones. The briefest of glances at his son told Kerim that the younger man's eyes wandered wantonly over the queen's body instead of those of her servants who would likely be offered openly. If daughters tended to look like their mothers as they aged, and Kerim knew that was often the case, his son would stay pleased by his wife's body for decades.

"I thank you, Queen Ilia. You are most gracious, but I am," Kerim paused his reply for just a moment, "disappointed that neither your husband nor your daughter is present to greet us. After all, it is my kingdom being joined to his, your daughter who is betrothed to my son."

"Let it not concern you, King Kerim. You have traveled many miles across the searing plains of Dulkur to be here now," Ilia replied, and a cool wave of calm seemed to wash over the king. She lowered her arms to hold them before her, and as she did so, the servants stood and approached Kerim and his retinue.

"My servants are here to take your burdens, and I personally will escort you and your son into my palace. Affairs of state will wait until tomorrow. Tonight, I entertain you, and I assure you that no want will go unrealized."

Before Kerim had realized what happened, her words swept his concerns away from the forefront of his mind. The strangeness of it struck him, for he'd negotiated with warlords, master merchants, pirates, and other kings, and never had one managed to calm him so easily. However, King Kerim also knew that he allowed it to happen, and if Kaimpur's queen offered rest, relaxation, food, drink, and pleasures for the night, he would accept it. She looped an arm into his left and simultaneously into his son's right, and he allowed Queen Ilia, Chosen of Nykeema and Queen of Kaimpur, to lead him into her azure palace.

The demands and threats of negotiations could wait until tomorrow.

10.

The kingpriest Mon'El paced across his chambers endlessly as the morning sun lit them from the east. A fluttering breeze whipped the curtains that partitioned his rooms, allowing him a view of the city. It always looked so peaceful from on high and so early in the day, before the people grew active like so many ants, their sounds carrying into the sky above them to his ears. For some reason, every time his gaze fell on Ilia, who sat breakfasting carelessly nearby as she always did, a burning flame grew in his gut. It threatened to overwhelm him, and only the pacing back and forth with the cool stone under his bare feet kept him from explosively unleashing his anger. He wondered if this was how it felt to be Chosen of Hykan. Is this how his arrogant, headstrong, stubborn, and infuriating daughter felt all the time?

At the sudden thought of Thyss, the fire threatened to burst into full conflagration, and Mon'El stopped his pacing. He hung his head, closed his eyes, and breathed in deeply, fighting to regain control of his emotions. Still there was no word of his daughter, but his eyes and ears in Kaimpur below told him that Guribda had returned to the city early in the morning, in a great rush, and was even now on his way to the palace. The man would only return so if he had news, and Mon'El needed whatever he knew before facing King Kerim.

"Calm," Ilia breathed from behind him, and he felt her will as it tried to flow over his.

He pushed it away, “I cannot until I know where she is. Only then can I meet with King Kerim.”

“And that is all that’s bothering you?” she asked.

Mon’El turned halfway around and beheld an impish smile on her full lips, and the baleful ire in his gut returned. He answered, “I think you want something to bother me.”

“Maybe I do,” she replied, as the smile fled.

“You play games, Ilia. I have never begrudged your appetites.”

She sighed and dropped a half-eaten melon onto a gilded plate, wiping some errant juice from her chin with the back of her hand. She said, “No, you haven’t.”

“I wish you to have everything you desire.”

“You do,” Ilia agreed before looking up into his eyes, “but this wasn’t about my desires. This was about your desires. I fucked him and then his son – a most debasing thing, I promise you – to further your wants, your schemes, your desires. I did it because you needed more time, and now that your answer is on the way, you don’t even care.”

Ilia pushed the chair back from the small table they shared every morning, stood, and lightly padded over to stand right before her husband. “I must wash,” she said, and Mon’El leaned in slowly, intending to kiss his wife when she struck him. Her hand slapped the flesh of his cheek loudly, a white hot sting that spread across his face, and then she stalked away, descending steps that would take her to her marble bath.

Even as his vision cleared from the surprise of the blow, Mon’El’s brow furrowed. He watched her disappear, trying to discern what had just occurred, as well as what he would need to do to rectify the situation. Perhaps he would commission a new necklace for her, or maybe a tiara, something that would accentuate her beauty and give praise to her god. She would appreciate that.

More footsteps sounded from another of the staircases, one reserved for his close advisors as well as messengers bearing important news. They echoed upward into his chambers as someone swiftly bounded up steps two or three at a time. After a moment, he realized that two persons approached from below, and Mon'El impatiently tapped a bare foot as he waited for their emergence. Finally, his faithful ranger Guribda appeared, followed by one of Mon'El's palace guards who huffed and puffed as he arrived several seconds behind to find his quarry already kneeling.

"I'm… sorry, Highness," the warrior gasped, almost doubling over, "he demanded… he come straight… away."

"I care not," Mon'El replied with a waved hand. "Stand and speak, Guribda."

"I know where she is, Highness," Guribda said before he even reached his feet.

"Where?"

"She is in the village of Calumbu, south of the desert."

"Calumbu," Mon'El repeated, squinting as he looked away, almost searching. Understanding struck him, and his face relaxed as he turned back toward Guribda. "In the jungles to the east."

"Yes, Highness."

"How do you know?" Mon'El asked, his eyes intently watching for any sign of duplicity.

"A story has traveled fast through the trade routes of a girl who emerged from the desert and was rescued by Calumbu's king," Guribda explained, carefully watching Mon'El's reaction at the mention of a mere village king. "There was a battle of some kind between Calumbu and some other tribal chief. It is said the girl fought for

Calumbu, burned her enemies where they stood, and engulfed entire squadrons of warriors in flames."

Mon'El listened, and as Guribda said these words, his sour demeanor lightened. A smile even touched the corners of his mouth, and he said, "The jungle tribes exaggerate, I think, but you have done well, Guribda. You were right to come straight away. It most certainly must be my Thyssallia. You know the fastest route to this Calumbu?"

"I do, Highness."

"Very good. Then at first light tomorrow, you will lead my army to it."

"If I may, Highness?" Guribda ventured.

"Speak," Mon'El commanded, and he felt eagerness to start on the journey rise, though the fire in his gut had vanished. Praise be to Aeyu.

"We must cross the river, a hundred miles of plains and then a jungle. An army would take two weeks to arrive, and by then we may miss your daughter."

"You are right, good Guribda," Mon'El replied, placing a hand on the tracker's shoulder. "You stay here and assist my generals with readying the army, just in case. I have a faster way to reach Calumbu and my daughter. I will return before sundown tomorrow."

Guribda nodded and cast his eyes downward at the floor as he wondered why the king hadn't just released him from his duties. Mon'El missed the resigned look on the tracker's face as he turned and said, "But first, I must meet with my esteemed guests, King Kerim and his son, the soon to be husband of my dear daughter."

Mon'El took a set of steps down into the heart of his palace, passing the levels at which he ran his kingdom, as well as his wife's floor where she no doubt bathed. He considered stopping to ask for her forgiveness, but he realized he had no bauble or trinket to offer her. While

Nykeema granted his wife calm quickly enough, now was not that time. He then paused on Thyss' level, momentarily, in consideration of the vacant emptiness that had settled in the air for the last six months while she adventured across Dulkur for reasons only the gods knew. Truth was that she loved nothing more than to raise his ire, to anger and irk him at every turn. He told his daughter many times of the importance of her marriage to Kerim'El, and the months if not years of negotiation that would lead Mon'El to rule most of Dulkur, passing that rule on to Thyss upon his death. She just wanted to try his patience, as always, and she would fall in line once he confronted her.

Three more levels of the pyramid he descended to emerge upon the level he had specifically designed for and committed to his guests' rest and enjoyment when he built the palace. A wide hall dominated the floor with mother of pearl wrapped columns flanking the length of an expensive, imported mahogany table the top of which was plated with gold. Dozens of matching chairs, their great arms carved to represent eddies and gusts of wind and inlaid with silver, surrounded the table, and they were upholstered with thick cushions of scarlet silk. A rug of the deepest blue lay underneath the table and chairs in homage to Nykeema, and two dozen rooms branched off the main hall – two luxurious suites and the rest more modest rooms, all of which had their own balconies and provided glorious views of Kaimpur.

Mon'El saw Kerim at the head of the feasting table, leaning backward most slovenly as he guzzled cool beer from an earthenware jar. Arrayed at the table before him, his warriors and other servants took in a late breakfast. Mon'El made certain that his own servants treated them lavishly with silver platter after silver platter of meat, fresh bread, and a generous supply of the oranges that only grew near Kaimpur, famous for how their taste started sweet and finished with pleasant sourness, to say nothing of their ample succulency. Mon'El noted the absence of the prince, but the grunts and moans emanating from one of the open doored suites left little to his imagination.

A few eyes shot King Mon'El's way as he approached, but if King Kerim took note or even heard Mon'El's footsteps, he showed no sign of it. However, Kerim also showed no sign of surprise when Mon'El said, "Good morning, King Kerim. I do apologize for not having met you sooner. Welcome to my kingdom and Kaimpur."

Kerim leaned forward to set his jar on the table, and its contents splashed over the rim, a few drops landing on the table and the rug underneath. Mon'El's eyes narrowed, and he fought to contain a sigh. That rug caused him no end of annoyance and aggravation. The guests always scooted their chairs across it, rather than lifting, damaging the fibers as they did so. Either that, or endless amounts of beer, wine, or greasy food ended upon it, staining or discoloring the deep azure hues. Regardless of the cause, Mon'El always went to great expense keeping that rug clean and in good repair.

"Kings are not used to waiting," Kerim grumbled.

"No, *we* are not," Mon'El agreed, "but I assure you that it was necessary. I endeavored to spare no expense on your comfort here."

"It is comfortable, but I'd have been just as comfortable in my own palace. My son, on the other hand," Kerim said, looking up at Mon'El's face for the first time, "has enjoyed your servants thus far. I suppose he has grown bored of mine and wishes to sow his wild oats in other lands further from home."

"Would you not rather he save his energy?" Mon'El asked. "Soon he will have a wife of pure blood, Chosen of Hykan."

"Will he?" Kerim questioned with raised eyebrows.

He slid the heavy chair backward on the rug a few inches, almost causing Mon'El to flinch with the motion, and he stood from it, the two kings facing only a few feet from each other. They were the same height, but where Mon'El's back stood erect, his muscles thin and fit, Kerim still slumped slightly. The crimson tunic he'd donned did little to hide the stomach that spilled over his girdle, and Mon'El doubted his rival king could even see his own cock. Mon'El's eyes, like those of his wife and daughter, had changed to silver when he was Chosen, but Kerim's remained brown, showing no favor of the gods. Regardless, Kerim's strengths lay not in his physical bearing or magicks, and Mon'El knew better than to underestimate him even from his slovenly appearance.

"That is the arrangement," Mon'El answered, nodding.

"An arrangement, an agreement that I understand you cannot meet," Kerim accused, his voice even. "Do you know, King Mon'El, what happens in my dealings when one cannot uphold their end of a bargain?"

"I am aware of the way you conduct business," Mon'El said, adding his own distaste for the word, "as I am aware of your kingdom's abilities to conduct war."

"Perhaps," Kerim acceded, "I know you have your spies, as I have mine, and mine have said your princess will not agree to the marriage. Further, she is not here, and you don't know where she is."

Mon'El fought to control his reactions to Kerim's words, not wanting to give the king any reason to doubt what he said next, "Your spies are incorrect. Well, partially. It is true that Thyss is not here at the moment, but I know precisely where she is. Tomorrow morning, I leave to retrieve her."

"Where?"

Mon'El shrugged, "Does it matter?"

"Yes," Kerim answered with a tone of finality. "I doubt you, Mon'El. I doubt that you know where she is, and I doubt that she will marry my son as we agreed. Chosen of Hykan are known for their… temperament."

"Calumbu," Mon'El replied without hesitation, expecting that such a quick and honest answer would put the other king's fears to rest. Seeing a lack of comprehension, Mon'El explained, "I'm not surprised you haven't heard of it. It's an unimportant village well to the east of my kingdom. She is there, and I will bring her back tomorrow. It is planned."

"What is she doing there?" Kerim asked, and the question honestly surprised Mon'El.

He shrugged again as he replied, "Who knows? She's involved in some minor war between villages. Thyss, like your son, likes to wander beyond all of the experiences directly available to her. I suppose we can agree that it is the nature of youth, but I do not remember it myself."

"Nor do I," Kerim agreed, and his keen eyes almost bored their way into Mon'El's, seeking any duplicity.

"Regardless, I leave tomorrow to retrieve her and will return by sundown. You are welcome to await our return."

"If I know the map of your kingdom well, Mon'El, and I assure you that I do, Calumbu must be at least a hundred miles away. How can you promise to return so quickly?"

"I am Chosen of Aeyu," Mon'El replied distantly, straightening his spine pridefully.

"Against my better judgement, King Mon'El, I will wait here with my son until sundown tomorrow. I prefer the comforts of your palace to the dust and heat of the road, and I'm sure my son will continue to enjoy what your servants have to offer, as well as your wife's… hospitality. But make no mistake – if you do not return with your daughter by sundown tomorrow, our agreement will be... endangered."

The sun hovered close to the horizon, having only just risen to cast its morning light across the plains of Dulkur. A bronze skinned man with silver eyes, climbed from the balcony of his great palace, a stepped pyramid that dazzled a deep azure to all of those on its eastern side. His muscles straining, he lifted himself from the balcony of his chambers on the top floor of the pyramid and heaved himself up until he stood on its apex. From here, he looked down upon the city of Kaimpur, seeing that his people already moved and bustled about their daily tasks, and he wondered if their thoughts had wandered far from the king of another land that visited and waited. The enormous shadow of the pyramid stretched almost two miles in the early morning light, bathing the entire city to the west, its shape reaching into the plains beyond.

Mon'El stood naked on the point of his palace, the physical creation that represented his achievements in bending Kaimpur and a hundred miles in every direction to his rule. He closed his eyes and lifted his arms straight from his sides to feel the gentle breeze of Aeyu as it threatened to ruin his balance and send him tumbling to his death. Of course, neither he nor his god would allow such a thing, and after the briefest moment enjoying the caresses of Aeyu, Mon'El allowed himself to tip forward off balance. He stretched his feet out behind him, pushing off of the pyramid to launch himself into the air, and as he plummeted downward, the kingpriest of Kaimpur felt his physical form dissolve away.

To someone down in the city below, if they had looked up at just the perfect time, it appeared that a bird perhaps decided to take flight from the top of the palace, descending downward to pick up some speed before disappearing altogether. In its place was a wisp of cloud, a whitish tendril of vapor that vanished from view as the winds blew it to the east.

11.

Thyss stretched her arms languidly. Spears of morning light shot across the main hall of Calumbu's palace, rousing her from her delicious slumber, and as her arms continued to reach outward, it caused her entire body to extend and sprawl, ridding her of sleep and bringing wakefulness. Harpalo's chest rose and fell slowly, evenly next to her, and a momentarily interrupted soft snore was the only sign that she disturbed him at all. It was the second night in a row she had stayed with him, and she wondered how many more there would be. Thyss sat upright with crossed legs, pulled a fur up around her chest, and looked over her shoulder at his prone, sleeping form. She considered that it was about time for her to go.

Harpalo's wound healed swiftly, either due to Déré's impressive and vast knowledge and skills or perhaps due to the king's own incredible constitution. Either way, Calumbu would have its king back in perfect health within another week or so, and Thyss felt something in her gut urging her on. It had nothing to do with Harpalo's skills as a lover, though most of it had fallen to her in his convalescence, and she had no doubt he would be much more vigorous in the coming weeks. That had no bearing on her decision.

A villager worked quietly nearby, setting a tray with food for Thyss and Harpalo for breakfast. Harpalo had spent the last few weeks in the palace at Déré's insistence, the healer checking on him two or three times each day at first. He felt that it would be easier to meet Harpalo's needs in the larger space, especially when others had to help him move about. Not that he moved much. Over the last two nights, Thyss had to make sure he moved as little as possible, which made for an interesting experience.

"Are you going to just stare at me?" Harpalo mumbled.

Thyss widened her eyes as if dispelling a veil that had been pulled over them, and it almost felt as if she had dozed off while just sitting there and ruminating. She leaned back on her left elbow so that she faced him where he lay still on his back, his eyes staring upward. She traced a muscle on his arm with a single finger.

"What would you have me do?" she asked.

"Kiss me?"

"Ha, you'll have to bathe again before that happens."

"I didn't mean," Harpalo trailed off, and he turned his face toward hers. "I thought, perhaps, you might feel enough for me to kiss me."

Thyss withdrew her finger and curled it into her hand, staring at him as he merely looked back. He blinked, sighed, and fixed his gaze back on the ceiling above him. She clenched her teeth and pushed herself up to her feet. As the fur dropped away, the woman setting their breakfast consciously averted her eyes from Thyss' naked, lithe body. The sorceress stalked around, retrieving her clothes, the tunic and leggings of Nekala's that had been gifted to her, and started to dress.

"I thank you for your hospitality. You saved me from the desert, and I saved you from Paddo," Thyss said as she pulled the tunic over her head and down to her waist. "I think our debts are even, Harpalo."

"Thyss," he called, "can we talk for a moment?"

"Don't think for a moment," she said as she affixed her scimitar to a leather thong on her belt, "that this was anything more than me feeling an itch I needed scratched."

Harpalo slowly and deliberately raised himself onto his right side and waived away his villager, who retreated with relief plain on her face. He said to Thyss, "Boarshit."

"Don't begin to think you know me, King Harpalo," Thyss said as she turned to leave him.

He called after her, "If that's all it was, there were plenty of readily available men in Calumbu who'd have gladly served your whims. No, it was something else."

Thyss had only made it a few yards away when she wheeled back around on him. Whatever she might have felt for this wounded king burned away with the anger that erupted in her chest, and Hykan's engulfing flames again burned in her eyes. She could almost hear him whispering to her, the god begging her to set Harpalo, his palace, his entire kingdom aflame.

She quenched it just long enough to say, "Don't fool yourself into thinking I care."

Harpalo opened his mouth to retort and then closed it again, flummoxed by the heartlessness of her tone and words. As they locked eyes, he wanted to say something to the sorceress. A heavy stone in his gut told him her words weren't true. His people told him how she exacted her brutal revenge on Paddo and how she carried the lifeless body of Nekala all the way home, refusing help. Though he was weak and fading in and out of consciousness during the funeral, Harpalo saw her shed a tear, and he refused to believe she didn't care. He steeled himself as he prepared to speak, knowing that what he next said could push Thyss over the edge into infernal violence, cause her to simply storm out of Calumbu immediately and forever, or perhaps, just perhaps, it might get through her stalwart exterior. Of the first two options, King Harpalo didn't know which would be worse, but either were worth the risk of getting through to her.

The doors to palace burst inward, spilling bright morning sunshine across the hall as Da'irda's massive form rushed inside, several other villagers in his wake. His entry drew Harpalo's attention, as well as Thyss' as she whirled to face the warrior. Da'irda came to a halt some fifteen feet away from them, and the expression on his face showed that he knew he had interrupted something between the two but also that he had important news.

Da'irda bowed his head briefly and said, "My apologies, Lady Thyss, King Harpalo. A man has appeared in Calumbu, and he is heading toward the palace now. He is naked, and…"

"Surely you've seen a naked man before!" Thyss interrupted, suddenly laughing at his expense with an innuendo much as he had done to her on the day Paddo attacked Calumbu.

While Harpalo chuckled softly, Da'irda's scowl did not change, and he explained, "Not one like this, Lady Thyss. He has your skin, a shaved head, and he came here from nowhere. The wind gusted cool across the streets, and then he appeared."

Thyss pulled a long breath in through her nose as she lowered her head, aiming a steely gaze at the floor just in front of the warrior's feet. Her skin almost began to crawl, and then the fine hairs across her body tingled as if they were burning. Her palms itched, and one ended on the hilt of her scimitar.

"What is it?" Harpalo asked from behind her.

"My father," she answered, her voice containing as much razor sharp, cold steel as her gaze.

"What?' Harpalo whispered. He raised his voice, "Da'irda, quickly. Listen…"

From the air as he traveled amongst the clouds and air currents, Calumbu appeared to Mon'El a medium sized city spreading across miles in either direction, but when he descended and solidified into his naked, bodily form, his opinion changed as his gaze took in the sights around him. True, hundreds or maybe even thousands of people lived here, but the city streets were dirt and the homes made of mudbricks. He saw no merchants, priests, or rulers of any kind, and no silver or gold shined its wealth in the sunlight. Most of the people wore basic linen or wool, the colors of their clothing in muted, earthy tones instead of the bright dyes one expected amongst prosperous people. They watched him as he strode through their streets, all their eyes locked on his brilliant, bronze skinned body, almost begging him to bring civilization, comfort, and security to their squalid existence. All told, Calumbu clearly had grown merely from large numbers of people simply breeding, and Mon'El pitied their poverty, even their very existence.

One building toward the center of Calumbu had stood out to him while he was still one with the clouds, a wide, single level edifice constructed of stone blocks instead of sundried mud, and this was his destination. The poverty stricken people parted swiftly for him, many of them bowing in reverence of his obvious godlike and monarchial status, and they whispered in hurried, hushed tones as he passed. Once he concluded his business with King Kerim, he would set himself to bringing these beggarly people into his kingdom to ease their burdens.

A gargantuan warrior with the dark skin so common to Mon'El's own bodyguards emerged from the crowds ahead, flanked by a pair of common servants. Everyone on the dust beaten street parted and moved to the sides as far ahead as Mon'El could see, obviously having been instructed to do so. The warrior approached, and Mon'El noted the immensity of the steely thews in his arms and legs, a chest and abdomen that rippled in muscle. Calumbu would provide an excellent source of strong warriors for his armies as well, and they would no doubt prefer a well-kept life of soldiery to this abysmal, abject existence. The warrior stopped some fifteen feet away and quickly kneeled before Mon'El, his face tipped down toward the ground, and his servants and many of the villagers followed suit.

"King Mon'El of Kaimpur," the warrior's rumbling voice announced falteringly in Mon'El's own high tongue, "welcome to Calumbu. We are honored by your presence. My name is Da'irda. King Harpalo is preparing to meet Your Majesty."

"Why has your *king*," Mon'El placed a peculiar emphasis on the word, "not come to greet me himself?"

"He sends his great apologies and regrets, Majesty, but King Harpalo is still healing from a wound received in battle. He requires more time than would be normal, and Your Majesty's visit was neither announced nor expected."

Mon'El nodded his head in acceptance of the explanation, though he channeled Aeyu's cooling breeze across the fire in his temper. To call the chief of such a wretched place and people "king", placing him on Mon'El's own level offended his sensibilities, but he reminded himself that he was here only to find his daughter. Besides, people's perceptions often dictated what they viewed as reality, as wrong as it may be.

Da'irda stood, and the sound of shuffling movement filled the air as dozens or even hundreds of others did likewise. He motioned to a servant behind him, a short girl of teenaged years, and said, "I have brought clothing for Your Majesty. I know they are not what Your Majesty is used to, but I think they may service for your visit?"

Mon'El eyed the folded linen held in the open hands of the girl and fought to hide his indignant distaste at the clothing's simplicity. He shook his head and said, "There is no need. I will meet Harpalo as I am."

"As you will, Your Majesty," Da'irda answered with a nod, "we merely thought nudity unbecoming of –"

Mon'El interrupted him, "I wish to be taken to Harpalo at once."

The warrior again nodded deferentially, apparently used to the commands of royalty, and he said, "Of course. This way, Your Majesty."

It was a brief walk to the stone building Mon'El saw from the air, an unimpressive and shabby affair that he assumed served as *King* Harpalo's palace. The warrior led him into a huge square that contained a bustling, but poverty stricken market. The vendor's stalls were little more than shacks, lean-to shanties, or canvas tents, and they exchanged their goods with each other without the glint of gold or silver. Mon'El heard of such villages about Dulkur, even liberated a few with his armies from their tyrant chieftains, communes of poverty full of the lower peoples of Dulkur as they struggled day to day to eke out a basic survival. The sight nearly brought tears of sorrow to his eyes. Da'irda led him around the pitiful market and to the plain stone palace at which point the two servants advanced and opened the doors. As Mon'El and the warrior passed through, the two servants bowed to the king.

They entered a wide but entirely unadorned hall, and Mon'El knew that no king held court in this place. No tapestries, sculptures, or golden or bejeweled works of art decorated the hall. It stood open and empty, and though the floor was at least made of stone and not dirt as he expected, no rugs or carpets cushioned his naked feet as he entered. At the least, Mon'El would have expected the floor to be covered with reeds or even straw, so common to feasting halls, but there were none of these either. It felt unused, as if the poverty stricken people he saw outside surely couldn't afford for their king to furnish it. He probably killed a hundred slaves just building the palace. A handful of torches flamed smokily around the perimeter, their haphazard, flickering orange glows pushed away by the bright daylight allowed inside by the open doors.

On the far side of the hall, some fifteen or twenty feet away sat a mountain of a man upon a wooden construct that Mon'El assumed passed for a throne. Even seated, he must have been five feet tall, and his brown skin contained monstrous muscles about his chest, arms, and legs. He wore nothing except a thick loincloth, which added to his image of perfect savagery, and Mon'El wondered how many of his own personal guard would be a match for this man that must be Harpalo. As he approached, he noted the stitched, discolored, and swollen flesh about the side of the chief's torso, the wound that the warrior named Da'irda had mentioned, and it wasn't lost on Mon'El that most men would have been killed by such an injury.

Despite it, the giant stood with significant effort from his meager, wooden throne, and towering over Mon'El, he nodded and intoned respectfully in perfect Highborn, "Great King Mon'El of Kaimpur, we of Calumbu are honored by your presence. I am King Harpalo."

Mon'El fought to hide his surprise that this Lowborn warrior, this mere chieftain of a jungle village (albeit a huge jungle village) who would dare use the title king spoke his own language without accent or inflection. True, the two languages of the Highborn and Lowborn Dulkurians had many similarities, their vocabulary almost completely interchangeable, but it was the pronunciations, accents, and inflections that made them differ. The fact that the head of this near feral village spoke his language so clearly gave Mon'El a moment's pause. Perhaps there was more to this man than he believed.

A slight shift of movement well off to his left caught Mon'El's attention. His eyes darted that way, and he squinted slightly as he attempted to make out the details of a gloomy corner of the hall. He saw a great pile of furs, wool blankets and what appeared to be linen bedclothes, and he surmised that King Harpalo slept in that heap. Mon'El's keen vision then made out a form, a woman thin and lithe and wearing all black, as she leaned against the wall near the bedding. A momentary burst of illumination from an undulating torch, and Mon'El caught a glimpse of silvery eyes, golden hair, and bronze skin. He gazed at her for a long moment before returning his attention to Harpalo.

"What can the people of Calumbu offer Your Majesty?" Harpalo asked.

"I seek the return of my daughter, Thyssallia," Mon'El replied, and for just a moment, he felt a burst of warmth erupt from the far corner at the use of his daughter's given name.

"If you mean Thyss," Harpalo said, "we are not holding her. She is free to go as she wills."

"Then come, daughter," Mon'El commanded, using his most authoritative tone, a resonance that was always obeyed without question.

Harpalo sharply inhaled and began, "I do not believe –"

But Thyss cut him off, having pushed away from the wall and stalked into the light, "I speak for myself."

"Of course," Harpalo deferred.

"I am not going," Thyss said.

Mon'El's anger flared, and this time it was his god whose power elevated as a brief, angry wind gusted in from outside. The torches guttered and almost winked out before he regained control, and he took a long, appraising look at his ever disobedient daughter. She set her feet wide in a defiant stance that both mirrored her attitude but would also give her a solid foundation should she choose to draw steel. Her hair hung loosely about her shoulders and back, her arms crossed over a formfitting and armless silken black tunic Mon'El had never seen before, and he noted that her right hand, folded under her left arm, lay mere inches away from a bronze hilted, steel bladed scimitar. Thyss stood some twenty feet away from him and equally distant from Harpalo, despite a sense of familiarity he felt between the two. Had she bedded with this Lowborn? He supposed it did not matter, but that was meant for Kerim'El.

"We've been through this," Mon'El said flatly, stating a fact he did not wish to repeat.

"And I said I was leaving," she replied, equally toneless.

"And I have never restricted you since the day you were Chosen. You are beloved of Hykan, but you are also my daughter. You have responsibilities to attend to."

Thyss spat to one side, the act causing Mon'El to tilt his face downward while fighting his temper by taking a slow, deep breath through his nose. Harpalo cut his eyes over at her, but Thyss ignored both men. She said, "I am no pig to be fattened and slaughtered as the king wills it."

"Of course not, but –"

"And I am no mare to be whored out to whatever stud you wish to mount me."

"The marriage is a symbol. You needn't even bed Kerim'El," Mon'El replied through clenched teeth, knowing that it was partially a lie – Kerim'El would have expectations, but that was the prince's problem. He glanced at Harpalo momentarily as he continued, "In fact, who you bed is your own affair, but the marriage will take place.

This arrangement is years in the making, and it moves our family one step closer to ruling all Dulkur."

The mere tribal chieftain, King Harpalo, bristled at these words, but Mon'El ignored his reaction. He had no time or care for the feelings of some Lowborn brute who styled himself a king, no matter how well the barbarian spoke Highborn. When this was all over, Mon'El fully intended to bargain with Harpalo to bring Calumbu into his empire so that its people might enjoy everything Kaimpur, civilization, and Mon'El's rule had to offer. The negotiations would be short, because the poor village couldn't hope to stand against Mon'El's gracious offer.

"Moves *you* one step closer. You have no family. My mother," Thyss stifled a chuckle, "if I ever had such a thing, is just a tool for you. The tool that solidified your grasp over the priests of Kaimpur, a tool that birthed me, the next tool in your grand plans. You think she loves you, adores you like everyone else in Kaimpur, and yet she seeks solace in the arms of anyone she can find. I'll not be your pawn, King Mon'El."

Mon'El reeled at the assault, and another gust of wind arose to extinguish the torches in the hall, leaving him standing amidst the column of light that peered in through the hall's open doors. The light ended at Harpalo, erect as he was before his meager throne, and the giant lowered his eyes, suddenly feeling like an outsider uncomfortably caught in the middle of a familial dispute. Thyss stood in darkness, difficult to see but for the fires of Hykan burning in the depths of her pupils.

"And have you found love in the arms of this primitive, this Lowborn?" Mon'El snarled.

Thyss ignored Harpalo's eyes upon her, keeping her gaze locked with her father's as she replied, "I plan on leaving soon, and I needed a fuck."

Mon'El glanced back at Harpalo who had turned his face away from both of them, and he struggled to define what he saw on the tall warrior's face. But the cold, heartless statement toward Harpalo emboldened Mon'El, and for a moment, he gloated victoriously with the realization that she was his daughter, through and through. He softened his tone, instilling his words with what sounded like reason.

"Come home, Thyss. You are powerful, and no one can control you. You've proven that. Come with me back to Kaimpur and take your rightful place. Marry Prince Kerim'El and help me forge the strongest kingdom in Dulkur. You will rule the entire land when I am gone, and your name will be spoken for a thousand years."

"Your dream, father, not mine," Thyss replied without a moment hesitation. "Why should I want this? To rule? Trade agreements and tax levies and mediating disputes and… *boredom*! I don't care about any of it. Keep it."

"And you'll what? Stay here with this pig?" Mon'El growled with a motion at Harpalo.

"I'll not suffer such insults, King Mon'El," Harpalo warned.

But the father and daughter ignored his clamor for their own, and Thyss replied, "I'll do as I wish, whether that means staying here or going elsewhere. If I suddenly desire to see Tigol or even Losz, then that is what I will do."

"You're coming back to Kaimpur with me."

"No."

"It is not your decision," Mon'El said, and he lurched toward his daughter, intent on forcing her out of the hall if necessary. Thyss hardly moved as he approached, and her gaze hardened dangerously as the air in the hall warmed.

But it was Harpalo that kept Mon'El from reaching his daughter, as the enormous brute interposed himself between them. Mon'El stopped short, his eyes level with the king's massive chest, and he looked up into a stony, stalwart face. Harpalo looked down into his eyes, two kings competing for dominance in a contest of wills, and he said, "Your daughter has said she will not return with you. You may be king in Kaimpur and for miles around it, but here you do not reign. In Calumbu, no one forces their will upon anyone."

"Out of my way, savage!" Mon'El's voice boomed throughout the hall, causing the two villagers by the door to cover their ears, but Harpalo remained unmoved, flinching only in the slightest. "She will obey me."

"She does not wish to, and she is her own woman."

Mon'El shouted, his voice a terrific gale throughout Harpalo's meager hall, "You will obey me, lest I visit ruin on your pathetic village!"

"I challenge you to try," Harpalo replied calmly. "Calumbu is more than this village. We are many tribes and villages, thousands upon thousands, who share an idea."

Heat flared behind Harpalo's back, an uncomfortable warmth that permeated the distance between he and Thyss, an infernal indication of the sorceress' volatile moods. He had felt it before in other circumstances, and her voice snapped behind him, "I do not need you to fight my battles."

Harpalo held an open hand away from him and said, "Peace, Thyss. I'm not fighting your battle. I am standing up for what is right. No one, king or otherwise, makes demands of anyone in Calumbu."

"She leaves with me now," Mon'El said, and his voice turned to a nearly inaudible whisper as compared to the thunderous scream on the wind just moments before, "or I will return and destroy your piteous kingdom."

"The mountain does not bow to the wind, no matter how it howls," Harpalo said, and he stepped away and turned toward Thyss, grimacing at his still healing wound. The heat abated once more as Thyss considered where she'd heard his words before, but she remained unyielding in her stance. Her right hand fingered the hilt of her scimitar, and her lips screwed up in distaste as she lifted her chin in defiance of her father the kingpriest of Kaimpur and probably the most powerful man in all Dulkur.

Harpalo nodded his assent, turned back to the darkly furious Mon'El, and said, "She has made her choice, and no one can impose their will on her here. You are welcome to stay as an honored guest, King Mon'El. We will feast and, perhaps, you will let me explain the ways of Calumbu to you."

Mon'El had locked his eyes on his disobedient bitch of a daughter, barely hearing King Harpalo's words as the larger man continued. A part of him felt a glowing pride at his daughter's self-agency, at her willfulness, but that was overwhelmed by the anger and indignance of her rebellion. If he did not present her to Kerim, it could mean war between their kingdoms, and he felt no wish to see the massive destruction that such would wreak. And who was this peasant king who dared speak to him as an equal anyway?

Without hearing another word, Mon'El turned on his heel and stormed out of Calumbu's stone hall. Once in the market, he ignored the seeking, curious, and frightened eyes of the Lowborn shits gathered around him, and he held his arms to the sky. An enormous gale arose, a wind so powerful and quick that it tore canvas coverings away from the vendors' stalls and even pushed over some of the rickety, wooden frames. After a moment, the outstretched form of Mon'El disappeared quite suddenly as his incorporeal self rose to join the scudding clouds above.

Harpalo waived at the two villagers still waiting by the hall's open doors, and they exited, pulling the doors shut behind them. He looked to Da'irda, who had stood by stoically during the entire exchange, and said, "I suppose King Mon'El will need more time to come around to our way of thinking."

Da'irda adopted a dubious expression, but it was Thyss who erupted from behind the king, "You are more of an idiot than I gave you any credit for! Have you already forgotten the lesson Paddo taught you? Were it not for me, all of Calumbu would have fallen to that man, a minor war chief of all things, and now you've angered the most powerful man in Dulkur! How could you be so stupid?"

Harpalo had turned to face her words head on, and he solemnly replied, "It is our way of life. He had no right to –"

"Your way of life will die by his hands! He cares not for you, Calumbu, your people, anything you care about!" she said, wanting to scream the words at him. Harpalo's face had turned to something she couldn't quite identify – perhaps indignance at her lack of gratitude? She wasn't sure.

"I do not want to fight your father," Harpalo said softly, "A man such as he does not rise to such a position without learning wisdom. I will send messengers to Kaimpur, inviting him to come talk. He will see."

"And again, you're an idiot. All he cares about is me, no, making me do what he wants."

"He has no right," Harpalo repeated, "and the people of Calumbu will not let him simply take what he wants."

Thyss dropped her eyes to the floor and shook her head vigorously. She couldn't believe what she was hearing from Harpalo, how he could be so blinded by his ideals to risk his own people. She fought the urge to lash out at him again, but some small part of her realized that it had done her no good so far. Eyes still cast downward, she said, "Mon'El rose to his position through power. Only after he crushed all of his enemies did he embrace wisdom, and even then, only when it benefited him."

She lifted her gaze to meet Harpalo, unsure how to deal with a sudden emotion she wasn't sure she could even understand, and said, "He is Chosen of Aeyu, God of Air, and while Aeyu grants wisdom, he can be no less destructive than Hykan. You cannot stand against him. When my father returns, he'll return with an army, and he will destroy everything you have built. Is this what you want for your people?"

"Of course not," Harpalo replied, and his face slackened with a sense of sadness. He tilted his head, turning it sideways as if to say something else, but Thyss interrupted him.

"The *only* way is if I leave. He'll be back in Kaimpur before sunset, but it will take him days, I do not know, maybe weeks to amass his army and invade. Send your messenger with a scroll I will write to my father. I'll tell him that I've left Calumbu and not to seek me here further, and I will leave tomorrow just after sunrise."

"There has to be some other way?" Harpalo asked, and his giant bulk seemed to shrink with the slight pleading in his voice.

"There is none," Thyss said.

She made to step past Harpalo to leave his hall, but the king reached out and lightly snagged her arm, just enough to bring her to a halt. Her head whipped toward him, anger rekindling in the dark depths contained by her silver eyes, and he felt the coiled tension in her muscles, a dangerous lioness ready to strike. Once again, Thyss the sorceress embodied deadly beauty.

"Da'irda, please go find a scribe for Lady Thyss," Harpalo, without breaking the unblinking gaze he shared with Thyss, said to his silent, stoic warrior, who made for the door to do as he was told. Bright sunlight again divided the darkness of the hall in which only one feeble torch still burned, and once Harpalo heard the door shut, again bathing the room in darkness, he asked, "Will you stay with me this last night."

Thyss let her arm slacken under his hand, and she closed her eyes, sighed, and nodded once.

12.

"I was afraid you would not make it, King Mon'El," Kerim called as the bronze skinned kingpriest emerged from his palace.

Kerim, his son, and their entourage had awaited on the street outside for over an hour, having chosen to be ready to leave as soon as possible. Somehow, Kerim did not believe that Mon'El would produce his daughter, or perhaps the line of consideration was whether or not he could, and Kerim took note that his opposite had no one with him but servants and bodyguards. Perhaps Mon'El had never planned on keeping his end of the bargain, and Kerim briefly searched the buildings around him for signs of ambush. But that was foolish. If Mon'El had wanted them dead, he would have had all the opportunity while they rested in his palace.

No, Mon'El clearly couldn't control his own daughter, and if that was in fact the case, he could never fulfill the agreement they had forged to bring their kingdoms together as one.

"My apologies, King Kerim," Mon'El began, allowing the wind to carry his voice – a show of power to be sure, but not an aggressive one.

Kerim had no interest in hearing more, and he interrupted his host, "I am leaving. You are unable to meet your obligations, Mon'El, and I have no interest in further excuses. It is not up to you to prove otherwise. In two months' time, my armies will march into your kingdom. I will take by force what should have been my son's in peace."

"King Kerim," Mon'El called soothingly, wishing his wife were by his side; she could always quench the fires of anger, whereas Mon'El usually fanned them. "There is no need for this."

"Two months' time," Kerim repeated, and with a motion from his hand, the muscled bearers lifted the snake carved chairs onto their shoulders.

"War will unnecessarily devastate both our kingdoms. I, too, have armies."

"My spies tell me I have twice the number of professional soldiers, trained warriors, and mercenaries. You have peasants and conscripts."

"I have the gods," Mon'El replied, allowing his voice to boom through the city street, echoing beyond.

"Two months," Kerim called again, and his bearers turned to carry him from Kaimpur.

Mon'El's rage boiled from in his gut, but he somehow controlled himself enough to keep from summoning a tempest that would knock King Kerim, his son, and their entire procession to the ground. He could kill them now, while they were in his city, but that would likely only bring the might of his enemies down upon him. The moment Kerim's loyal generals learned of his murder, they would form up and invade. At least this way, Mon'El had some time, and all may still be saved. He turned back to his palace, stormed inside, and began to climb the steps.

After a few minutes, a deafening gale tore through the halls of Kaimpur's largest pyramid. A force before which no one could stand, the power of a god channeled through his most powerful avatar in Dulkur, would have swept everything and everyone before it away to be shattered against the buildings or paved streets of the city below. However, the servants, guards, and slaves of King

Mon'El of Kaimpur long learned to recognize his moods, especially when his old temperament took charge, and the hallways of his palace through which the wind ripped stood empty.

The howling tempest reached its destination – a set of dark lacquered wooden double doors, banded with cold wrought iron. Wood creaked and iron screeched as the doors began to bow against the deific force brought against them. Iron rivets popped with a clang as wood planks warped enough to free them from their prisons. Finally though, it was the doors' massive bronze hinges that gave way as a rending of metal sounded throughout the corridor outside the doors, and they fell inward with an echoing slam. The wind abating, Mon'El walked into his daughter's chambers, standing atop the doors his powers helped him defeat. He would later admit to himself that it would have been simpler to find a steward and have them unlocked, but his pride demanded that he destroy the offending obstructions. Mon'El didn't know what he expected to find here or even why he intruded so, but it gave him some small satisfaction, as if invading Thyss' rooms gave him one small victory over his obstinate, pigheaded daughter.

He looked around the suite that occupied nearly an entire floor of his palatial pyramid, wandering through it room by room, sometimes running a finger through dust that accumulated over the course of… How long had she been gone? Weeks? Months? Outside of a few small sculptures and other offerings to Hykan, as well as a handful of discarded silk robes, almost nothing indicated anyone ever lived here. There were no items or trinkets of personal value – the things people collected over time that reminded them of certain events in their lives or places they had visited – anywhere in any of the rooms. Rich furniture such as silk cushioned divans, intricately carved tables and chairs, and silken hangings and curtains abounded, all expensive furnishings Mon'El knew since he had paid for them, but none of it meant anything to his daughter. The rooms suddenly felt empty, but the harsh reality struck Mon'El that Thyss had never truly lived here. And when she left, she took nothing with her except some gold, a heavy water skin, and that damnable sword of hers. Mon'El considered that the steel scimitar, taken years ago from one of her bodyguards, meant more to her than any of the luxuries he had provided over the years, and he fought back the urge to have the fury of Aeyu take and carry it all away from his sight.

No. Now more than ever, Mon'El needed control over his emotions, over the elemental chaos that being Chosen often imposed on one's will. He must show his daughter, Chosen of Hykan, God of Fire, that ambition, calculation, and strength of will meant more than burning the world to the ground for the pure havoc of it, that responsibility towards one's destiny carried more weight and importance than frenetic wandering. Tomorrow, he would lead his armies east, and his daughter and all the people of Calumbu would bend to the order of his will.

13.

A blazing heat permeated Thyss' very being as she drifted from a deep, dreamless slumber into that state where one finds the strangest and least rational of dreams. Were she not Chosen of a god, or were she not dreaming, the broiling she felt across her body would sizzle fat away, split and blacken skin, and instantly sear meat to inedibility. She reveled in the glory of so much warmth, idly wondering where she would find such magnificence except for, perhaps, the pit of a volcano, the surface of the glowing disk of the sun, or in the loving embrace of Hykan Himself. She had known men of course (one slept soundly beside her), but if this all-encompassing fire that burned within her heart and across her flesh was what it meant to love the god of fire, she would know no more.

Something drew her closer to wakefulness – a sound. She couldn't identify it at first, but its repetition… No, its continuous bursts, pops, and crackles, random noises without pattern or reason pulled her further from sleep. She sat upright in Harpalo's makeshift bed, rubbing her eyes with one hand as she lay her other on the slowly rising chest of the king beside her, and the deific warmth faded from her body. She glanced at his slumbering form and then scanned the hall in search of what sounded increasingly like a campfire, something that made less and less sense to Thyss the more alert she became. When they retired for the night, Harpalo's hall lay dark with just the glow of a few dying torches to illuminate them, but now a small fire burned without smoke some fifteen feet away toward the hall's center.

"Come," a rasping voice beckoned.

Thyss disentangled her legs from a white linen sheet and, nude, approached the tiny flames which cast a sputtering light across the taut muscles of her arms and legs and the definition of her abdomen. As she came closer, she noted that the fire cast no light beyond a few feet, and when she glanced over her shoulder, she saw that Harpalo, his bed, and even his entire hall had vanished into blackness. She stopped a foot or two away, her naked feet on a smooth, cold floor that she could not see, and despite the lack of light cast by the fire, heat again infused her entire body. She wrapped her arms around herself, her hands caressing her upper arms as she bathed in the warmth of Hykan.

"You have chosen a dangerous path," the fire flared for just a moment, the flames rising as it did so, "but I expected nothing else. Behold."

As Thyss watched, a soft red glow came into existence beyond Hykan's fire, and as it grew, Hykan Himself shrank to nothing more than a candle's worth of flame. The luminosity increased, eventually becoming a blood red illumination, a garnet aura that consumed the darkness and enveloped Thyss and all around her. As the view coalesced, the colors continued to brighten into molten hues of oranges and reds.

She blinked, and then Thyss found herself in a cave. No longer naked, she now wore the black silk tunic and leggings that belonged to Nekala, and hard sandals separated the soles of her feet from a smooth, scorching stone floor. Though she had never gone spelunking, or otherwise shown any interest in caves at all, the cavern felt quite large to her. The varied and uneven ceiling stood some twelve to fifteen feet overhead, undulating contrarily to the relatively flat floor, and spikes of stone rose and fell from the floor and ceiling like the teeth of a great beast or dragon. The air tasted toxic and smelled of rotten eggs, and even though Thyss didn't truly breathe that foul air, she fought the urge to cough and expel the foulness from her lungs. Immense heat, as well as a bright orange glow, emanated from a calm pool of lava on the far side of the cave, slight eddies and currents churning the molten rock. Thyss quickly turned to glance behind her, finding a tunnel entrance, a yawning dark portal that led vaguely upward.

Before she turned back to the cave, a question rising to her lips, a clanging sound brought her attention back to it fully. A monstrosity, a creature standing so tall that it almost bumped its head on the roof overhead stood in profile as it brought a large, flat rock down upon a glowing metal blade set upon a makeshift workbench of solid rock. The thing, male by its obvious anatomy, had a squat, muscled torso atop long, bony legs, and its arms, to include hands with long fingers and vicious claws, measured at least eight feet in length. Hairless, a thick and leathery skin of mottled browns and muted greens covered its entire body, and while Thyss couldn't see its face, she got an impression of a protruding, lantern jaw and a mouth full of teeth. She suppressed a shudder, guarding herself against any similarities between this thing and the *d'kinde* of the northern jungles.

"Feghul," Hykan hissed. For a moment, the creature stopped its pounding and straightened its slightly hunched back as it listened unmoving to the air around it, and fleetingly, Thyss feared the monster turning her way. Somehow, she knew she was safe in Hykan's presence, that the scene played out before her happened a great distance away, certainly in miles or even perhaps in time.

Satisfied that he heard nothing, the creature, Feghul, continued to strike a great, curved piece of metal, not unlike Thyss' own scimitar. Sparks flew from the collision over and over until, and with a cracking and tumbling of rock, his stone shattered and fell apart. He grunted, bent down, and retrieved another to resume his primitive smithing. The blade's glow cooled into a dull red that soon only showed itself in the center of its widest part. Feghul lifted it into the air as if to inspect his handiwork in the light cast by the lava, and the metal shined an alien green unlike any steel Thyss had ever seen. With another grunt, he turned, the blade held lovingly against his leathery hide, and stalked toward the lava pool. Thyss watched in awe as the creature named Feghul gingerly stepped straight into the volcanic flow and moved deeper until he was half submerged. He set the blade down in the molten rock and then lowered himself down into it as well, leaving just his eyes and nostrils exposed to the air.

Thyss was about to pose a question, but Hykan's murmured voice stilled her thoughts, "Patience."

Feghul rose from his infernal resting place, apparently no more bothered by what would mean instant death for a human as a baby was by a warm bath. He held the blade in between his claws, and it glowed brilliantly. He set back to work, smoothing imperfections in the metal and then running a large chunk of quartz up the curved edge repeatedly, occasionally stopping to inspect his work. As the metal cooled, Feghul finally stopped his work and touched a clawed thumb to a razor sharp edge. He inhaled swiftly, a whistling and horrible wheeze as a fine cut slit his flesh, black blood oozing from the wound, and he grunted again as he set to work fitting an irregular, hexagonal piece of bronze onto the blade. A quick in and out rumbling sounded from deep within Feghul's monstrous torso, and Thyss had the distinct impression the creature was laughing.

Mere seconds later, though Thyss felt like it took hours, the creature Hykan named Feghul turned to face Thyss and her god, and he swung before him a brilliant and deadly scimitar. As it flashed before back and forth, all agility and strength without skill or discipline, its vaguely emerald hued blade would cut through flesh and bone easier than any bronze or steel weapon, perhaps even steel itself. Its shimmering arcs mesmerized her in their lethal splendor, and she knew she must have the weapon.

"Feghul has a new claw. The sword sings to him," Hykan whispered as the cave, the lava, Feghul, and his sword faded from view, and as the blackness once again consumed everything but the lone, miniscule flame that was her god, Thyss felt a terrible longing in her heart, a sorrowful cavity that needed filling.

"I must have it," she breathed, her naked chest rising and falling rapidly with the pumping quickness of her heart and lungs.

"Yes, you must," Hykan agreed with flaring flames, "and while you will need my gifts in the time ahead, you will need to look to others if you desire Feghul's Claw."

"What does that mean?" Thyss asked, but Hykan did not answer immediately. She dropped to her knees, feeling them painfully strike a cold metal floor she could not see, and she held her hands out in supplication to Hykan, offering herself in any way the god should so desire. She repeated, "Please, what does that mean?"

Thyss awoke sitting upright with her hands held out before her, early morning sunlight barely diffusing the gloom of Harpalo's great hall. It sat empty and silent, no sign of a cave, a subterranean creature, or her god, and Thyss dropped her chin and gritted her teeth in annoyance. Some small part of her should have felt gratitude for the visitation, but most of her essence railed that if the gods were not going to be more helpful, they should stop meddling in the affairs of mortals.

“I will ask you one more time to stay here with us,” Harpalo insisted, but Thyss shortly shook her head even as he spoke.

She gazed off to the southeast, toward a series of mountains rising above a jungle in the distance and replied, “No. If I stay here, my father will most assuredly kill or enslave you all. It is safer for you if I leave. Besides, Hykan showed me something last night, and I must retrieve it.”

They stood on the southern edge of Calumbu, less than a hundred feet from where the jungle fought blade and flame to encroach on the city-village. Da’irda and N’tuli attended them, the former helping the still healing Harpalo with the short trek from the palace, while N’tuli led a mule by a leather cord. The animal was laden with supplies – several water skins, bags of dried meat, nuts and even some fruit, and a small jug of *palua* water.

“What is it?” Harpalo asked, genuine interest plain on his face as no god had ever deigned to show the giant anything. He knew the Highborns and the Chosen loved their gods, but never had he spoken to one who admitted to actually speaking with a god.

Still staring into the distance, Thyss said with an absent tone, “A sword, forged from strange metal by a monster living in a cave.”

“A Grek,” Harpalo grumbled, and he spat off to one side, “a fool’s errand.”

“What is a Grek?” Thyss asked, returning her gaze back to the king.

“A beast from before our time. Huge and strong, they live in the volcanoes,” Harpalo explained, pointing to where Thyss felt her gaze pulled. “They come out sometimes for food, and I thought they were mythical until I saw one a long time ago."

Harpalo stopped a moment and brought a thoughtful gaze back to Thyss before he continued, "But I've never heard of one having a weapon, much less forging one."

Thyss found herself again staring into the distance, following Harpalo's outstretched finger, and she pulled her attention back to his face. She couldn't explain it, but she could almost hear something beyond the horizon, a faint humming tune played low under the sounds of Harpalo's voice, the jungle before her, and the village behind. It soothed a burning anxiety she didn't realize she carried, but also begged for her to come, causing that tension to build and then crash down like a great wave. She needed to go.

She shrugged at Harpalo and said, "It is there. I will find it."

Thyss reached for the leather thong by which N'tuli held the mule, but the athletic warrioress raised a hand and said, "Hold, I have something for you."

N'tuli, dressed in her leather jerkin and skin leggings as always, shrugged her way out of a black coil that had looped many times about the right side of her neck and under her left arm. Thyss, so preoccupied with her vision of Feghul's Claw and her desire to leave Calumbu, had failed to notice it until the woman held it out to her. It was a rope, perhaps a hundred feet long based on the number of coils but weighed next to nothing, and it matched the tunic and leggings Thyss wore – black silk, apparently, with strands of silver woven throughout.

"It will hold many times your weight," N'tuli said as she offered it.

"I hope I am never many times my weight," Thyss replied with a lopsided smirk, receiving one in return. Haltingly, she asked, "Did this belong to…?"

"No," N'tuli shook her head, "this is mine, and I give it to you in thanks for your service to Calumbu."

"I thank you," Thyss replied, "but I didn't do it to serve Calumbu."

"The reasons do not matter," N'tuli said with a shrug, and she held the rope even closer to Thyss.

Wordlessly, Thyss accepted the rope and looped it around her neck and shoulder as N'tuli had. She then took the mule's lead and turned to face the three warriors who escorted her to the edge of her village. N'tuli appeared sad, while regret shown clearly in Harpalo's eyes, and Da'irda watched stoically as he continued to support his king. With nothing more to say, Thyss nodded her goodbyes to them and led the mule away from them and into the jungle.

Harpalo's booming voice called after her, "Calumbu ends at Nganozu Enzu. Travel safely, Lady Thyss!"

14.

Thyss followed a well-traveled cut through heavy jungle reminiscent of what she recently went through in the north, but it was a different kind of jungle. The village of Calumbu had tamed it and forged relationships with other villages nearby. Between trade and, apparently, Harpalo's high minded ideals, Calumbu had grown into a real city despite its poor appearance, and the name became synonymous with a nation of people who lived peacefully. She passed some of these people as she tracked south-southeast. She thought she recognized the dark faces of some of the city's inhabitants, but also, she saw so many more that they had to be from the other villages or towns or whatever they were. Peasants – well, those dressed in the Lowborn manner which she was accustomed to – passed her heading toward Calumbu, many of them carrying goods she had seen in the city's marketplaces. It seemed that anything from melons and vegetables to bronze weapons and leather armor made their way there to be further distributed across Harpalo's kingdom. Thyss even passed one overweight fellow, leading a mule much like her own, the animal laden with black silks that shimmered with silvery steel strands woven throughout. For a moment, she considered stopping to ask the merchant how he made them or from whence they came, but he seemed to be in no mood for conversation.

She certainly wasn't. She felt almost sick at the thought of leaving Calumbu behind, knowing the depths her father's anger could reach, but the message she'd sent off just after his visit should do the trick. As much as he sometimes channeled elemental fury, she knew he also valued wisdom and reason, and Mon'El wouldn't make war on a people for no reason. Harpalo may have injured her father's pride, but he had much larger problems to deal with. No, Calumbu and its people would be safe from him, especially if she weren't among them. If by some chance her father did come back, Harpalo would fight to defend her right to make her own decisions about her life. He'd fight to the death. His death. And everyone in Calumbu.

Thyss rarely cared for anyone else. Most people were a waste of time, and caring for others often just opened the door for them to harm or take what they wanted from you. Such was the case with her mother, who at some point genuinely loved Mon'El, and Thyss watched as Ilia had been nothing more than a piece in his boardgame for years. She vowed the same would not happen to her, and the people of Calumbu deserved better. Those she saw now often smiled or nodded politely, even if they had never seen her before, and Thyss further resolved herself that she would not be the cause of their torment, even if she believed their way of life foolish amidst a world where wealth, strength, and power ruled all.

She reached the first village in the late afternoon as the sun headed inexorably for the horizon, bathing Thyss' road in shadow. Commoners and travelers on the road thinned out as the day grew hot but became more common in the mile before the jungle opened upon a picturesque town. Unlike Harpalo's city-village, which was built from mudbricks harvested from the nearby river, this place looked more like a town she might find in the north of Dulkur with all of its buildings constructed from hardwood. While she saw only one two story building, a home of the local leader or elder perhaps, the town with its wide array of brightly dyed and painted wood homes almost assaulted the eyes, a vibrant and polychromatic contrast to the stark and utilitarian city some fifteen miles or so away.

But there were similarities as well. The streets and alleys here also were not paved, just dirt hard packed by the stomping of hundreds of feet, and the people smiled openly with each other and even toward Thyss, despite the obvious differences in her appearance. Her Highborn status, steel scimitar, and odd clothing – Nekala's clothing – drew no concern, reproach, or distrust, and the people made offerings of food, drink, or supplies to her as she passed no differently from the others around her. People were plentiful, though they didn't choke the streets as claustrophobically, and Thyss tried to count as she traversed the town. She gave up at three hundred, sure that at least a thousand called this place home, even as the population thinned out on the far southern side as the town gave way to sprawling farms.

The ancient mountains that were her destination hovered in the distance, great rows of ridged, gray mounds lording over the jungles surrounding the kingdom of Calumbu so far away, and her first day's travel seemed to bring the range no closer. For a moment, Thyss cursed her errand and even Hykan as she considered she had no idea where to find the Grek named Feghul or, more importantly, his sword. She dispelled the thought, knowing that she dared not lose Hykan's favor for what was yet to come.

Standing on the edge of this town, Thyss looked to the sky to judge how much more daylight remained. She had no interest in being caught in the jungle overnight, but every hour she spent traveling away from Calumbu took her closer to her goal and further from Harpalo's ridiculous sensibilities. If he thought there was any chance she remained in his lands, he might just try to convince her again to stay. Also, such a fact would further drive her father, and she would not give him reason to destroy Harpalo and his people. She continued.

As the jungle swallowed her, its canopy overhead blocking the heat and light of the sun, she pondered Hykan's last words to her. What did it mean, that she would need to look to others to possess Feghul's Claw? Thyss did not seek other people for aid. Between her god's favor and the steel at her hip, she had little need for other people. Even in the northern jungles as she faced the *D'kinde*, none of those with her who had attempted to kidnap and enslave her provided her any aid, and with her time in Calumbu Thyss had already done enough looking to others as she could handle for a lifetime. The thought of Nekala and Harpalo suddenly brought a torrent of emotion that she both hated and chafed against. No, she would accomplish everything on her own as she always had and as she always would.

She covered the miles easily, her body completely rejuvenated and rested from the ordeal in the north, and the jungle grew gloomier as the fading light of the sun struggled further to break through the foliage and trees overhead. Jungle sounds grew more prevalent – large numbers of insects serenaded each other in a cacophony of clicks, predatory night birds awoke and called out their presence, and even a great cat yarled somewhere out amongst the ferns and leafy plants.

Thyss picked up her pace and was rewarded with another settlement, much smaller than the last. Some few persons watched her as she entered the village, while most others busied themselves with moving their goods, children, and other family members indoors. She noted that the homes were built from both wood and stone, a brownish stone like that of Harpalo's palace. She approached the closest villager, a tall man whose dark skin appeared almost black in the failing light, and he eyed her with curiosity more than suspicion.

"Am I still in Harpalo's kingdom?" she asked.

"You are, stranger," he replied with a nod. "This is the village of K'watu, the last village of Calumbu to the south."

"Am I nearing Nganozu Enzu?"

"You are. Follow the road southeast from K'watu, and you will pass through it on the way to Berak'a."

"And what is Berak'a?" Thyss queried, uncomfortably aware that she virtually begged help from this Lowborn villager.

"Berak'a sits at the base of the mountains. We trade with them for stone."

"Is Harpalo's palace built from this stone?"

"It is. You know King Harpalo, then?"

"I do," she said with a slight nod.

A wide smile split the villager's face, his teeth shining brightly even in the failing light, "Then come stay as a guest in K'watu. We can find you a place to sleep, and you can continue your journey in the morning."

Thyss hesitated, seemed about to decline the offer, and he said, "You must not stay in the jungle overnight. The jungle here is extremely dangerous, much more so than around Calumbu itself. We will hear no refusal." He called to a passing woman, older and dressed in a simple white, linen robe, "Akili! Would you prepare a place for one of King Harpalo's guests?"

The woman turned as he spoke, and Thyss looked her way as she listened, nodded slightly, and turned to go about her task. Her first impression of Akili was incorrect. The woman wasn't older, but one of the eldest people she'd ever seen with heavy cracks and creases around the eyes and on the forehead from squinting in the sun. Deep lines wrapped her mouth from either smiling or scowling, and the corners of both her eyes and mouth sagged downward to point at the ground. Yet, she moved quickly and with purpose, and Thyss started to wonder how many elders lived in all of Calumbu. There were many she remembered seeing, but she was sure she had ignored many, many more, her eyes wandering past them without interest no differently than if they were a plain piece of furniture.

"Please, follow Akili," the villager said, whose name she didn't know and hadn't asked. "She will make you comfortable for the night."

Within minutes, Thyss stood in a simple stone bothy with a single room and a plain door made of nearly pure white wooden planks. Inside, the stone had the same light brown hue as outside, shown by a single lit torch whose smoke vented through a covered break in the slanted wood roof overhead. To enter, Thyss descended four or five stone steps, where the villagers had dug down and a stone foundation laid snuggly into the hole. The lower two feet of the stone walls were covered by the ground itself, and she wondered at the need for such construction.

The old woman, Akili with a head full of gray and white hair that sprung in all directions unrestrained and unfettered in any way, stacked a few blankets on top of a wide netting that stretched suspended across the width of the single room, its ends anchored into the stone walls. As if reading Thyss' mind, her gravelly voice explained, "The ground helps keep the room cool."

"Where do I sleep?" Thyss asked, eyeing the contraption that looked more at home in the fishing boats of the River Thyssallia with apprehension and no small amount of skepticism.

"The sleeping net," Akili said with a shrug and a slight gesture of one hand, a tone of condescension in her voice. "You Highborns know so little of how to live simply."

Indignation and the gnawing heat of fiery anger erupted into being in Thyss' heart, and her eyes blazed with the desire to act. Her brief captivity as a prisoner to Lahn and Ulinae before coming to Calumbu had taught her the value of patience, the value of waiting for the right time to strike, but there was no need here. This ancient bag of flesh and bones meant nothing to Thyss and offered her no danger. She could set the woman aflame or lop her head off in one smooth motion before Akili realized her misstep, but as Thyss' eyes narrowed on the old woman's face, she saw a keen intellect reflected in those elder eyes.

Perhaps it was Harpalo's kindness and Thyss' respect for him, being that she was still in his kingdom, which stayed her hand.

Akili's mouth edged up in the smile of one who knew she had won a contest, but her words said, "My apologies. Never mind an old woman. You are Chosen. Who is your god?"

"Hykan is my Patron," Thyss said simply, seeing no harm in answering a simple question.

"Ah, God of Fire. A dangerous and powerful god, to be sure. Beware, Princess, lest you allow his fires to consume you. Temper your desires with wisdom and clarity."

"Who are you to speak to me so?" Thyss anger flared again, a wave of heat rolling off her body.

Akili shrugged, said, "Lay one of the blankets across the net to keep the rope from rubbing your skin," and she turned to leave.

Flummoxed at the woman's entirely uncaring attitude toward the difference in their positions, Thyss seemed at a loss for words. The confusion warred with her anger, and it seemed that confusion would win the day. As Akili opened the door to trudge up the steps into the cooling night air, Thyss called after her, "How did you know I am a Princess?"

Akili pulled the door shut behind her and replied without even looking back, "Sleep well, Princess."

The sleeping net would have been more comfortable if it were anything else. As Thyss stretched her sore muscles and worked out cramps in her neck and back, she gazed balefully at the charred remains of the device that was clearly meant more for torture than sleeping. It surely seemed pleasant at first, and the sensation of lying suspended in midair was surprisingly relaxing. But Akili was right, after a short time, the netting seemed to bite into the flesh, leaving horrendous hashmark indentions across exposed skin. And it rubbed. And it itched. Thyss took the advice and laid a blanket, the thickest one they gave her, across the interlacing strands of rope or whatever the damnable thing was made of, but the damage had been done. No matter what, her skin hurt, and no matter how she laid, comfort was not to be had. To say nothing of, in an attempt to turn onto her side because her preferred sleeping position on her stomach bent her neck back at an unnatural angle, the net swiftly and remorselessly deposited her on the stone floor. She incinerated the nightmarish thing and curled up on the floor, using the blankets to provide a miniscule amount of cushion.

And all the hijinks left her with a lack of sleep, soreness, cramps, and knots. She wanted nothing more than to go back to sleep, but all of that would subside with activity. Normally she would prefer to sleep late and rise when the whim found her, but that just wasn't the case as of late. Her sandals clapped on the stone steps outside the hut as she climbed up into a bright and unusually warm morning sun. Just exiting the cool shelter, she already felt a fine mist of sweat on her forehead, though she enjoyed the buildup of the heat on her skin and black clothing.

"I wanted to be near when you awoke," a voice rang out, and Thyss looked up to see the man from the previous day walking toward her. "Will you be leaving?"

"I will. Thank you for the shelter," Thyss said, and only later as she traveled to Berak'a, would she realize how few people she had thanked in her life.

He shrugged and said, "It is nothing. All are welcome while in Calumbu. Do you have supplies enough?"

"Yes, though I might refill my waterskins. Nganozu Enzu is the end of Calumbu's lands?"

"Yes, it is not far, and Berak'a is beyond that."

"How will I know when I reach Nganozu Enzu?" Thyss asked.

Puzzlement ran across his face for just a moment, followed by realization, and he patiently explained, "I am sorry. I did not think that the name may not translate to your high tongue. It means 'land of many colors'. I promise you'll know when you reach it. Do not stray from the road in Nganozu Enzu. There is much danger there, but you will be safe if you stay away from the plants."

"I thank you," Thyss said again, wondering at this newfound gratitude she felt toward this man. They should give her whatever she needs just for virtue of her obvious higher station, for being Chosen. She pushed the feeling away and asked, "What is your name?"

"Rafuki," he answered, his face breaking into the enormous smile she saw last night.

"Thyss," she said and offered her arm. Rafuki took it as if they were old friends or perhaps close comrades of some past conflict.

"Will we see you again soon?"

Thyss looked past the canopy of trees toward the mountains that did seem larger today than they had yesterday. Larger meant closer, and if she could note that difference, she was getting close. Or perhaps it was all a hopeful illusion.

"I cannot say," Thyss shrugged, and then she adopted an impish grin as she considered how angry it would make her father to find her back among the people of Calumbu after he had come and gone from their lands, "Maybe. We will see."

"May that day come soon. The well is in the center of the village, and it is for all. Go safely, Thyss," Rafuki offered, and they released arms.

15.

The jungle ended abruptly, the sky opening up before Thyss over a picturesque valley that ran on for miles. The road wound through this vale, flanked on either side by ferns, flowers, and plants she had never seen before and could never identify. There were so many colors, hundreds of shades and hues that varied subtly from the simple descriptions of green, blue, or red, so many different tints and tones to be as many as there were stars in the night sky. She had never seen so much vibrancy, and it went on for miles.

And the mountains loomed ever closer.

She took a step and found the leather cord leading her mule to be stretched to its limit. The animal refused to take one step forward. She cursed at it, cajoled, pleaded, and begged, and yet it would not move forward, its eyes wide as it stared into the chromatic plethora of plants. Cursing again, Thyss took her waterskin and a sack of supplies, and looped them over her shoulder. As she turned from the mule, it began to wander back into the jungle, never straying from the road.

As she started into Nganozu Enzu, the road traveled vaguely downhill, down into the valley, and Thyss fought to control her curiosity. She had never before seen blue and yellow fronds on a fern or bright scarlet flowers almost the size of her head shaped like a pitcher. She watched as a bee landed on one of these and climbed through the aperture to find the sweetness inside the flower, and she nodded and sighed in understanding as the opening closed behind the insect. She watched as other plants closed on hapless insects not unlike the devices trappers used to catch animals, and some distance away, she saw a vine whip through the air in an attempt to catch a bird in flight! Thyss tilted her head slightly to one side as she thought about it – she knew of toads, spiders, and snakes that were dangerous and identified by bright colors. She supposed plants could be just as deadly and marked just the same.

She stopped as she neared a cluster of ferns with bright orange fronds wrapped in dark green on the right edge of the road. The group of plants was almost six feet across, and it rustled and gyrated incessantly as if some animal within them detected her presence and could not decide whether to attack or flee. The frenetic stirring continued as she watched, and Thyss decided to put as much of the dirt road between she and them as possible, stepping cautiously down the left side as she passed.

And then a figure popped out from the middle of a group of giant pitcher plants only a few feet to her left. She caught a flash of utterly discombobulated gray hair and white linen, coupled with a boisterous crooning of, "Hello, Princess!" and Thyss shouted her surprise as she half stepped, half jumped away. Her feet caught on each other, her ankles crossed, and Thyss fell hard backward, right into the orange and green ferns that moved of their own diabolical volition.

"Oh, no!" she heard a muffled voice exclaim, followed by, "Hold on, Princess, I'm coming!"

The orange and green engulfed Thyss, and she landed flat on her back, hitting the ground hard as her head bounced off a cushioned lump of foliage. A huge puff of brown and black exhaled around her, as if she had fallen on a giant mold puffball, and she instinctively held her breath, as most people would when confronted with breathing in something other than air. As she struggled to regain her senses and rise, she got the acute feeling that her skin was literally crawling, or rather, something crawled all over her skin. Panic ensued, and her arms flailed.

"Don't fight so!" Akili's voice shouted in annoyance, and a strong hand gripped her wrist. She reciprocated the grip, as the old woman hauled Thyss out of the ferns and back onto the dirt track. Thyss looked in disgust and dismay at the hundreds, no, thousands of miniscule spiders that crawled all over her body. Before she could get past the immediate revulsion, Akili came at her with a bucket of water that was hidden in the foliage, drenching Thyss and washing most of the offending arachnids away. She dropped the empty bucket, reaching for another when Thyss screamed something unintelligible, and a pillar of flame exploded, enveloped her instantly, incinerated the spiders, and evaporated the puddling water with an instant hiss of steam. Akili put her hand up and turned her head to shield herself from the blinding heat, and then it was gone, leaving Thyss and her clothing spider free and yet impressively intact.

"That was unnecessary, Princess," Akili chided. "The second bucket would have washed most of them away and spared the spiders as well."

"I have no need to spare the spiders," she hissed back.

"You invaded their home, not the other way around."

"If a stupid old witch had not been hiding in carnivorous plants awaiting the opportunity to startle passersby, it would not have even happened," Thyss accused, though she felt her ire abating quickly.

"Old? Yes. Witch? Maybe. Stupid? I think not," Akili shot back angrily, but then she softened her tone,

"Though, I admit I may share some blame in your misfortune. You have my apologies, Princess."

"Stop calling me that," Thyss snapped. "Why were you hiding about anyway? I was told the plants are dangerous."

"They are," Akili confirmed, "to you, but not to me. The plants and I have… an understanding. Anyway, I have what I came for, so I am going home now. I'll escort your mule back to K'watu. He'll be there for you whenever you return."

"I don't know if I will return."

The aged woman smiled and loosed a rasping chuckle that sounded like something horrific moved about in her chest. "Of course, you will, Princess."

Akili picked up her buckets, one empty and the other full, and hobbled her way past Thyss, walking only slightly faster than the mule who was slowly rambling away. In all the disquieting activity, Thyss hadn't before noticed the heavy leather belt wrapped around the old woman's waist with dozens of pouches hanging from it, out of some of which poked sprigs of plants, flower petals, and even insects.

"I think I hate you," Thyss said after her, "I could end the world of your vexing existence right now."

"You could," Akili agreed with a nod, and she half turned back toward the sorceress, "but you won't."

"And why not?"

Akili's face broke into a smile full of yet more vexing, irritating mirth as she shrugged, "Because I'm harmless. Remember, Princess, fire isn't the answer to everything. Sometimes water will do just as well."

Thyss watched in bewilderment as the elderly witch shuffled and tottered into the jungle, chasing after the mule as she did so. Given the old woman's higher rate of speed, she thought Akili might just catch up to the animal right about the time they reached her village. Thyss shook her head, aggravated that someone could be so purposefully annoying and yet so pointless to kill, turned, and followed the road through Nganozu Enzu.

She climbed from the shallow valley only a few hours later, and it seemed that the pulsating vibrancy of its foliage ended just before the ridge that Thyss now stood upon. It gave way to a savannah that stretched ahead for miles, a flat plain covered in waist high grasses and dotted with acacia and marula trees. Wildlife abounded – a group of gazelles just a few hundred paces to the east, a herd of buffalo lumbering at a riverbank a half mile to the west, and even a few lions resting lazily in the shadow of a sparse tree. The road straightened, shooting like an arrow to a city nestled right up against the mountain range only a mile or so away.

The afternoon sun behind her, Thyss noted that the entire city seemed built of brown stone, and she was certain the blocks would be uniform, quarried from somewhere nearby. A wall perhaps twenty feet tall, though she admitted that it was hard to be sure of the height at this distance, surrounded most of the city to provide obvious protection from attackers, and dark specks stood and moved on top of them. There appeared to be farmsteads outside the wall, but she doubted they provided enough food for the walled city which she thought must have at least two thousand inhabitants. Doubtless, the city leaned heavily on hunting parties, for game nearby seemed plentiful. To add certainty to this observation, a dissonant chorus of honking growls sounded from the direction of the river as hippos grunted their displeasure at the nearby buffalo, the latter of which trotted up the riverbank to escape the cantankerous creatures.

She set out for Berak'a immediately.

As she closed the distance, the farms spread further from the walls than she realized, especially along the riverbank. She could see that the wall did not entirely enclose the city, as one side of it stood open to the river upon which dozens of tiny boats floated as their one or two man crews fished the freshwater. The occasional marula trees had been cultivated into an orchard bordering the city's north, and figures moved through its shade picking the tart, yellow fruits the trees grew. And true to Thyss' original thoughts, groups of hunters ranged beyond the farms and the orchards, picking off select animals to bring home for slaughter and allowing the rest of the herds to move on.

She realized now that she underestimated the height of the walls from a distance, as they towered well over forty feet in the air with occasional peaks rising above that, and men with bows walked these, paying little attention to what happened below. She noted other differences in her original observations as well. The houses amongst the farms were not houses at all, but rather wooden buildings clearly meant to hold livestock, grain, seed, and all the other sundry supplies one needed for such a bucolic profession. She assumed the workers lived inside the city, safe behind those towering walls, but it wasn't just farms she passed. She saw several butchers, the thunking of heavy blades sounded as they chopped through flesh and struck wood underneath, and the yards around these shacks were drenched in blood or perhaps permanently stained red. Off to one side, a tanner worked with several young men plying his trade, the noxious fumes being swept away by the light breeze toward the river.

Foot traffic picked up the closer she came – hunters with their prey slung over their shoulders or tied to pole stretchers, persons pushing wagons full of fruits and vegetables, or cloudlike puffs of harvested cotton. There was an obvious destination for many of them. A black iron portcullis provided the only entry into the city other than the river, through which she heard the familiar clamor of merchants hawking wares.

The activity, the array of chaotic voices, and the stone of the city itself eased a tension Thyss did not realize she'd been holding onto. It had been months since she left Kaimpur, most of that time spent traipsing through the wilderness with all of its unknowns, to say nothing of what happened in the northern jungle. And even this was just a temporary stop as she prepared for yet another foray into the unknown, this time into caves she didn't even know the location of to face a creature she didn't know how to fight. Thyss swaggered through the gate and into Berak'a, the known dangers of civilization of more comfort than the softest bed.

The stink of life assaulted her. Unwashed bodies, rotten meat, and the animal smells of livestock filled the air and mingled to form the miasma of existence she had come to expect from every city other than Kaimpur. The streets were paved with stone, their alleys and corners where they met buildings filled with refuse and stinking of piss. The towering walls kept the freshening breeze from clearing the air. She almost wondered if she had lost some of her eyesight, as everything around her seemed to be a shade of the brown stone from which the city was built, excluding the clothes of some of the city dwellers, but even they varied only towards grays and whites. People pressed all around her as they pushed their way toward their destinations, most of them uncaring or uninterested in anyone or anything other than their tasks. There were others, however, that watched everything, and Thyss felt gazes from above on the wall or dark alleys and doorways boring into her like a carpenter's or stonecutter's drill as they watched the Highborn weave through the throngs of people. Whistles, hollers, the solicitous call of vendors and whores, squeals of pigs, chiming clangs of a smithy, and all manners of sounds that blended into one deafening tumult filled her ears, and Thyss smiled at the chaos of it all.

And underneath all of it, a soft melodic humming drew her attention to the mountains that loomed over the city of Berak'a. Hykan told her the sword sang to the abominable monster Feghul, but she now wondered if it sang also to her, its longing for blood and the impact of steel giving it strength to serenade her even from miles away.

The city sprawled ever closer to the mountains, and as Thyss moved her way through it, she found that it spread closer to them than she realized. It was built on top of foothills and abutted against a vertical escarpment. Where there had once been steep slopes and inclines of hills, the city added narrow, precipitous stone staircases that connected lower level streets to those above them. Many of these were slick with waste, animal and human, and Thyss watched her step everywhere she went. Even though she avoided most of it, she still resolved to at least rinsing her feet and sandals wherever she stopped for the night.

Unlike the jungle bound villages of Calumbu, Berak'a refused to sleep as the sun sank behind the green canopied horizon to the west. Vendors closed their stalls, workers returned home, and the great portcullis dropped with a grating and clanging of iron, but as the day's work ended, the night's revelries began. Music, dancing, and drinking filled the night as watchmen walked the streets igniting torches. While she did not partake, Thyss enjoyed the entertainment – jugglers and jesters, dancers and bardic voices, foppish gamblers and iron thewed wrestlers – and watched it all with the knowing smile that many of the people of Berak'a would awaken tomorrow with throbbing heads and much less coin.

She retired early, the gold she'd taken with her from Kaimpur those many months ago dwindling dangerously, but she had no intention of staying in the city long. Tomorrow, as soon as she awoke, she would range into the mountains in search of the foul Grek named Feghul and his wicked claw and may the loving caress of the scimitar's ballad lead her to it.

16.

An army marched into the pitiful village on the western edge of Calumbu's border. Over ten thousand strong, Mon'El's host was over half conscripted peasants with just enough training to know which end of the pike was dangerous, but he also brought mercenaries, professional soldiers, and his elite guard. He rode a black stallion at the front of the army, without concern at all for any Lowborn's ability to harm him, and behind him followed three priests, one Chosen by each of the other elemental gods. Truth be told, Mon'El hated riding smelly beasts, but it was necessary that he be at the head of his army. At least the weather had been fair, and his silk robes, dyed blue so light as to appear almost white, flowed comfortably in the breeze.

As they invaded the lush savannah that well preceded the village, the wilds turned to cultivated lands. They approached primitive farms, small orchards, and even rickety corrals, and dozens of dark skinned Lowborns dotted the signs of civilization. One by one as they noticed the force, or had it pointed out to them by others, the workers deserted their places and sped away on foot to the east. Mon'El's troops, despite being peopled by so many Lowborns, were well disciplined and knew what was expected of them. They did not chase the escaping villagers, but marched inexorably onward, driving rodents and other small animals before them and crushing wretched crops into the dirt and dust.

The village looked like so many others across the savannahs of Dulkur, many of which served under his rule. Only a few hundred called the place home, Lowborns all of them with skin tones ranging from browns to near ebony, and his eyes swept their deplorable existence. Children ran naked, gathered by parents or elders, most of the latter of which wore little clothing themselves. The homes were built of wood, likely gathered from the jungle, the edge of which Mon'El saw on the far side of the village. A well stood in the center, a squat circle of stones that stood just a couple of feet tall, and a wooden bucket with a long rope tied to its handle lay haphazardly next to it. There was no gold, silver, silks, or sign of wealth of any kind, but he did see spears and swords, some of steel and most of bronze.

As his army reached the village's edge, he held a hand aloft, and the voices of sergeants and overseers echoed almost as one behind him to bring all ten thousand to an immediate stop. Many of the villagers fled indoors while some idly edged toward weapons in a vain attempt to be inconspicuous in their actions, but neither were the cause of Mon'El's command. He watched as dozens, hundreds of warriors clad in leather or skins emerged from dense jungle, each of them armed with a sword or even two, daggers, and several spears each. At their head marched their giant king, Harpalo, and Mon'El also recognized the thick muscled warrior at the king's right from his brief time in Calumbu. Though, he couldn't remember the other man's name, nor did he care to. Mon'El waited patiently, his eyes roaming over the much smaller force, the sun glistening on the sweat covered bodies of a thousand warriors as they entered the village from the east. The kingpriest of Kaimpur also noted many of the villagers surreptitiously fled into the jungle or joined Harpalo's warriors as they stopped just past the well at the village center, only a hundred feet or so from Mon'El's own army.

"Good King Mon'El," called Harpalo, his heavy voice easily carrying, "again I welcome you to Calumbu, but I would ask that your army stay on the plains."

"Ask nothing of me, Lowborn," Mon'El replied, and he spoke in a soft timbre, allowing the winds of his god to carry his words to every man, woman, and child in the village. "I am here for my daughter."

"I am sorry," Harpalo replied, and though he kept his tone light and neutral, his expression betrayed his feelings about the way in which he was addressed, "Lady Thyss is not in Calumbu. She left days ago, but you know that already. She sent you a message."

Mon'El ignored this. He received the scroll, of course, and it angered him so that he summoned a gale that lifted the hapless villager who brought it and tossed him out of his abode atop the pyramid. The poor soul fell over fifty feet before he landed on the steep, lapis lazuli façade of the palace with a shattering of bones, and he then proceeded to slide down the exterior, smearing blood across it before he landed in a tangled heap of bone and flesh. Mon'El had felt a twinge of regret about that, even though the villager wasn't the subject of his ire, and it took workers hours to clean all the blood off the lapis.

"Tell me whence she has gone, and I will leave your… *kingdom* in peace."

Again, Harpalo fought off the offense of Mon'El's words, and he said, "I cannot."

"You shall," Mon'El said, and a short gust of wind carried his voice in a sharp boom across the village.

"I cannot help you. She went her own way."

"You *know* where she went, you ignorant savage, and if you do not tell me, I will slaughter your people and raze Calumbu to the ground!" Mon'El screamed his fury. A crash of thunder split the air overhead as dark clouds suddenly scudded across the sky to block the sun, pushed as they were by an unseen force.

"Peace, King Mon'El," Harpalo called, placatingly with open hands before him. "There is no need for bloodshed here today. Thyss has no desire to be a part of your rule, and here in Calumbu, we believe that people determine their own fate."

"You're a fool," Mon'El whispered, raising a hand in the air.

"Please, join us, and truly see Calumbu for what it is," Harpalo implored. "With you and your strength with us, we can build remarkable things across Dulkur. Peace and cooperation are the way."

"Kill them!" Mon'El's voice crashed like a destroying wave across the savannah, the village and even into the jungle trees as he dropped his hand. "Slaughter all who fight, take those who do not!"

Troops surged forward and around Mon'El and his priests, driven by his thunderous command and the vocal and whipping urgings of their sergeants. The conscripts crashed into the village, and Harpalo's warriors rushed to meet them with thrown javelins and the flashing of bronze blades. Men cried out in pain and horror, death cries filled the air, and within minutes the dirt of the village's alleys clumped and ran with blood. Mon'El's conscripts fell by the dozens to Harpalo's better trained warriors, and even Harpalo himself slaughtered them with abandon, their corpses falling swiftly to the ground like tall grass shorn by a scythe.

Mon'El watched with bored eyes, and as his sea of pikemen died quickly and horribly, he busied himself with smoothing several creases in his robes. They appeared while riding, and it was not worth the effort of correcting them until he stopped. He glanced up noting that despite the death being dealt to them, his enlistees slowly enveloped Harpalo's warriors and brought them down one by one with dozens of stabbing spear wounds. A javelin with a bronze tip whistled through the air directly at his face, and Mon'El lifted his left hand to waive it away. A forceful puff of wind deflected it, and men shouted their surprise as it whistled past him and into his mercenaries. His hand still open before him, Mon'El noted some grime under his fingernails and set about working to clean them.

The number of bodies strewn about the village grew, and the coppery, sickly scent of spilled blood permeated the air. Mon'El noted with satisfaction that at least half of Harpalo's fighters lay dead, and some had broken away to flee into the jungle. He did not bother to count how many pikemen lay dead. It didn't matter. There were always more.

A voice interrupted his thoughts, and he looked down at the captain of his personal guard, a hulking Lowborn that could almost lift a horse by himself, who said, "Majesty, should we not send in the *kopishi*?"

Mon'El turned in his saddle to view his mercenaries, three thousand men and women he had gone to great expense equipping with bronze studded leathers and steel scimitars in addition to whatever they brought with them to his service. They watched the battle intently as many of them licked their lips or stood with hands on sword hilts, and all of them appeared as if they might leave their own skins behind, jumping so swiftly to join the battle when the order was given. He turned back to the sounds of combat, noting in annoyance that Harpalo and his survivors seemed to be holding well against the waning bloodlust of Mon'El's own spear wielding peasants.

"Very well," Mon'El sighed. "Send them. Do not pull the conscripts until the *kopishi* are engaged. I want no one to escape. That one," he said with a pointed finger, "their king, I want him alive."

"Yes, Majesty," the captain half bowed and turned to relay the orders.

Mon'El sighed again. He hated to slaughter all of the people of Calumbu, but he would if they continued to fight. They didn't understand how valuable they were to him. People were one of the most undervalued resources in Dulkur, but he would brook no trouble from the peasants that called this piteous land a kingdom, especially Lowborns.

Harpalo fought like a lion, losing count of the number he cut down, and his people made him proud as they fought with him for something more than land or gold. They had reached an equilibrium of sorts, fending off the prodding spears and still dealing death when the swordsmen appeared, their steel scimitars hacking through leather armor and destroying the bronze blades of Calumbu's warriors. Harpalo had fallen under the press of the attack as a blade sliced through his hamstring. Da'irda and others fought to their king, maiming his attackers brutally before helping him to his feet, but it was to no avail. Their defensive circle shrank increasingly as more of their fighters went down. Harpalo lost his enormous two handed sword and engulfed a man's throat in his massive hand, crushing it as the corpse convulsed. He retrieved the dead man's own scimitar and turned just in time to see N'tuli's head fly from her shoulders with a spout of blood and flashing steel. He screamed unintelligibly as he waded into a group of three, dealing death and dismemberment, but a slash cut through the triceps of his right arm. He again lost his weapon and brought his left fist about to crush a warrior woman's skull. Harpalo bent over to take her weapon and rose to come to Da'irda's aid, but he was too late as the man went down under the hacks of a half dozen swordsmen.

Before long, there were no friends left, none of his people to aid or turn to, and Harpalo stood surrounded by enemies who seemed somehow reticent to make him join his people in death. He heard high pitched screams as Mon'El's troops found villagers who had not fled their homes, and his rage exploded at the meaning of those cries. He attacked as well as he was able, but as blood dripped and flowed from a dozen shallow wounds, his muscles slowed. His clumsy assaults were avoided or parried, and finally, a swift kick to the back of his good leg brought Harpalo down hard in the blood soaked dirt of the village. He had nothing left to offer. He couldn't find the strength to lift a sword, or even to roll over to stand, and the enemy took him.

They bound his hands at the wrists and tied silk rope around his arms to tightly bind them about his body. They kept his legs free to allow him to walk, and a healer or physician bent over him just long enough to make certain his wounds were not fatal. It seemed that Mon'El wanted him alive. They fit a gag snug into his mouth, and a leather cord was tied about his wrists and attached to the back of Mon'El's saddle.

"We lost over two thousand of the draftees, Majesty," Mon'El's captain reported, and if Harpalo could have spat their way, he would have.

"How many slaves did we take?" the king asked from the back of his horse.

"Only twelve. Several women and some children. The rest either died fighting or ran into the jungle."

Mon'El sighed, "Very well. We must try not to kill all Calumbu's people, as they are my people now, but we will not tolerate anything other than surrender. We go east into the jungle." He paused as he turned a meaningful gaze on Harpalo, though he continued to speak to his captain, "There are nine villages of Calumbu. This was the smallest. We shall take every single one. Those who wish to join us may do so. Those who fight will die, and the rest come as slaves. We take everything of value, burn the rest, and then return to Kaimpur."

The captain merely bowed, and the host set off into the jungle. True to his words, Mon'El destroyed everything in his wake. Harpalo's people fought, or at least they tried to, with swift attacks on the flanks, throwing javelins into the invading army before melting back into the jungle. Though surprising at first, the effect was minimal as the army rotated more armored men to the flanks, protecting the skittish conscripts. Scouts were sent to locate the ambushers before they struck, and Calumbu lost more defenders.

Over the following days, Mon'El and his army swept through every one of Calumbu's villages and towns, destroying each of them in turn. Harpalo already lost most of his warriors in the initial combat, but still he held out hope that the people could kill enough of Mon'El's troops to force the kingpriest to return home. He stumbled about behind Mon'El's horse, weak from loss of blood and lack of food, and on the occasion that Calumbu put up a stiff resistance, he felt energized with hope and pride, only to have it drain away when another village went up in flames.

Eventually it ended at K'watu, Mon'El apparently aware that Nganozu Enzu marked the edge of Calumbu, and the invaders found only two remnants of its population, the rest of them having either run off or already died helping defend other parts of the kingdom. There was only an old woman with a hunched back and unwashed gray hair arrayed in dozens of directions and a mule that grazed boredly nearby. The elder spat and cursed the invaders, shouting at them in a tongue none of them knew, regardless of whether they were High or Lowborn. She threw a glass vial at Mon'El who merely ducked the missile, and the shattering of glass behind him brought with it exclamations and then writhing screams of pain.

"Kill the witch," Mon'El sighed, having grown almost indifferent over the dull tedium of conquering Calumbu.

The woman stood her ground, and to her credit, she neither begged nor cried as death approached her with an unsheathed sword. As the blade lifted and reflected the sun's radiant light, she cackled horribly, a laugh apparently comprised of two large rocks grinding together deep in her chest. The terrific humor ended abruptly, and Harpalo fell to his knees, unable to withstand the trial any further.

"I commend your strength," Mon'El said softly, and Harpalo looked up to see the kingpriest had dismounted from his horse. "I thought you would have died before now."

Harpalo said nothing, not that he could have as they only removed the gag to allow him to drink enough water to keep him moving. A terrible emptiness gnawed in his stomach, and his arms hung limply at his sides as he knelt on legs folded underneath him. He had no strength left.

"On the other hand, what manner of king are you to be able to watch your people suffer so? You believed in yourself so much that you allowed me to kill, rape, loot, and take at will. Are your ideals so important? I will weep for your people."

Harpalo retorted then, but it came out as a muffled concoction no one understood. At a halfhearted wave from Mon'El, his captain cut the gag with a curved dagger. Harpalo licked cracked lips for a moment, fighting to work up enough saliva and energy to speak again. Finally, he said, "I weep for you."

"Don't be ridiculous," Mon'El almost laughed. He suppressed an arrogant smirk and asked, "And why would you weep for me, king of a lost kingdom?"

"Because she'll come for you," Harpalo's strangled voice eked out from a parched throat, "and you will be lucky to know only the pain you visited on my people."

Mon'El did laugh then, a mirthless knowing chortle that carried on the winds of Aeyu throughout K'watu, the rest of Calumbu, and even across Nganozu Enzu. He eventually reined it in enough to look down into the exhausted and defeated eyes of Harpalo, and he explained, "I'm counting on it."

"Decapitate him," Mon'El commanded.

Not even waiting to see if the order was carried out or caring to watch the execution, he turned toward one of his saddlebags. As he fished around inside of it as the sound of steel coming unsheathed rang out, followed by a sickening thunk and the sound of a body falling to the ground. Mon'El turned back to the prone body of Harpalo and picked up the dead king's head by the hair from where it had bounced a few feet away to set it next to the body. He reached down to where blood poured with decreasing flow from the stump of Harpalo's neck into the village's main avenue, wetting his finger in the redness. Mon'El ran his finger across a piece of unrolled papyrus, writing a flowing script in Harpalo's own blood, dipping his finger once more as the ink went dry. He motioned for a dagger from one of his guards, and once it was in his hand, he plunged it into Harpalo's back, pinning the scroll in place.

He mounted his horse and announced, "Home to Kaimpur!" to the assorted cheers of his army.

17.

Smoke curled and wafted into the air as long dead brambles mixed with weeds and spider webs burned away from the irregular hole atop the southern facing ridgeline. Thyss wondered at what made the gap, for it didn't strike her as a normal cave entrance, and while she admitted that she had very little knowledge of caves or mountaineering, this particular ingress into the mountain itself had the aspect of something having punched through, as if some titan with the height of a hundred men had brought its gargantuan fist down onto the ridge to break through into the caves below. Once most of the obscuring brush burned away, the remainder of it tumbled down into a dark cavity, and she lost count of how many breaths she took before she heard a light splash below.

Thyss swiftly realized upon hiking into the range that she had no mountain climbing equipment at all, not that she would have known what to do with it if she had. She carried a leather pack with a handful of basic supplies – food, water, a few torches – as she scrambled her way from path to path, ledge to ledge until she could go no further and backtracked. She entered passes that inclined upward to end at sheer rock faces, some of which were short and easily climbed, but others towered overhead. By the second day, she had found several caves, but most of them were shallow, little more than cubby holes some predator called home. One large entrance looked promising with its size, but the pile of human bones within coupled with the fact that, only ten or so feet in, it shrank into a tunnel she would only be able to wriggle through like a worm warned her away from it.

On the third day, she was almost ready to turn back to Berak'a and find a guide, the only thing preventing her from doing so being her lack of coin. The city was like most outcroppings of civilization – its denizens did not share the high minded ideals of Calumbu. No one would help her unless she paid for the assistance, and then there was no guarantee they wouldn't try to take more. Calumbu's way of life felt so at odds with everything she held true, and a strange sensation tingled in the bottom of her heart when she considered that. Was it shame? Regret? She couldn't quite understand it; it was so alien to her very being, and yet it somehow seemed wrong to her that she understood implicitly the wickedness of the people of Berak'a and all the rest of the world.

She churned these thoughts and feelings over and over as she made her way up a tall but sloping ridgeline on the southern edge of a series of peaks in the hopes that, once she stood atop that ridge, she would have a clear view over miles of foothills and mountainsides. Loose rock fell away under her feet as the slope inclined steeper, and she resorted to dropping to all fours, her hands steadying her advance by taking ahold of solid bits of rock. The morning sunlight shined brightly on her face, and the air was notably cooler than the city, savannah, and jungle below. Thyss felt renewed vigor as she made her way up the knife's edge of the ridge, and it was close to the apex of the ridge, where it turned almost perfectly vertical toward the mountain's peak that she very nearly fell right into the hole, having missed it due to the scraggily, dead vegetation that filled its maw. As she regained her balance, narrowly avoiding falling through the thorny brambles and into the abyss beyond, she cursed herself for not paying more attention.

Now clear of detritus, Thyss wondered how she missed it at all. Not only was the hole longer than most men were tall, but its edges also made a concave impression in the rock. As she looked at it, she became more certain something had punched through the rock from above. Uncaring for the wonderment of what caused such, she peered down through the opening, but the sun struck it so that the light dispelling the gloom below cast a cylindrical column at an angle so that it ended at a cavern wall. Glancing at the sun, Thyss decided that she would not have to wait long before it was directly overhead, and that's when she would make her descent.

She shrugged off her pack and then the rope gifted to her by N'tuli and studied her surroundings for a likely candidate. An outcropping of rock stood only a few yards away, pointed boulders jutting from the base of a rockface like the lower teeth of the Grek she knew she must face, and she picked one that was uneven and larger toward its terminus than the base. She looped the rope around it, tying it tightly around the bottom of the rock and then leaned backward with all her weight. The knot shrank as it tightened, but the protruding boulder gave no sign of give at all. Thyss turned and tossed the remainder of the rope coil down into the entrance. There was no sound but the slightest movement of air for a few seconds before she heard it splash in the water below. She shrugged with the knowledge that it couldn't be more than a hundred feet through the darkness to whatever underground lake or river, and Thyss removed a hard biscuit from her pack, chewing absently as she waited for the sun to climb overhead.

It was only as she sat in total silence, ignoring the wind and the mountainous vistas around her, that Thyss realized how she knew this was the place she had sought. The silent humming tune she had heard since Hykan had shown her the subterranean vision, the soft hymn of a lilting voice singing in a language she didn't understand, had grown clearer as she climbed up to the ridgeline, and as she had peered moments ago into the depths of the hole in the cavern ceiling, she could almost make out specific words. While they had no meaning to her, she recognized the pauses common to languages across the world where one idea stopped, and another began. The scimitar with the otherworldly green hued steel, Feghul's Claw, was somewhere down in that abyssal darkness, somewhere even deeper where lava flowed.

The sun shone cheerily overhead when she again peered into the opening, and she saw that her rope hung loosely, its end having disappeared in a pool of murky water. It appeared that the remainder of it had just sunk down into the water, but its coloration prevented her from seeing if the rope reached the bottom or not. At least there was no sway or movement in the silk indicating swirls or eddies in the water… or living things. Thyss couldn't make out the edges of the pool, but she had the sense that it was a massive underground lake.

Shrugging, she slung the pack over one shoulder, took a firm grip on the rope, and backed toward the cavern's mouth until her legs were levered against it. The silk felt so dainty, so fragile in her hands, and she couldn't help but question whether it would hold many times her weight as N'tuli promised. Trusting the warrioress, Thyss leaned backward over empty space and peered downward before she pushed off. She swung backward a few feet, and her weight pulled at her. She had the sick feeling of panic as the silk slid through her tight grip, but as she fell, Thyss wrapped her legs around the dangling rope. The callouses on her palms from swordplay protected the flesh of her hands somewhat, and her descent slowed and then stopped.

Thyss dangled in midair some twenty feet from the cave's mouth and at least forty feet from the lake, swinging like a lazy pendulum from left to right as she peered around. Her eyes slowly adapted to the darkness, though the swaying in and out of the column of sunlight felt at once blinding and comforting. She looked across an underground lake that she assumed formed from rain collecting in a low point of the cavern, though it appeared to be at least eighty feet across. Roughly circular, over half of it terminated against the cavern walls, and a sort of rocky, inclined shore exited the lake only four or five yards from where the rope disappeared into its depths.

Thyss still swung a few feet in either direction, and that gave her an idea. She released the pressure on the rope to continue descending, though in a far more controlled fashion. As she became more comfortable, she lowered herself by grasping the rope hand over hand instead of letting it slide through her grip. Hanging just a few feet over the cloudy lake, the putrid scent of stagnant water filled her nose, and she became ever more convinced she did not want to fall into it, regardless of its depth. She augmented the faint back and forth of the rope's sway by leaning into it, and after a minute or so of effort, she swung like a living pendulum, ever closer to the water's edge. Once, then twice, Thyss hesitated as she was over the dry cave floor, but on the third such swoop, she released the silk rope, keeping the lightest of grips with one hand. Her feet shot true, and when she hit the cave floor, she bent her knees and rolled forward, away from the foul lake. In a maneuver much practiced while sparring, she tumbled and sprang back to her feet, the black silk rope still held in one hand.

Smiling in satisfaction, Thyss crossed the cavern for a stalagmite, pulling the rope from the lake as she did so, and then she wrapped it around the rock formation a half dozen times. Setting down her pack, she pulled a torch from it. She stared at its end for a few seconds, and a lively, orange flame erupted from its end.

The subterranean vault felt almost grand to look about. With its high ceiling, and generous width, it impressed her more than Harpalo's palace. Many colored stalagmites and stalactites that pointed towards each other like so many giant teeth, and strange, four pointed crystals spotted the walls and glowed with a faint purple light. The air chilled her exposed skin, substantially cooler than it was on the ridge above, and nowhere and everywhere at once, she heard the faint dripping of water as if it both plinked right behind her and at the same time echoed from far away. The effect was most disconcerting and caused the fine hairs on the back of her neck and arms to stand on end, as if an unseen predator was watching her.

She'd had enough of that in the north to last her a lifetime.

Several crevasses and tiny crawlspaces exited the cavern at various places, and Thyss suddenly prayed to Hykan that she wasn't looking for some tunnel deep in the putrid water pit. Finally at the far end of the cavern, she found a gaping hole hidden behind a large outcropping of rock. An apparently natural tunnel twisted and turned away into darkness, vaguely dropping downward. As she considered it, she noticed a most peculiar aroma, so very minimal that she wouldn't have noticed it if she hadn't stopped to peer into the passage. She wrinkled her nose as it reminded her of rotten eggs, and she noted the air wafting from the natural tunnel warmed her ever so slightly. She shifted her torch to her left hand, drew her scimitar with her right, and cautiously stepped inside.

A labyrinthine jumble of tunnels and caves followed. Openings appeared everywhere, some scarcely larger than a cat while others would only accommodate her if she stooped or hunched. The main passage continued ever downward, turning and twisting back the way it came. Sometimes she found a dead end and had to backtrack to previous intersections to progress. Often, she was presented with the choice of multiple directions, and she always chose that which appeared to lead downward more than the others, unless she was too tall to walk it comfortably. She reasoned if she was too tall, the Grek would be unable pass through such a tunnel as well. She trusted her nose, always deciding if the air in one tunnel seemed fresher than another, it was the wrong direction. The tunnels grew warmer.

Time lost all meaning deep in those subterranean passageways. Thyss could have traversed through them for hours, or even days, with the only sign of time's passing her grumbling stomach. She only stopped when she could not ignore it anymore, and even then, only long enough to eat a single hardtack biscuit, choked down with a mouthful of water so that she could continue her exploratory spelunking. It happened with growing frequency. Perhaps she really had been down here for days, though she hadn't felt the desire to sleep, or maybe the cold, stone caverns and tunnels simply bored her.

She hoped she could retrace her steps.

Her torchlight licked outwardly and showed the end of her tunnel ahead, but two gaping mouths opened to either side. She inspected the left closely, finding that it angled steeply upward into cool, crisp air. Foul fumes emitted from the hole to the right, as well as hellish heat, and the passage glowed with an orange light as it descended steadily and turned off to the left out of view. A dull roar, sounding from a source she couldn't identify seemed to fill the way downward, and underneath it, the soft hymn she'd been following sang more clearly than it had ever before.

Thyss quickly and as silently as she could manage stamped out her torch on the cave floor and ducked into the low opening of the tunnel. If the Grek named Feghul was down there, she didn't want to announce her presence, and she took several soft steps before she realized that she held her breath. Loosing it in the heat, she took in air slowly through her nose, and began to choke on the noxious fumes. She stumbled backward, out of the passage, into the cooler tunnel from whence she came, and struggled to gulp down cleaner air. It took all of her self-control to keep from having a coughing fit to expel the poisonous vapors.

Her breathing slowed as she recovered, and Thyss sat on the cold, damp cave floor and leaned against a wall as she considered her options. Certainly, she could hold her breath as she descended further, but she had no idea how far down the cut went. Perhaps Feghul was just around the corner, lounging in the heat with his blade laying nearby. Could she just dash in, grab the sword, and escape before he could react? She had no reason to think such a shoddy plan would work, because the longer she stood exposed there, her eyes burned from exposure to whatever noxious emanations filled the stony conduit.

Thyss' mind wandered as soreness and lethargy set into her limbs. The journey into the caverns drained her muscles more than she had realized, and her eyelids grew heavy the longer she sat against the cool rock. As so often happens to one in that state between wakefulness and sleep, images and thoughts passed. Brief ideas came and went before she could take ahold of them and decipher their meaning or purpose. She felt herself drifting deeper, and Hykan's blazing voice echoed through her head, "you will need to look to others…" Thyss felt herself wondering again why her god had said such a thing to her, but it vanished before she could truly think or voice the question.

Her eyes flew open as understanding struck her like lightning, and Thyss nearly jumped to her feet, new energy infusing her limbs. She could not go further, for the poisonous air would choke her, but perhaps her father's god, Aeyu, would show her some small favor. She had never before called on him, but she asked for precious little. Thyss closed her eyes and called a silent prayer to He Who is the Sky and Winds, beseeching him for only the smallest aid. Before she even completed her mute but earnest plea, a cool draft of air from above made its way down the tunnel and enveloped her before continuing into the passage heading downward.

"Many thanks, Lord Aeyu," Thyss whispered, and she again ducked into the tunnel's mouth.

As she hoped, the gentle current of cool, crisp air led her down. It cleared the toxic fumes, the permeating scent of sulfur, and even helped fight off the heat that grew as the tunnel dropped, twisted, and turned. The dull reverberation grew in intensity until it vibrated the cave walls and floor, or perhaps it only seemed to do so as it overpowered the near silence of her breathing and footsteps. Eventually, she came to one final turn, and beyond it radiated immense heat. Thyss took a quick glance around the bend, and seeing nothing of the Grek, she sauntered arrogantly right into the cave she had seen in Hykan's vision. The blazing temperature would have almost immediately dropped a lesser person, but between Aeyu's and Hykan's blessings, Thyss ignored it.

Her eyes swept across an incredible vista, a spectacular panorama of deific brilliance and power. An enormous lake of lava boiled and eddied around itself for dozens, hundreds of feet within the mountain, and Thyss knew she reached a place where the powers of Hykan, Lord of Fire, and Goelgar, Lord of Stone and Mountain, clashed to create something just as holy as it was destructive. For a moment, she regretted dismissing Goelgar so swiftly when all the gods presented themselves to her some eight years ago, but there was no changing that now. She was Chosen of Hykan, and she adored His fiery magnificence, the pure embodiment of chaos.

Pulling her attention from the majestic grandeur of the underground volcano, Thyss scanned the cave as there was no sign of either Feghul or his Claw. Assorted bones of past meals littered the area, a few random bits of clothing and other personal effects laying rotted and singed, and she noted some of the rocks and other tools the Grek had used to forge the blade in her vision. The cave floor dropped off some twenty feet or so ahead, dipping down into a shallow pool of lava that the volcano's currents kept moving only enough to keep it molten, and her eyes covered the edge of the pool, remembering what she saw. And there he was, mostly submerged with just his eyes and nostrils protruding from the molten rock, and if she hadn't known exactly what to look for, she likely would have missed him. She made no sign that she noticed him, and he stayed perfectly still.

The creature likely held the sword in one of his clawed hands, and Thyss needed a way to bait him out of the lava. She considered, briefly, turning and exiting back into the tunnel, but she quickly dismissed the idea. If the Grek chose to rush at her, getting caught in a narrow passage with the monstrosity was not a pleasant prospect. She stepped a few feet further into the cave and poked around the aged, discarded detritus of those long dead, but neither did she find anything of interest and nor did Feghul budge from his position. She crossed the cave to the flat stone outcropping that served as his anvil and kicked at the rocks he had once long ago used as tools, but still he made no move from his hiding place. Thyss pursed her lips and turned as if to leave the cavern, but just before she would have stepped into the tunnel, she turned and stared intently right into the Grek's eyes.

Feghul rose, his thick hide of mottled browns, greens, and grays apparently impervious to the hellish temperature of the molten rock, and he climbed up fully to stand at least two feet taller than Thyss. He held the scimitar in his clawed right hand at the end of a long, dangling arm, and Thyss' eyes rested covetously on the blade. The Grek seemed to understand then, that this soft, tasty human had come for what was rightfully his, and rage filled his reddish orange eyes. He roared a challenge and charged.

Pure instinct took over, and Thyss extended her left hand. Calling on Hykan's aid, blue flames – perhaps the hottest she had ever conjured – shot from her fingers, and a raging azure inferno enveloped Feghul. The creature had not expected the attack, and he stopped as suddenly as he had charged in apparent confusion. After a few seconds, Thyss felt the strength drain from her magick, and the flames encasing the Grek changed from blue to red and then to orangish yellow. The fire ceased, and the creature advanced, that horrific laughter like the grinding of stones rising through his torso to emit from his vicious mouth.

Thyss stepped backward toward the cave entrance as fear began to rise in her gut. This was the second time in as many months that she faced a creature impervious to Hykan's gifts, and she suspected that her sword would be equally useless. Even if her skills outclassed the Grek's she doubted she could match his strength or speed, and she knew his blade would cleave her steel scimitar more easily than hers could cleave bronze. She considered running for it, but it would give chase. It knew the caves far better than she, and in her haste, it would only be a matter of time before she tripped or turned an ankle.

She could try to climb the cavern wall, but that was not an escape. To claim the sword, she would have to come down, or fall to her death into the volcano. And besides, she was no spider. *The spiders. Fire isn't the answer. Sometimes, water will do.*

Thyss crossed her arms in front of her body, a hand resting on each shoulder, and again she begged a god for aid. But it was not Hykan, Aeyu, or Goelgar, but instead she sought out Nykeema, Goddess of Water and whom her mother was Chosen of. She felt the water somewhere up above her, that fetid lake of cold, dark fluid that laid fallow and unmoving for countless years, and she pleaded that Nykeema grant her dominion over it for just a few short moments. She sensed its immensity, its murky depths, and then its movement as it rose from its resting place, and the entire lake poured itself into one of the tunnels adjoining its own immense cavern.

A distant rumbling began to build, the sound and a rush of cool air pouring out of the cave passageway behind Thyss, and it grew in intensity until the floor itself began to shake. Feghul, who slowly approached to savor the brutality of his killing stroke, again stopped his stalking advance to cock his head in apparent confusion. The clamoring rumble rose to a crescendo, and Thyss dove to the floor to her left as a veritable river of gelid water exploded from the cave tunnel behind her. Feghul froze in place, his hundreds of years of life having never prepared him for this new experience, and the water collided with and surrounded his form. A great, explosive hissing of steam erupted from behind him as the water met the magma, but his hide, brought up to unfathomable temperatures from both the lava and Thyss' attack, also hissed as the frigid liquid enveloped him. After a few moments, the water had all but dissipated, immense amounts of steam filling the cave, and Thyss looked up to behold the Grek.

He stood almost over her with a light shining from his eyes that she might have considered fear were he human. He grunted and then whined as he began to move his arms, but his very hide shed a sound much like the stretching or flexing of leather. His flesh began to split, spidery cracks spreading across his legs, torso, and arms as she watched, and then the Grek apparently had the thought to retreat to the lava. He tried to turn, but his feet refused to obey. His upper legs and torso turned toward the crusting magma pool with a shattering not unlike glass, and then it broke from his lower legs to fall to the cave floor to shatter into thousands of pieces.

Thyss stood from where she had thrown herself to the cave floor and brushed dirt and dust away from her black tunic and leggings. She gingerly stepped around the gory bits of the Grek that littered the area and reached down to retrieve the beautiful, alien scimitar. The clawed hand of the Grek still wrapped the hilt, part of his forearm attached, and taking ahold of its irregular hexagonally shaped guard, she uncurled the creature's fingers from the weapon. Some of these broke as she did so, and she shook the rest of Feghul away from her new scimitar.

Thyss marveled at the weapon for an indiscernible amount of time, but eventually, she felt the air again becoming thick with poison. She drew her steel scimitar from its place at her belt and dropped it with a clang to the floor, replacing it with Feghul's Claw. She bowed her head for a moment in reverence to Hykan and all the elemental gods before turning to climb her way out of the cave.

18.

Thyss awoke to a cool breeze sweeping across her as the sun climbed the eastern sky. Thyss squinted at the sun, and noting its distance to the horizon, she slept later than she had wanted to. The previous day sapped much more of her strength than even she realized. Finding her way back to the lake cavern and her rope had been hard enough as it was, but that final climb out took everything she had. Pure will drove her up that rope and into the refreshing night air, as she would not dare sleep in the caverns. True, she found no signs of other Grek or any subterranean dwellers, but she would take no chances. As she lay down the night before, her drifting mind was aware of a soft hymn that lulled her to sleep.

She closed her eyes, grimaced, and rolled away to face west, away from the morning light. Maybe an hour passed by before she sighed heavily and forced herself to pack up her belongings and start retracing her steps to Berak'a. The return hike was faster as she already knew what paths, cuts or slopes led where, and she could choose the easiest and most direct route. By the late afternoon, she crested a ridge that looked down upon the city, and she smiled at the knowledge that she wouldn't have to sleep on the rocky ground another night. She started a southerly course down the ridge, and once at the bottom, she could turn due east and circumvent the city. It would be close to night then, and Thyss knew she would curse the city for having only one gate.

Three men emerged from cover somewhere down the slope, and as they closed the distance in a sort of echelon with one in the lead and the other two arrayed behind and to either side of him, Thyss searched them thoroughly. The leader stood about six feet with a fit frame, and he had light brown skin and hair indicative of a Highborn parent or grandparent. The man to his right was even taller with hulking corded thews on full display as he went without a tunic, and the third stood closer to her own height and was thin, though she thought his clothing hid deceptively wiry musculature. Both of them showed dark brown skin and black hair, mixed Lowborns both, and all three were armed with steel swords. Their greedy eyes never strayed from her form, and Thyss stopped and loosened her new scimitar as they formed a triangle around her.

"I told you she'd come back eventually," the leader said, first eyeing her body appreciatively and then her sword. "There's nothing in these mountains to find, and there's easier ways to cross them."

"Have you ever seen a sword like that?" breathed the shorter man to her right as he rested his hands on his hips near twin daggers.

"Nyam'a, what are we to do with him?" the leader asked the brute to her left. "Here we have a fine piece of fuckable Highborn, and all Sogiro cares about is her sword!"

"Not all!" Sogiro protested to the mocking laughter of his cohorts.

"Have you ever fucked a Highborn, Nyam'a?" the leader continued.

The brute whose body so reminded Thyss of the massive Da'irda replied in a voice so deep it almost weighted the very air, "I have not."

"It's quite the experience!"

"Careful, Kongozu," the shorter Sogiro warned, "do you see her eyes? She is Chosen."

Thyss immediately commanded, "Let me pass."

"Ha!" blurted the leader, Kongozu. "Not a chance. We've waited two days for your return."

Thyss' eyes narrowed, and an edge came to her voice as she said, "You followed me?"

"We tried to," he admitted with a nod, "but we wanted to stay out of sight. It's not often one sees a pretty Highborn traveling all by herself, no servants or guards in sight, so when you came into the mountains, we knew that was our chance. We were curious what you were looking for, but you kept double backing."

"Doubling back," the shorter man, Sogiro, corrected.

"Yes, whatever," Kongozu said with an eye roll and a quick shake of his head. "Anyway, we hid from you, but we grew bored. By the time we decided to just take you, you'd disappeared into the mountains. So, we decided to wait."

"Let me pass," Thyss repeated, "or Hykan will take you all."

"Highborns and your gods," Kongozu mocked. "Maybe Hykan will enjoy the show."

"There will be no show with your manhood lying bloody on the rocks for the buzzards," Thyss warned as her pack dropped from her shoulders, and she confidently raised Feghul's Claw into a defensive position, the muscles of her exposed arms going taut.

"Do you know how to use that big sword, little girl?" rumbled Nyam'a as he drew a two handed scimitar from a leather sheath on his back.

"Come find out, whoreson Lowborn."

"Don't make this hard, girl," Kongozu said, and his voice almost sounded reasonable. "I'd hate to kill you. I'm sure you'd hate for us to kill you. It could be fun. Nyam'a here is renowned for his stamina and, um, other attributes. Women actually pay *him* for his services. So, why don't we just make this easy."

"He will be servicing no one after this is over," Thyss said, and she spat toward Kongozu, spittle and phlegm landing on rocks near his sandaled feet.

"All right," Kongozu sighed as he drew his own sword, a plain, steel scimitar with a bronze handle, "let's try not to kill her before we have our fun."

"Don't worry," Thyss said while inwardly asking Hykan for aid.

She stepped backward up the ridgeline, careful not to misstep on loose rocks or turn an ankle as she kept her eyes on their leader, expecting that her peripheral vision would warn her of impending attack from her flanks. The men moved with her steadily, maintaining the short distance between her and each of them, and they clearly had done this many times before as calm and collected as they stayed. Thyss began to consider if she would be better off on the attack, but a flurry of movement to her right caught her eye. She saw Sogiro coming close to her, a curved dagger in each hand, and as she adjusted to face this threat, a warning shout exploded in her mind.

Thyss dove forward and to the right and somersaulted between the smaller man and his leader, much to their surprise. As she vaulted to her feet, she brought her empty left hand up, and blazing heat exploded as a ten foot tall and wide wall of flame separated her from the Sogiro and the massive Nyam'a. At the same time, she brought her scimitar around in a wide slash meant to cut their leader in twain at the waist, but as powerful as the blow was, it was also obvious. He jumped backward and made to parry with his own steel. The two swords clashed, sparks flew, and steel rent with a terrific cry as the man's steel scimitar came away from the collision horribly mangled. He suddenly flung the bent and torn blade at Thyss, and the move was so unexpected, she instinctively dropped flat to her hands and knees. He reared back a sandal to kick dirt into her face, and only Thyss raising her hand over her eyes at the last moment saved her from being blinded.

Knowing that she had mere seconds before the other two shook off their surprise and circumvented the flames, Thyss rolled away to her right to avoid another kick and regain her feet. As she did so, an iron grip yanked at her ponytail, and she cried out in pain and surprise. Her neck wrenched backward, Thyss kicked and slammed her shin right into Kongozu's groin. She felt his breath blow out of his lungs and across her face with a spray of spittle, and he released his hold on her hair. He realized his mistake too late as she brought Feghul's Claw around, its blade reflecting an alien green in the afternoon sunlight. He backed away a step and even raised his forearms defensively, but the scimitar sheared right through flesh and bone, leaving stumps that jetted blood from halfway between his elbows and wrists. The tip of the sword slashed across his neck, and Kongozu fell to the ground, gurgling as he tried to staunch the lifeblood pouring from his neck with nonexistent hands.

Just then, Nyam'a came around that side of her flame wall, looking down on his dying leader, and the massive man roared a challenge and charged. Thyss smiled and met his sword with her own, and sparks dazzled the combatants' vision. By the gods, his strength was impressive, no doubt something of a legend in his city of Berak'a, and every time their weapons met, his great, steel scimitar lost pieces as Feghul's Claw wrecked it. Thyss' arms ached with the impacts of their duel, but soon the warrior's scimitar would be useless where her own had not a scratch.

Again, a warning shouted out to her, a star that burst in her head to remind her of something forgotten, and before she could react, Sogiro had come around behind her. Her magick that garnered her countless valuable seconds was now useless, and it faded away as a jab bludgeoned her back. She cried out with the pain of it, and Thyss turned while stepping backward unsteadily. Nyam'a allowed her retreat, a wide and cruel smile splitting his face, and she saw Sogiro just as he plunged a dagger into her gut. As had Kongozu before, so now Thyss expelled all her breath as the punching jab penetrated her, and she knew then that she'd lost. She had forgotten about an enemy, so focused she was on those before her, that she now died to one behind her.

Thyss stumbled backward, and an odd clarity took ahold of her. She would have thought that, as she bled to death, confusion and darkness would overtake her vision, but that wasn't the case. She ran her free hand over her belly where Sogiro's blade impaled her, but she found neither a tear in the fabric, nor was her hand hot with blood. Sogiro looked at his daggers in confusion, as if concerned that he had forgotten to sharpen them, while his compatriot looked at him. The pain in Thyss' back and belly subsided somewhat, but bruises from the jabs would hurt for days.

Sogiro jumped backward as Feghul's Claw almost decapitated him, and sudden flames engulfed Nyam'a. The warrior screamed and screamed as he ran at first, arms flailing like a miniature windmill, before he fell to the ground. He rolled across the rough terrain, leaving bits of charred flesh scraped off onto the rocks beneath him, but the infernal flames would not abate. Thyss chased the agile Sogiro with lightning quick strikes of her sword, and the brigand, now realizing that he could only kill Thyss if he could get his knife to her neck or head, just managed to retreat away as steely death sang for him through the air. The constant attacks stressed Thyss' muscles to the limit, and she let the flames consuming Nyam'a die out so she could conserve that strength. Even still, Sogiro's quickness evaded her.

"Just die!" she shouted as he danced away from her sword yet again.

Finally, she had enough. Thyss brought her sword around again, and knowing he would back away from it, she conjured another wall of flames just behind him as he did so to avoid his death. He fell through the flames and screamed as his hair and clothes ignited instantly. She dismissed the flames as quickly as she summoned them, and Sogiro lost his balance and fell hard onto his backside, the rocks under him abrading his palms as he lost his daggers.

Thyss loomed over him, ready to deal death, and he begged, "Please! Please! I have no choice. I do what he tells me, or he'll kill me!"

"And now I kill you," Thyss sneered, and she brought her scimitar straight down, cleaving his head in half down to his neck. She yanked the sword free and wiped the blood and gore from it on the dead man's singed clothing.

As she caught her breath, another sound caught her attention, a ragged, struggling breathing, and she turned to see that Nyam'a was still alive a dozen feet away. The man laid there and wheezed terribly. His hair had been burned away, revealing a scarred scalp and the white of bone beneath that. A range of pink and reddish hues adorned his body, the dark skin mostly gone, and the air around him stank of charred flesh. Thyss knew he could never survive this, and she was tempted to leave him there to die. In the end, she brought her blade down swiftly and decapitated him. As his head rolled slowly down the slope, she questioned if it was an act of mercy or an act of wisdom. It was unwise to leave an enemy behind you. Especially one that you wounded so and still lived.

Suddenly aware of her lack of coin, she searched the corpses of the three men, a somewhat grisly task when it came to the scorched Nyam'a. Between them, she recovered a dozen pieces of gold, enough to buy food and shelter at one of Berak'a's inns for a short while. She also found around the neck of Kongozu a blood covered gold chain with several attached gemstones, and this she buried in her pack. It wouldn't do to sell it in Berak'a and invite revenge from someone recognizing it. Their steel weapons, though plain and lacking anything to distinguish to whom they belonged, had value even as mangled as the scimitars were, but she had no desire to weigh herself down with them.

She was about to retrieve her pack when a sudden thought struck her, and she reached fumbling hands to where Sogiro's dagger should have dealt her a killing blow or at least ruined a kidney. As she tentatively touched her back, pain flared at the point of impact, but the black silk of her tunic had not been rent by the weapon. She realized that she would likely develop a nasty bruise there that may hurt for days or even weeks, but the silk itself had held up as well as steel, preventing the dagger from fatally wounding her. She wondered if the merchant she saw in Calumbu realized his wares would be worth not only his weight but also the weight of his wagon and pack animals in gold to other kingdoms in Dulkur.

Dropping her hands, Thyss bent to reclaim her pack from where she'd let it fall and started her way back down the sloping ridgeline toward Berak'a. Her muscles tingled with life and excitement. She felt as if she could set the world on fire and laugh as it burned to the ground, whereas usually after such a struggle, she felt drained, and her muscles burned from the effort. She thought of her new sword, and she questioned who she should thank for the newfound strength, the weapon or Hykan. In the end, she received no answer, and she hummed a delightful tune she didn't know as she neared the city.

"I am sorry, Lady, but I have no rooms available," the woman, middle aged and somewhat round from numerous childbirths, said from behind the bar. "You should check with some of the places further in the city."

Annoyance flashed across Thyss' face as she argued, "But I just stayed here a few nights ago. How is it you now have no rooms?"

The woman cringed slightly, unused to the ire of a Highborn or perhaps she saw fire in Thyss' eyes. Making herself small, she gestured across the common room and eked out in reply, "Even the floor is full of K'watu's urchins, Lady. While I am full, there were not so many. I am sure you will find a place, a much nicer place at that. Try Giatha's inn a half mile up the road. Tell him I sent you, and he will surely have a room, probably at a discounted price."

But Thyss had already stopped listening to her words as she looked around the inn's modest common room. The room was full of Lowborns, over a score in fact, and about half of these stared back at her as if they knew her. There were two families with five children between them and several elderly persons as well. The dust and dirt of travel stained their clothes and faces, and most of them looked as if they had no possessions at all. She locked gazes with one, an old woman, and the flesh around her eyes was swollen, the eyes themselves reddened from weeping. As some of them looked back at her, she couldn't ignore the feeling that she had seen many of them before.

She turned back to the inn's mistress and asked, "What is this of K'watu?"

"It is a village to the north, part of a kingdom known as Calumbu. We trade with them sometimes."

"Yes, I know of it. Why are people from K'watu here."

"My apologies, Lady! You're right. I should usher them out and make room for Your Ladyship."

"Damn it, woman," Thyss snapped, and sudden heat emanated from her being, causing a fresh round of contracting and shrinking away from the innkeeper. "Why? Are? They? Here?"

"I'm sorry, Lady, I assumed you knew," the woman squeezed out, her hands covering her face in terror. "An army marched on Calumbu and destroyed it. Some of the people in K'watu fled here to Berak'a."

"What?" Thyss breathed. "What army?"

"I," she stammered, "I do not know, Lady, but it is said that a Highborn king led."

Thyss fell into dark thoughts as she attempted to make sense of the news. There could be no doubt as to who attacked and destroyed Calumbu, and if it was indeed her father, there would be nothing left of the kingdom in payment for the slight against him. As she gazed back across the people in the common room, she whispered, "No, it cannot be. He didn't. I left so he wouldn't."

"What is that, Lady?"

The question broke her from her thoughts, and Thyss looked back at the woman for a long moment. Thyss reached into a purse she'd scrounged from Kongozu and removed half of the gold from it. As she dropped them on the wooden bar, the coins clinked, and one coin fell onto its edge, rolling away a few inches before it lost its balance and fell over. It rang softly as it wobbled and settled flat, drawing the innkeeper's attention.

"Put these toward the people's upkeep," Thyss said.

"Of course, Lady," replied the innkeeper as she prepared to sweep the coins off of the bar and into an open hand.

Thyss caught one of the woman's wrists and squeezed the bones painfully, not enough to break them, but the act caught her attention. Thyss growled, warming her hand uncomfortably to accentuate her point, "I mean it. This should pay for them to stay here for a week at least. If I hear otherwise, or find they were mistreated in any way, I'll come back for you personally."

Wide eyed, the innkeeper bobbed her head up and down. "No. Of course, Lady, it will pay for them. No problem at all," she said, the avarice having disappeared from her eyes.

She released the woman's wrist, who immediately pulled it back protectively against her round belly, and Thyss turned to stalk toward the door that exited into the street beyond. She ignored the questioning, thoughtful, or even thankful gazes of those inside as she entered a night illuminated by torches out on the streets and lanterns in windows. While the bustle of legitimate business had died, Berak'a stayed busy at night, and Thyss stormed past the seedier aspects of humanity. Whores who plied their trade in back alleys during daylight now did so openly on the street, and rogues gathered and talked in hushed whispers like conspiracies of ravens. Two of these broke away from their group and followed her after Thyss stormed by, but she was having none of it. She turned toward them suddenly and stared them down frightfully, the flames of Hykan dancing in her eyes, and the two men turned down an alley as if that was their intended path all along.

She reached the city's gargantuan gate and found it closed and barred against the night. A handful of guards, dark forms whose details she couldn't make out, stood atop the towering wall, braces of javelins close at hand as they kept a watchful eye on both the savannah beyond and the street below. The street's haphazard torchlight barely reached that far, and they had no light sources atop the wall itself, likely so as not to disrupt their vision as they looked into the night.

Thyss reached down within herself and summoned her most imperious nature. She raised one hand to her mouth and loosed a sharp, night piercing whistle that caught several guards' attention, and she commanded, "Open the gate. I am leaving."

Laughter met her words, the deep chuckles of several men reaching her ears, and they added fuel to the fire that burned in her very soul. As the laughter died down and the men realized she was completely serious, one of them called down, "The gate stays closed. It's dangerous out there."

"I said open it!"

"There are lions and cheetahs and hyenas out there," the voice chided, and at just that moment, a lion roared somewhere past the wall. "Do you see? It's death out there. No one goes out at night."

"I am going," Thyss declared.

"Then, I hope you can swim," replied the disembodied voice, receiving amused snorts and chortles from his cohorts for the effort, "because the river is the only way out."

Thyss sneered a disgusted hiss toward the wall and turned to leave, but the guardsman's voice called out after her, "But if the hippos don't get you, the crocs will!"

These last words stopped Thyss in her tracks. She wanted to explode in fury, reign fiery death on everything and everyone around her, but it was only due to the frustration of being trapped within the city for her own safety. She fumed and waves of heat rolled off her body, and anyone within ten yards of her moved away and disappeared into homes or darkened alleys to avoid the hellish wrath she could visit on them. She stood still, forcing the air in and out through her nose until, finally, her breathing slowed enough that the heat subsided, and reason took hold of her mind again.

Thyss strode away into the night in search of Giatha's inn.

She awoke early, questioning whether or not she even fell asleep as she tossed her legs over the side of the bed. The hay filled mattress squished down, as if it might fall through the rope suspension when she pushed herself upright, and she rubbed the back of her neck as she twisted her head back and forth. She tossed and turned all night, and if she managed to lay still enough that she dozed, some imagined sound brought her senses screaming back to her. The only proof in her mind that she had fallen asleep were the fading memories of dreams and the faces of Harpalo, N'tuli, and others.

The sun had crested the mountain ridges to the east when she stormed through Berak'a's open gate. The city had just awoken, and farmers, merchants, craftsmen, and workers of all kinds started toward their daily tasks, some of them refreshed while others stumbled from a night of drink or debauchery. She stopped only long enough to purchase some bread and jerky, purported to be crocodile meat, before leaving the stone walled city and its surrounding farms behind her.

In only a few hours, she reached Nganozu Enzu, the flamboyantly vibrant valley seemingly hidden from human's view were it not for the road that cut through it, and she wasted no time continuing her journey. At any moment, she expected the crazy witch Akili to appear from amidst the deadly foliage, and the thought of it made Thyss smile despite her feelings of disdain toward the ancient woman. After a moment, the smile fled her face as the somber understanding that the witch wouldn't be found here drove the image away.

Well into the afternoon, Thyss arrived on the edge of K'watu, and she felt the urge to rush headlong into the village. She forced herself to slow her pace, drawing Feghul's Claw, as an eerie silence hung over the place. She listened to every sound in the village and nearby jungle. Her eyes darted between stone huts and across the packed down dirt streets and alleys, but she neither saw nor heard anyone within the village itself. It hadn't rained in days, and she saw the signs of hundreds of sandalled or even booted feet had made their way through K'watu. If not for the occasional spatter of blood flung across a stone hut's wall or a broken spear or sword, one might not have even deduced the reason for the desertion of the village. Of course, Thyss knew. Buzzards flew overhead, and one swooped down toward the village center and out of sight. Where such birds went, one would find carrion, and Thyss picked up her pace.

She slid between a pair of stone huts and into a wide avenue, in the middle of which stood a trio of dogs surrounding something in the street. At her appearance, two of them turned their heads away from a lump of flesh and viscera to stare her down and growl while the third continued to tear at its meal. She recognized the shaggy coats and brown spots of hyenas, and she braced herself as they began to turn her way. Thyss took in a deep breath and sighed in frustration, aggravated at yet another meaningless obstacle, and she flung her hand outward toward the animals. Flame arched forth and struck the ground right between the two hyenas, and they yipped and yowled as they ran away through the village, their third companion chasing after them with its laughing cries.

She approached the corpse, knowing from the stench it had been dead for days. She didn't want to look down at it, but she felt the need to know. The body was too mangled for her to be sure at first, as the torso and belly had been rent open and feasted upon by the hyenas and gods knew what else. The flesh and skin of the face was mostly gone from the swarming ants that covered it, but it was the unwashed, crazily arrayed gray hair that told her who it had once been.

Thyss looked up and away and suddenly wished she hadn't as she spotted another corpse in the road just near the village's center, two vultures pecking at it. She gave Akili's body a wide berth as she approached this second corpse, its huge size causing a sickness in her stomach. She swung her sword idly as she neared it, and the two vultures squawked their displeasure before tottering and winging away. The ants and other insects hadn't yet worked as extensively on this body, and if somehow Thyss hadn't recognized Harpalo's face on the severed head next to it, she would have identified the enormous, still healing scar in the torso's side. A dagger stabbed into Harpalo's back pinned an unfurled papyrus scroll to his body, and Thyss reached down to retrieve this, the blade cutting through the papyrus as she tore it away. She looked down at the brown characters, drawn in long dried blood, and stared at them for minutes or even hours as time lost its meaning.

A burning slowly replaced the malaise in her gut, searing it away as the flames of white hot rage grew within her. Her breath came and went forcefully as raw rage took her over, pure chaos feeding a wrath the likes of which Thyss had never felt before. Never had she felt hatred so fully, and her entire body – her skin, flesh, every wiry sinew, and even her bones – accepted the blazing intensity.

She wanted nothing more than to join that terrific entropy, than to scorch her will with pure unadulterated flame on an unsuspecting world, and it called to her as surely as Hykan's voice whispered in her ear when she was a child. There was never any choice than for her to be Chosen by the fire god, and He wanted her to show the world that His strength and will was unmatched. She felt her own will, her ego, everything that made Thyss a person and not pure destruction, balance dangerously on that precipice as she leaned over the edge, prepared to lose herself and everything she had ever known in that existence. At the last moment, her mind returned to her, and she almost collapsed backward, her arms wrapped around her body as if she had truly pulled herself away from a cliff's edge.

Thyss raised her face to the sky and screamed, her roaring, primal voice echoing throughout the village of stone and off the trees of the jungle surrounding it. Distraught by the unexpected disruption, birds took flight and rodents scurried into holes. A blazing inferno, a pillar of living flame exploded from Thyss at that moment, rising dozens of feet into the air where it split into two. Each curl blasted back toward the ground and consumed a bloated, half eaten corpse that lay in the streets of K'watu. They burned flesh, organs, and bones away for an interminable amount of time, and they ended as abruptly as they started with Thyss collapsing to her knees before a scorched ground.

She sighed softly and hung her head in a quiet repose. Her eyes closed as she breathed slow and deep through her nose, and her thoughts wandered as they so often do when one begins that lazy drift into sleep. With the calm, Thyss realized that another emotion lingered down in the depths of her soul, but she refused to display it to anyone, even herself. Or perhaps, Thyss, Chosen of Hykan, didn't understand how one released sorrow. She had no time for it; it was not part of who she was. A thought occurred to her, and she formulated a plan.

A soft thumping in the dirt sounded off to her left, and Thyss opened her eyes to behold a mule as it idly grazed on scraggily grass between a pair of the village's stone huts. She suppressed the sudden urge to laugh, which then threatened to turn again to intense grief, something so alien to Thyss that she didn't trust herself to give in to it.

Because Akili had known. Somehow, the witch had known.

Thyss stood from her knees and approached the mule, who lifted its head in anticipation, as if the creature understood that it existed purely to assist her on the next part of her journey. Thyss removed her pack, tied it to the mule's back, and led the animal by the leather cord west out of K'watu. She wasn't headed north, for there was no need to see what further destruction her father had wrought in Calumbu. Instead, she intended to leave Calumbu and then skirt the southern edge of Mon'El's lands to the west.

As Thyss walked, her thoughts returned to the message inscribed in blood on the scroll, Harpalo's blood she was sure, and it was just as surely written by her father's own finger. As they sounded over and over in her head, driving her west and fueling another slow building rage, they were spoken in her father's voice. They echoed incessantly and coldly, an accusation without a hint of humanity within them.

You did this to him.

19.

Dozens of torches burned smokily, their guttering, flickering light filling a great hall built of uniformly masoned granite blocks, each a full yard in every dimension. These indomitable walls were plastered inside and covered with vibrant, colorful frescoes depicting King Kerim in a variety of scenes. He led armies into battle to conquer those who would not submit, he brokered contracts that brought him mountains of wealth, and he bought the loyalty of thousands and thousands of citizens and mercenaries. Unlike his rival King Mon'El, there were no paintings or carved reliefs giving thanks to the gods, as Kerim had built his kingdom with blood, sweat, cunning, and wealth, not gods. The stone floor had been covered with smooth marble and feldspar in a variety of hues to create a mosaic of impressionistic beauty, and a dozen gilded stone pillars held the vaulted ceiling some forty feet overhead. The hall was flat and level with several doors and arches on the flanks leading to other parts of the palace.

At the far end from the grand entrance, which was a pair of gilded, twenty foot tall double doors, several marble steps led to a raised dais. Kerim's solid gold serpentine throne, the model for his gilded, wooden travelling throne, sat upon this. This throne stood fifteen feet tall, and it was known that it had to be crafted in place, for no one hundred men would have been able to lift it. Chairs of silver, no less ornate, of the same humanoid snake in design but half the size flanked the golden throne, one for his son and the other for Kerim's dear, long departed wife, whom he had never replaced. All though, it was well known that the king had sired many bastards in his house in the fifteen years since she had been poisoned by one of Kerim's own mistresses.

The mistress, whose name no one dared speak, died horribly for that offense. The king had her coated in honey and then tied naked to a stake out on the savannah during a scorching summer day. Her screams of torment as the insects and wild animals consumed her echoed throughout the day and hours into the night, and young parents who were but children at the time told their own children of her spirit and what she did to children who would neither eat, nor clean up after themselves, lie, or cause other mischief.

The torches' murky smoke rose toward the ceiling, where slotted vents had been worked into the stonework by Kerim's engineers. The smoke exited into the cool night air beyond, but hoods on the vents prevented rain from entering through them. The king was not on his throne, but instead stood at the head of a trio of four foot wide and twenty foot long wooden tables that had been placed side by side. A canvas map had been laid out across this huge plane, showing the vast details of all his lands, as well as King Mon'El's to the east. Figurines representing men on horses, warriors in armor, or even simple peasants carrying spears dotted the map and were moved around with wooden poles by the men assembled around the table. The king's son, Kerim'El, stood on the far end from him with a bored disposition, occasionally sighing his displeasure, and Kerim intended to speak to him about it behind closed doors.

"My company will arrive by sundown tomorrow, Majesty," reported the man to Kerim's right, one of six commanders arrayed to either side of the map, and he slid an ivory icon from the northeast to the city of Tajoru.

King Kerim nodded toward him and said, "Very good, Sawraka. Ready to march the next morning?"

"As Your Majesty sees fit. My fighters are strong and disciplined," Sawraka replied. He was not the image conjured by most people when they thought of warrior generals, standing under six feet with the dark skin of a Lowborn and shaved head, but under his bronze studded leathers was a wiry, iron body with the quickness of a panther. His free company of mercenaries had roamed Dulkur for over twenty years, fighting for the highest pay, until he fell in with King Kerim, who was at the time just the lord of Tajoru. Showering gold on Sawraka and his fighters, Kerim went from a lord to a king, and Sawraka's company grew fourfold to an army.

"When we meet Mon'El's host, your men will be held in reserve at the rear of my armies," Kerim said, and he noted how the commander bristled at this.

"As you wish, Majesty, but the men and *women*," he explained with emphasis on the fact that he also employed consummate professionals of what most considered the fairer sex, "under my command will not be happy about being kept from the fighting."

"I pay you to do as I will."

"True, Majesty," Sawraka agreed with a deferential nod, and he fell silent.

"However," Kerim continued, softening his tone, "I understand that your people have been on a forced march from the northern border for a week. I want them to conserve their strength and act as my personal guard. There are none I trust more."

The Highborn men around the table shifted uncomfortably, finding slight in the trust shown by their king in someone born beneath them, but they could say nothing. Sawraka caught his king's eyes for just a moment, and his back straightened proudly. He nodded again as he said, “Thank you, Majesty.”

Kerim returned his eyes to the canvas map, upon which the entire landscape of western and central Dulkur had been painted. The lands around Kaimpur under Mon’El’s control for at least a hundred miles in any direction were colored in the kingpriest’s signature almost whitish blue, whereas his lands from the plains east of Tojaru all the way to the sea were shaded in gold. Mon’El’s kingdom was larger, and he had twice the number of statuettes arrayed around Kaimpur, but Kerim knew most of them were little more than peasants with sharp sticks. He nodded appreciatively even as his son released a long yawn, drawing eye rolls and exasperation from the other men. He picked up a wooden dowel, a thin pole over two yards long, and he tapped a wide savannah just past the border into Mon’El’s kingdom.

“This is where the battle will take place,” Kerim mused. “Our force is smaller, better disciplined. We will cross the miles faster than Mon’El. This affords us the chance to pillage supplies as we move, as well.”

As he spoke, his commanders and generals moved their respective statuette armies to the indicated plain over a hundred miles from the city of Tojaru, and once done, they then moved Mon’El’s to the same location. If the map was accurate, and none of them doubted the fact based on what Kerim must have paid for it, the battle would take place closer to Kaimpur than Tojaru.

“I am outnumbered almost two to one, but I do not think Mon’El’s conscripts will hold well against my mercenaries and soldiers. Mon’El has less than half the number of professional troops at his disposal,” Kerim continued, receiving grunted assent or nods from the others. “Still, we fight in Mon’El’s kingdom. His people’s morale will be bolstered, believing they fight for their homes.”

"They are but farmers and serfs, Majesty," said a Highborn named Ahknet, a near giant of a man who commanded the army of Tojaru itself. "They are driven by the whip, and if they do not agree to die at our hands, they die at their own king's. I doubt they will be so motivated."

But there was yet one other concern on their minds, and Kerim saw it plainly on their faces as they stared down at the map. Finally, one of them spoke up, airing out the anxious worry most of them held, "And what of the priests, Majesty?"

Kerim nodded his recognition of the problem and replied, "The Chosen are dangerous to us. We cannot match their power, but it waxes and wanes like the ocean tides. They will grow tired quickly, so Mon'El will not dedicate his priests to the battle until he is sure he must."

Sawraka filled the pause, "Which he *will* have to. His rabble is no match for our armies."

"Indeed," Kerim agreed, "once he does so, it is imperative that we reach them, and cut them down, quickly."

"I will handle that," Kerim'El announced, his first contribution to the gathering in hours.

He came around the corner of the table to one of the sides, the men making room for him as he did so. He placed a five inch tall golden figurine on the map just to the west of the two armies. It depicted a man on the back of a rearing horse, scimitar in one hand as his other held on to the animal's mane. Detailed craftmanship astounded the eyes as the rippling muscles of both the horse and rider could be seen in the statuette.

Kerim'El explained, "The Kujari will ride with me."

"Nomadic savages," sneered the Highborn Ahknet, receiving muffled agreement from two other men.

"I have spent my life learning their ways. You will find no better horsemen in Dulkur. Their means of pleasure and sport would cause your skin to run pale, Ahknet," Kerim'El replied, channeling the insult against the Kujari into one against the Highborn. "They are as fierce as any, and I will lead them to attack Mon'El's priests. Two days before we reach the plain where the armies will meet, the Kujari and I will ride off to the south. We will keep messengers riding back and forth to keep my father aware of our position and progress. When Mon'El's priests join the battle, I will lead the Kujari in to attack. Mon'El will not be expecting it, and his conscripts will melt before our charge."

Kerim beamed proudly at his son. The plan was sound, for the nomads feared nothing when their bloodlust took hold, even the magicks of the Chosen, and to have enlisted them in this cause was no mean feat. Perhaps the boy had his knack for negotiation and persuasion after all.

Sawraka politely asked, "Highness how will you know when it is time?"

"The Chosen wield the power of the gods – air, earth, fire, and water. When the very ground shakes and when a great storm strikes up from nowhere, its lightning splitting the sky to strike those below it, I will know the time has come."

"My son," King Kerim grinned, "the warrior, and now both a statesman and a poet! Very well, we –"

A clamor interrupted him as steel clashed outside the oversized double doors that exited the hall into the streets of the city beyond. The men turned expectantly, most of them with hands on weapons, and the screams of dying added to the cacophony. Before any of them could draw steel or move toward the giant, gilded doors, Kerim held one hand upright, calling for patience. He had no doubt they could handle whatever caused the commotion, and the ringing of steel ended with an unidentifiable *whump* and a momentary flash of orange light through the crack separating the doors. A few seconds later, the two doors slowly swung inward with a mild squeal of bronze hinges, a lithe form with golden hair leaning into them from the other side as she pushed through. Behind her, Kerim could just barely make out the fallen forms of several of his house guard, including a smoking lump that he suspected had once been a person.

"Princess Thyssallia of Kaimpur," Kerim called, his voice echoing about the hall as she passed between the doors, the opening just wide enough to accommodate her.

Thyss eyed the eight men arrayed around the tables, noticing that five of them seemed ready to jump to the attack, but their muscles itched with nervousness. Only a Lowborn immediately to the king's right appeared calm and collected, while the king himself looked on in curiosity. She also recognized that his son followed her every movement with bright eyed, almost ravenous alertness. She sauntered directly for the end of the wide table, which she realized were multiple set side by side, keeping her hands confidently on her hips and away from her sword.

"No longer," she disagreed. "I am Thyss, Chosen of Hykan. I am no princess of any city."

"So, you are not here to present yourself for marriage to my son?" Kerim asked with raised eyebrows and a face slightly tilted to his right.

Thyss laughed raucously, a deep guffaw that arose from deep within her belly, and the almost arrogant melody filled the hall as it echoed in on itself. "Of course not! Would you not have expected my father to be with me were that the case? Would I have had to burn and slay the ignorant curs outside these doors if I were here to offer my hand in marriage to this whoreson?"

Kerim'El's face screwed up in anger, and he started aggressively toward her, prepared to draw his scimitar as he approached. Ahknet, the Highborn general, placed a warning hand on the prince's shoulder, causing the latter to almost whirl toward him. "Patience," the general whispered.

"Take care with your words, Thyss of Hykan," cautioned Kerim. "He is my only son, begotten in marriage with the only woman I ever loved."

"Only son begotten in marriage, you mean," Thyss scoffed. "Everyone knows you have mixed born children all over this city, Majesty, but it doesn't matter. I apologize if I have given offence."

King Kerim searched her eyes for what felt like an eternity, something he learned to do in mere seconds in decades past. It was a valuable skill, being able to investigate the depths of a rival's, challenger's, or opponent's soul and see what was truly there, and it served him well as he built a kingdom. Though he clearly heard the disdain and insincerity in her voice, he found honesty in her gaze, as well as an intense, burning desire for something yet unexplained. She wanted something more than she had ever wanted anything before, and the hunger for it threatened to consume her. He could feel it.

"If you are not here to marry my son, then for what have you come all this way?" Kerim asked, apparently deciding that a more forward approach may yield better results than subterfuge.

"I am here to help you kill my father."

Reactions around the map covered tables ranged from quiet thoughtfulness to shouted disbelief. Three or four voices all spoke at once, engaging yet more into the chaotic discord, and neither Thyss nor King Kerim understood where the various commanders stood on her bold statement. They picked out words from the overlapping, echoing spew of course, but nothing that resembled a cohesive thought shared by multiple people. In the end, only the king, the sorceress, and the dark skinned Lowborn said nothing further. After a minute or two, Kerim grew tired of the shouted opinions and arguments, and he started calling for quiet.

When no one took notice, Sawraka slammed a fist on the table and shouted, “Silence!”

All fell instantly quiet, and Kerim continued to gaze into Thyss’ very soul as he said, “Why should I believe you? Why would you want your father dead?”

“My reasons are my own.”

“It is more likely, Majesty,” said one of the Highborns, “that she will wait for the opportunity and then slay you for her father.”

This received mumbled agreement, but before Thyss could reply, Kerim said thoughtfully, “No. No, I don’t think so. If she wanted me dead, she would have already struck. She could have summoned a wave of flame to crash down upon us all at once, claiming victory for her father King Mon’El.”

“She would have died trying,” snarled Kerim’El.

“Do not underestimate Chosen, my son,” Kerim lightly admonished, “especially with what is to come.”

“Yes,” Thyss agreed, her voice piercing the air of the hall, “you should not underestimate Chosen. You are about to meet them in battle, and you cannot hope to defeat them.”

“Our soldiers are far better trained, disciplined, and experienced than any pathetic farmers your father can conjure,” Kerim’El shot back, taking offense at Thyss’ words.

“Perhaps,” Thyss replied simply, conceding the point.

"*And*," he continued aggressively, "I have thousands of Kujari ready to ride with me into battle. We will strike your Chosen from their flanks, trampling them under thundering hooves or sending their heads flying in an arc over their peasant soldiers with blades shimmering in the morning sunlight before they even know what has happened."

Thyss stared back at him, unmoved by his words. She shrugged and replied in a simple, matter of fact tone, "You cannot win."

Kerim cut off the defensive, disbelieving shouts with a raised hand and a warning glare before they erupted. Certain that no one else would speak, he looked back at Thyss and asked, "Then why are you here?"

"Because with my help, you can win. I am more powerful than any of my father's priests. I will help you defeat them, and I will help you kill him."

"I am still waiting to know why you would do this?" Kerim asked pointedly.

"I demand…" Thyss' voice trailed off, and she looked down at the map for a moment as she searched for the word. It was revenge, to be sure, but the term felt somehow lacking. She suddenly looked back up to the waiting eyes of King Kerim and said, "Justice."

The intensity of her gaze and the all-consuming hatred burning in her eyes convinced Kerim at once that she hid no duplicity, that her words held more honesty than perhaps any he had heard in his entire life. He had but one concern, and he voiced it then, "And if we destroy your father, his priests, and his armies, what then? What will you do?"

"I will ask for some gold and provisions, and I will move on."

"I will control half of Dulkur, including your homeland, and you will just move on? A Highborn with no wish to rule?" Kerim questioned.

Without hesitation, Thyss said, "If I wished to rule, I simply would have married your son. I have seen the lives my mother and father live, and I'd rather die in combat. Or live a penniless beggar in a foreign land. Or any number of other existences that at least leave me to decide my fate."

"Seems hard to believe that you would visit death upon your own father and then would just walk away from everything that could be yours," Kerim replied.

"And yet you know I speak the truth."

"Indeed," Kerim said softly. "Very well, Thyss of Hykan. If this is your desire, we are honored by your presence. We leave at sunrise the day after tomorrow, and I would have you ride alongside me as we march to glory."

"I want to make myself clear on one thing, Kerim."

Kerim stirred slightly, his eyes narrowing, as he was used to neither being addressed so informally nor having expectations placed upon him, but after a moment he simply asked, "And that is?"

"No one kills Mon'El," Thyss answered as her eyes burned darkly. "That honor is mine."

20.

Thousands of feet stomped as they marched to the beating of drums, the first elements of the host kicking and stirring great clouds of dust as it marched east into the lands beyond Tojaru. The deep thrumming of the oversized drums helped twenty five thousand warriors keep time with each other, so their feet fell on the ground as one. It allowed them the most efficient march possible, and it shook the ground as they approached and passed. As they entered the wild plains and savannahs between Tojaru and Kaimpur, they drove all manners of animals before them, even great prides of lions and big, stupid, armored rhinos. Even the latter feared men in large enough number. The army flattened the tall grasses of the plains, and eventually the clouds of dust settled to be trampled underfoot.

Even Thyss was impressed. She remembered her father going to war, but when he did, his armies looked nothing like this. She looked across hundreds of tight packed rows of men and women as they marched in unison, the corded sinews of their arms and legs rippling and glistening in the blazing heat of the sun overhead. Almost all carried steel scimitars – relatively common in the more civilized parts of Dulkur, but still extremely expensive to equip an army with them – and many also had steel tipped javelins strapped to their backs. The warriors wore bronze hauberks and bronze plated legguards connected by thick leather, probably tanned rhino hide. Her father would have at least twice their number, but King Kerim clearly spared no expense when it came to training and equipment, and Thyss hoped it would make the difference.

Of course, having steel swords and even armor was easier for a king that controlled the Iron Mountains, Dulkur's largest and best source of raw iron ore. Bringing them under his reign was incalculable to Kerim's wealth. He could control the sale of steel across the continent, not to mention tax it heavily when sold to his challengers.

Truth be told, it was her presence that would make the difference. Kerim's mercenary soldiers would make quick work of her father's peasant army, but his Chosen would revisit the same back again. It would be up to her to bring down the priests as fast as possible. As they began to fall, the Lowborn conscripts would lose heart and flee.

Thyss thought about Lowborns and Highborns as she looked around her, because she rarely saw them as intermingled as she did in Kerim's army. The mercenaries varied so much, with Highborns marching alongside their lessers, and there were more of mixed blood among them then of either caste. Most of the generals were like her, Kerim, and his son – Highborn – but more officers had the dark skin of Lowborns than the bronze of Highborns. It seemed King Kerim's most trusted general, as well as almost all of Sawraka's troops, were of low birth, and they served as Kerim's personal guard, marching all around the king as he rode. She couldn't help but realize that since she had left Kaimpur, she found that the strict divide between people that was law in her father's kingdom was largely ignored everywhere else in Dulkur she had been.

And then there were the Kujari, those savage nomads that roamed the lands of Dulkur and took what they felt they were owed. She watched as they rode like wild bandits around the flanks of the army as it marched, dashing off and returning back again. The riders enjoyed taunting the professional soldiers, most of whom responded with eye rolls, grumbled complaints, or stoic silence, but occasionally an officer had to bring one of the mercenaries back in line. The Kujari laughed at the disturbances they caused, riding away before anything could be said to them only to return hours later to harass the same warrior who hadn't kept their calm. When the army stopped at night, Thyss watched with smiling interest as the nomads played a deadly sport, riding in circles as they tossed curved daggers at each other. She grew up believing these men and women to be little more than animals and perhaps even a savage scourge to be wiped out when encountered, but they fought, played, laughed, and loved every minute of their lives. Her father taught her they were muddled half-breeds, impure of blood, thought, and deed, but Thyss disliked nothing about them the more she observed. They just… lived, and she found herself edging closer to their camp.

After the second full day of marching, the army encamped and cookfires burned in the cooling night air. A warm westerly wind carried the warriors' voices across the camp, and those voices, as well as the spirits to whom they belonged, rose when the daily ration of wine arrived to thirsty hands. Songs, games, and merriment abounded, but Thyss had no interest in any of it. She wandered to the edge of the tents and looked out to where the Kujari riders hobbled their four thousand horses. Seven foot bonfires shone brightly, each one illuminating cadres of hundreds of the nomads, and Thyss' eyes scanned them, interest reflected in her eyes as much as the roaring flames of the bonfires.

Some hundred feet away, four or five dozen rode in a wide circle. A heap – of what she couldn't discern – lay in the middle of the ring as the desert people whooped and hollered. Steel flashed here and there, the blades catching the firelight as they tossed daggers across the circle. Sometimes, the blades clanged as they met in midair, but more often they flew into the night. Thyss knew they would be recovered later, but her brow furrowed as she tried to make sense of the game or contest or whatever it was.

"They are impressive to watch," a man's crisp voice said in accented High Dulkurian.

Thyss hardly moved, and the voice certainly didn't startle her. Despite his obvious attempts at stealth, she heard the soft footsteps behind and to her right as he approached her. He stayed about two yards away, which was close enough for her to know that she was his intended destination, but distant enough to seem respectful. She turned her head and saw the dark form of Sawraka. The Lowborn was almost invisible in the night but for the fires illuminating his outline.

Thyss returned her attention to the Kujari and only nodded, prompting Sawraka to say, "They are the best horsemen in Dulkur, even better than the Shet I think."

"Shet?" Thyss asked.

"A people from the great plains of Tigol."

She tore her eyes from the spectacle and looked back to Sawraka, who had edged closer but kept his arms almost pinned to his sides. She asked, "Have you been to Tigol?"

"No, but I have heard stories of the Shet," Sawraka replied, and she returned her attention to the Kujari. "I met one once in Port Dulkur. He was a sailor of all things. The Shet are horse lords but of a different sort from the Kujari. Horses are sacred to the Kujari, and every one of them has their own. If a warrior's horse dies, the tribe provides another. To the Shet, horses are purely a measure of wealth."

"Interesting," Thyss replied, but her tone indicated boredom.

A cry of pain rang into the night, and a crowd of Kujari watching the game gasped and shouted their displeasure as a horseman separated from the ring. Thyss could see little of him in the dark, but the spectators jeered while making aggressive and unsavory hand gestures as he rode away with slumped shoulders.

"What just happened?" Thyss asked.

"I'd say his dagger hit another player."

"That is bad," Thyss stated, though there was an unspoken question in the words.

"Do you understand the game?"

"No."

"It is called the *hankmet*," Sawraka explained, "and it is a sport of agility, horsemanship, endurance, and precision. The contestants ride in a circle and toss their daggers across the circle at each other."

"Dangerous," Thyss commented, and her eyes glittered in the dark. "How many daggers?"

"Each player gets just one. Striking an opponent disqualifies the player, and striking a horse, Gods forbid, exiles the player from the tribe."

"What is the point then?" Thyss huffed, her usual impatience bubbling to the surface.

"To shear the hair from your opponent's head. The winner makes the closest cut without drawing blood."

"Ridiculous," Thyss grumbled as she watched the Kujari, their horses' hooves thundering, "no one could be so accurate."

"They are," Sawraka said simply and fell silent.

The horses neighed and whinnied as they were driven around and around at a gallop, the animals first flattening and then smashing to a pulp the savannah grasses underneath them. A haze of dust and dirt arose and encircled the dervishes in their maelstrom of man, beast, and steel. Several more cries shouted into the night, and every time it happened, a Kujari would split from the group to receive tongue lashings and sometimes a beating or two from his or her tribe members. Finally, no more steel blades caught the moon or firelight, and the tornado of horse warriors slowed to a stop as winners and losers were selected, congratulated, or slunk off to their tents.

"How do they know who won?" Thyss asked. "I could make out nothing amongst that chaos."

"They know. Each one of them knows who they marked and who marked them."

"What stops them from lying about it?"

Sawraka's silence caused her to turn towards him, and he answered, "Their honor. To lie about anything also means exile. Look, the winners divide the spoils."

He pointed back toward where the game took place, and Thyss watched as a dozen warriors approached the nebulous mound that was at the center of the ring. Some reached downward as if to take something and then left, while others lifted larger items for inspection. One, a woman from her smaller, lithe figure, held up a skin of some sort before nodding her head and taking it with her. Another hefted a sword, curved and at least four feet long, though Thyss could make out no details of quality or workmanship in the dark at a distance. He walked toward one of the bonfires, and as he stepped into the light, Thyss noted it was King Kerim's own son.

"Kerim'El," Thyss said with a jut of her chin, "he participates in the…"

"*Hankmet*," Sawraka supplied. "Yes. In fact, he spends more time amongst the Kujari than he does with his own father."

"He often wins?"

"I assume. He has unified over twenty tribes," Sawraka said, and then a wide grin split his face. "And now they collect their other winnings – the first choice of who shares their bed tonight."

Kerim'El and the other Kujari winners, men and women, began to select from a group of waiting and willing spectators. Some of them embraced and kissed sensually before leading one another off to a tent, while others immediately ran off together into the night. Kerim'El boisterously scooped up a willing Kujari woman, who squealed with glee, before turning and heading to a nearby tent. He stopped for just a second, his eyes gleaming in the night as they fell on Thyss, and she felt her face flush for just a second.

"Enough of this," she spat and turned away to find another flask of King Kerim's fine wine, Sawraka trailing in her wake.

For days, the army advanced across the land. The weather, though hot as was normal in Dulkur, stayed fair, and rain, though cooling, would slow their march and grind on nerves of both the king and soldiers alike. It was well known in both kings' lands that a great battle approached, and most of the farmsteads or small villages that dotted the savannahs stood empty. Commoners stood from doorways and waived the army on, wishing the warriors good luck against the scheming King Mon'El and showering them with other benedictions or small gifts. Spirits stayed high even as they crossed a shallow river and into Mon'El's kingdom.

More than once as she rode near King Kerim, Thyss looked to the sky, certain that she felt eyes upon her. She recognized a familiar tingle at the base of her neck, often felt by prey just before the predator strikes, and sometimes the fine hairs on her arms stood on end. Of course, there was nothing to see there, and she knew there wouldn't be. But she couldn't help wondering about a thin wisp of cloud that seemed to pace the army's march east, while the prevailing winds drove its larger, billowy cousins west. Her father spied on them from the clouds, and she wondered if his eyes had found her.

As it forded another shallow river, the army began to cross yet another savannah. Acacia and baobab trees dotted it as far as the eye could see, and while these usually provided some small amount of respite for game from the beating sun overhead, there were no animals to be seen. Every man and woman in the march knew they had crossed into Mon'El's kingdom, nervous energy of the coming battle filling every step, and even the wildlife of the plain felt the conflict coming in the stifling, stagnant air. Thyss noted the lack of a cooling breeze that had benefited them for several days and wondered if this too were her father's doing.

Another five miles took them into the afternoon, and a Kujari rider sped his way toward the army's ranks. He drove his horse relentlessly in the heat, and sweat poured off of both man and beast. King Kerim called for the host to halt, and the lumbering mass of soldiers and mercenaries came to a swift and efficient stop as the horse galloped relentlessly toward them. They parted ranks just enough to let the Kujari through, his intent to report directly to the king plain enough, and he pulled up his mount in a storm cloud of dust mere yards away from King Kerim, Sawraka, and Thyss.

"You have something to report," King Kerim stated as the horse huffed.

"Yes, *Harphoa*," the rider replied succinctly. Thyss had heard the word once or twice before, and she assumed it was the Kujari's own title for Kerim. The man held his horse's reins tightly as he spoke with a heavy accent that sounded as if he was trying to produce phlegm, "We spotted the other *Harphoa* and his army encamped five miles west. Half a mile from it is a single tent of plain canvas, perhaps large enough for a dozen men."

"Is there no one around the tent?"

"No, *Harphoa*."

"King Mon'El offers us parlay," Kerim considered aloud. "Do you have a count on the other army?"

"No, *Harphoa*," the man replied. "*Keha Khan* wished not to alert the other *Harphoa* to our presence."

"*Keha Khan*?" Thyss whispered to Sawraka.

"War leader," he replied.

"Kerim'El," she concluded in a hushed tone, receiving Sawraka's nod as confirmation, and she noticed King Kerim watched them, waiting for them to finish before he spoke again.

"Wise. Tell him –," Kerim began, but his words were cut off by Thyss' derisive snort. He turned to face Thyss and said, "You disagree."

"I'm certain I've seen my father amongst the clouds several times the last few days. He joins with them, and he has seen our entire army, including the Kujari."

"He has such power?" King Kerim asked, and he received a nod from Thyss, her face twisted in arrogance and condescension. "Why would you not tell us this?"

"I assumed you knew," she shrugged.

"I knew he could travel like the wind, but to observe and see for miles?" Kerim asked with interest. He quickly shook off the awe so that none of his subordinates would see it, and he returned his attention to the Kujari rider. "Tell my son that we will march to one half mile from the tent, and he is to join me here when we halt. In the meantime, I want the Kujari to scout the enemy army. Do not attack or harass them in any way. I merely want a count."

"Yes, *Harphoa*."

"Go," Kerim commanded, and the Kujari turned his horse about and hasted back through the ranks of soldiers.

"What are your orders, Majesty?" Sawraka asked crisply.

"We march to a half mile from the tent. I believe Mon'El will have a message for us by the time we get there," King Kerim replied gravely.

21.

The canvas billowed as a soft, cooling breeze blew through it. Of course, the tent kept the sun off Mon'El and the five men with him as they awaited King Kerim and whatever entourage he chose to bring. The message his slave bore to the opposite king was simple – bring up to five and no weapons – and Mon'El languidly gazed at those he had selected. He had of course brought a Lowborn servant to serve as a scribe, who fidgeted endlessly with anxiety, Guribda, and the three priests who marched with him on Calumbu. These last three were all Highborn and Chosen. Each represented one God with Mon'El Himself of Aeyu, and the priests reflected the mannerisms of their gods as they too waited. The Chosen of Hykan let off his annoyance at being kept waiting in waves of heat, which Mon'El swept away in the breeze, while Nykeema's priest simply stood with shuttered eyelids, calm, cool, and collected. The priest of Goelgar stood between them and kept them apart as if to separate their very auras lest they cause a catastrophic explosion of competing magic.

The tent's east facing flap opened, spilling bright sunlight inside as Guribda said, "They are coming, Majesty."

Mon'El chose to keep the tracker in his service, much to the man's chagrin he knew, but he proved himself too knowledgeable, too resourceful. The kingpriest hired him to track Thyss across her jaunting adventures but had found the man to be so much more than a simple tracker.

He had eyes and ears almost everywhere across the continent, a true spymaster, and Mon'El chose to retain his services as exactly that. It was because of Guribda's vast network that Mon'El had known about the unification of the Kujari under Kerim'El long before Mon'El himself had spied their four thousand horsemen from the air.

He shot a look across his priests, a warning gaze to keep their elemental tempers in check, for he had some small hope that war could be avoided, the pact somehow salvaged. For a moment, a grin touched his lips as he considered the irony in that. He had made this deal with King Kerim years ago to merge their kingdoms on the marriage of their children, a deal that had immensely more cost to him than the loss of his only legitimate child, and King Kerim's reputation to holding to, and holding others to, his deals was legendary. Mon'El was certain he intended to murder Kerim, his son, and all of their wedding guests the moment the nuptials concluded, and now that he was faced with a straightforward war that would accomplish the same ends, he found himself eager to keep the agreement together. Perhaps, it was because he had spent so much time, energy, and wealth on it.

"How many?" Mon'El asked, straightening and smoothing his light blue silk robes.

"Only four," Guribda said, "King Kerim, his son, a Lowborn, and your daughter, and they are all armed, Majesty."

Mon'El fumed inwardly as he straightened the circlet about his head, made of solid gold of course with sapphires and diamonds and inscribed with a prayer to Aeyu. He couldn't have been any clearer in the message he'd sent – he was prepared to negotiate, and if Kerim was as well, he should come to the tent straight away with an entourage numbering up to five. Mon'El made certain that his group, even Guribda, brought no weapons, and now his rival ignored such a simple expectation. As the tent flaps opened once more, Mon'El sought calm and pushed the aggravation away, recognizing that Kerim often employed such tactics during his dealings to disrupt his opponents' balance.

The first figure through was a Lowborn, the late afternoon sun silhouetting him blindingly as he entered. Though unimpressive of height at under six feet, his body was strong and fit with not an ounce of wasted material. Scars shone as lighter or even pink streaks against his dark skin, his trophies from countless battles, and he wore a bronze chain shirt that was belted at the waist. A steel scimitar adorned one hip, a pair of daggers the other, and he surveyed Mon'El and his group briefly before bowing slightly and saying, "King Mon'El of Kaimpur, I present King Kerim and Prince Kerim'El."

He then stepped out to hold the tent flap open, and Kerim then stepped through with his son in tow. The prince wore light skins and leathers, common to the nomads with whom he rode, and they did little to hide the strong athleticism of the young man. Kerim wore armor similar to his Lowborn slave – or bodyguard more likely – and even the metal links did little to hide his soft, fleshy form. They stopped just a few steps in, keeping about eight feet between themselves and Mon'El in the tent that grew rapidly crowded.

Almost as an afterthought, the tent flap opened one last time, and Mon'El caught a glimpse of golden hair clasped into a high ponytail. A bronze skinned woman came to stand at Kerim's left hand, opposite Kerim'El on his right, and Mon'El scarcely recognized his daughter, despite having seen her only weeks before. Thyss stood with her feet spaced widely in arrogance and her arms crossed in confident defiance, both something Mon'El had come to expect from his daughter over the years, but there was something else that made her almost alien and unknown to him. A strange sword, an impressive weapon with green hued steel the likes he'd never seen, hung at her side, and she wore the odd, black silk tunic and leggings he'd seen in Calumbu. But even these weren't the cause of his disquiet. Thyss radiated strength, power, and conviction in a way he'd neither felt from her before, nor anyone he had ever faced, and he wondered if he caused that same apprehension, that same unease in those he faced. As Mon'El locked eyes with his daughter, he felt the hatred in her eyes burn into him.

"Mon'El," Kerim began, "I am disappointed that your wife is not here to greet us. I found her company most... agreeable last time we met. What is her name again?"

For just a moment, Mon'El's jaw hardened, and the muscles flexed under the skin of his face. Kerim had struck a first blow, wicked and like a striking serpent, and Mon'El wasn't even sure why it angered him so suddenly. He and his wife had often bedded others during their marriage, but she hadn't allowed him, or any of her other lovers, near her since the other king and his son visited the palace in Kaimpur. It was no matter, Mon'El decided as he shrugged it off. The assault was only another tactic bent toward giving the merchant king an edge, and Mon'El summarily dismissed his own indignance at the comment.

"Greetings, King Kerim," Mon'El started grandly with a bow, "I thank you for meeting me so that we may yet resolve this peacefully, but I am concerned."

"By what, Mon'El?" Kerim replied coldly.

"You are armed, and as you can see, my servants and I are not."

"Are you not?" Kerim questioned, keeping his voice level and even, without a hint of inflection. "Then I am to assume that you and your Chosen left your powers in your tents?"

The Lowborn snickered, and a smile jumped to Thyss' face before she suppressed it. Before Mon'El could respond, Kerim continued, "I was not ready to march so quickly into this tent to my death, and I know our steel could not deal yours before your magicks ended us. To level the field, I brought my own Chosen."

Mon'El glanced back at his daughter for just a moment before returning his gaze to Kerim's face, which was cold and solid as granite. He said, "With my daughter's appearance at your side, it would seem that our bargain is concluded."

Thyss snorted derisively and opened her mouth to reply, but Kerim raised a single hand to call for her silence. Even still, she turned her blazing, unblinking stare on him for just a moment as he said, "There is no bargain, Mon'El. Thyss will not marry Kerim'El to consummate our deal, and that was the final part of your end of the bargain. Since you cannot meet your responsibilities, I am here to take your kingdom from you."

"And yet she stands with you," Mon'El said.

"She stands with me –," Kerim began to answer.

But Thyss interrupted him, and waves of heat rolled off of her, causing even Mon'El's own Chosen of Hykan to shift uncomfortably, "For reasons of my own. I have come for vengeance."

"Vengeance for what, for who, my child?" Mon'El asked with a sigh, and the cooling breeze increased.

"You know who," Thyss sneered.

"That Lowborn savage you took as a lover? He was little more than a petty chief! Why would you seek to avenge someone so low, so unimportant? People like him are meant to be used, discarded if they are of no use. There are so many more to replace him," Mon'El scoffed, his words driving Thyss' ire to new heights as she breathed heavily through her nose.

"Such a great king. You once told me we take only what we need from those beneath us, but you meant only so long as they serve us. You're a fool, a stupid fool, blinded by your own arrogance! I'm not here to avenge *my lover*," she shot back, deadly edge to her words. "I'm here to avenge the only people who were ever truly kind to me, and you killed them all."

Mon'El inhaled sharply as she spoke, taken aback by the words that spilled from her mouth. It wasn't just the reminder of his own words or his hypocrisy. His mind reeled, but neither from her insults, nor from her admission that she had bedded the giant chieftain. Mon'El's thoughts tumbled and somersaulted over an idea he could not seem to grasp – she was angered, angered to the point of violence and murder over that tiny jungle kingdom he'd found her in? He didn't even remember its name!

"Yes, father," Thyss continued, "I am here to kill King Mon'El of Kaimpur. The people of Calumbu aided me and asked nothing. They were good people, who only wanted to live and help one another, but I knew their way would never survive. I knew that one day, some ruler of shit such as yourself would come and destroy them for no reason other than they would not serve you. I warned their king of it, but he would not listen. You murdered them, and now I am going to kill you for it."

Mon'El regained his composure and looked on his daughter, his eyes full of sadness as he shook his head slowly. "You do not understand, Thyssallia. I didn't kill them. You did that when you opposed me. They stood with you, and I had to show you how wrong you were. And now, I will do the same to Kerim, his son, and his entire army. You cannot win, daughter. Your will shall bend to mine, as surely as the winds of Aeyu shall put out Hykan's flames."

"Never. Hykan's flames are only spread by the winds. You shall burn, fucker!" she screamed furiously.

Mon'El's priests tensed with the outburst, seeking their gods for aid, and a slight rumble shook the ground as nearby lightning split a cloudless sky. The scribe and Guribda huddled for cover behind the priests, prepared to run out the back toward their army any moment. Kerim, his son, and the Lowborn's hands all shot to their scimitars, ready to fight, but they were only stayed from drawing steel by the calming, upraised hand of Mon'El himself.

"King Kerim, I beg that you excuse my daughter," he said. "Obviously, she and I have some… issues to work out, but we can still salvage our agreement and keep the peace between our kingdoms."

"Indeed, we can," Kerim agreed with an understanding nod. "It is quite simple. Have your peasant army return to their farms, send your priests back to their pyramids, and abdicate the palace to my son, Kerim'El. I offer you a life well cared for, every whim indulged, assuming of course your daughter lets you live, but you will never rule again."

"Unacceptable," Mon'El breathed.

"Very well. Tomorrow morning, we will meet on the field," Kerim replied without hesitation.

The Lowborn stepped out of the tent, holding the canvas aside for his king. Kerim waited a moment, as if expecting some last word from Mon'El, but seeing one was not forthcoming, he exited the tent with his son just behind him. Thyss had not followed them out, and she stood perfectly still, her infernal gaze working to burn a hole right through Mon'El as he turned to look back at her.

He opened his mouth to speak, but she cut him off, saying, "And tomorrow, I will sever your head from your body and leave both for the vultures, just like you did to him."

Before he could form a reply, she strode out of the tent without so much as a glance over her shoulder.

Kerim dismissed his generals early in the night, a mere two hours after the sun set, to let them walk amongst their troops, review plans with their officers, or perhaps attempt to get a good night's sleep. There was nothing more to go over, for their plans had been reviewed almost every night since leaving Tojaru, and there was nothing more to say. The Kujari had confirmed the number and makeup of Mon'El's army, and it was precisely as expected. The plan was simple, because no complex plan would ever stand on its own once Mon'El's Chosen joined the battle. It was clear to all that success against their magic relied on the speed and skill of the Kujari and Thyss' own power.

And her thoughts wandered while she nursed a wineskin that she'd snagged from the supply train, even though no one was to get drunk on the eve before battle. There was wisdom in those orders but seeing her father had left her with a need to drown in wine. Truthfully, it was the only way she could keep herself from charging across the open plain and outright challenging him before both armies. She had wanted to do exactly that, but King Kerim was adamant that she stick to the plan. "You will get your chance," he promised, his words echoing in her ears. After only a few swigs of wine, she tossed the skin aside with a sigh of disgust. It did nothing to assuage her anxious desire to burn her father to ash.

As it had almost every night, the savannah carried the whoops and shouts of the Kujari into the army's camp, and the joyous celebration of life starkly contrasted with the solemnity of a professional force preparing for tomorrow's battle. Thyss emerged from her tent into the cool night air. The army was deadly quiet, the only sounds being the sounds of smiths repairing weapons and armor, the neighing of horses, and the quiet roar of campfires as the soldiers gathered around them in silence. After tomorrow some, maybe none, of them would leave the savannah alive, and this evoked a time of silent reflection. Thyss had no use for it, and she quietly stalked her way between legions of warriors, some of whom watched her with bright interest, some of whom observed sullen eyed, and many who paid her no mind at all.

She reached the empty stretch of plain that separated the Kujari camp about a hundred yards from the rest of the army, and she moved toward the edge of the nomad camp. It seemed over half of the horsemen were involved in *hankmet*. Whirlwinds of steel flashed amidst the clouds of kicked up dust by the thundering of hooves, and the camps themselves stood almost empty as those who were not at play watched.

With a notable exception. Prince Kerim-El sat near a campfire, surrounded by several of his chiefs, silently staring into the flames. The movement of her approach, though only illuminated by a half-moon, must have caught his eye for he glanced up at her some fifty feet away. His brown eyes stared into hers for a long moment before he mumbled something she could not hear, and the prince stood from his place by the fire and padded quietly toward her. He wore a plain, white linen shift that fell to just above his knees instead of the open leather jerkin and leggings the nomads wore on horseback. His bare feet aided his quiet approach, though he made no attempt to keep himself hidden from her.

"Good evening, Princess," he said softly as he grew near enough for her to hear his faint voice.

Her eyes narrowed at the title, while she considered if he meant it sarcastically. But after a moment, her ire cooled, and she replied, "I've told you all not to call me that."

"My apologies," he mumbled. "Did you come to observe me or the *hankmet*?"

"What would make you think either?" she demanded.

"Because I have seen you watching us almost every night on the march."

"I find it interesting," she admitted, but then her tone grew harder, "and my interest has nothing to do with you."

"Oh, no? I apologize."

"Do you? Did you apologize to my mother?" Suddenly taken aback by such a bold question he hadn't expected, Kerim'El didn't know how to answer. He stood in shocked silence for a moment as he turned and looked back longingly at his camp as she continued, "Oh, I have heard. An army likes to gossip, and I've heard the whispers of the degradations you and your father heaped upon my mother. Kerim all but confirmed them this afternoon."

After a long silence, Kerim'El asked, "What would you have me say?"

"You have a great reputation among the men in your father's army, and I saw you take a woman to your tent the other night. So, I ask you, Prince Kerim'El," Thyss paused for a moment before posing her question, "are the whispers of what you and your father did to my mother true?"

Kerim'El looked away across the empty expanse between the army and the Kujari, and he thought he could feel her eyes burning his skin. He glanced up to the moon as he sought an answer that would keep him alive, and finally, he turned back to Thyss and softly said, "I… I had not realized she was your mother."

"Is it true?!" Thyss screamed at him, causing a shockwave of unbearable heat that washed over him and was gone in an instant, and two of his chieftains stood from their place around the fire to stare at him.

He raised a hand toward them to indicate that all was well, sighed, and whispered, "Every word. My father said Mon'El sent her to distract us, and he hoped to sow discord between –"

"Enough!" Thyss howled.

She turned and stormed away toward her tent, heedless of the various eyes that watched and unaware of the near silent sigh of relief that Kerim'El released as she left him. Men and women, warriors and mercenaries all, stayed out of her path as she tramped back to her tent, and those nearest Thyss felt the hellish heat flowing from her. For a moment, she thought she might explode as she had in K'watu, but through her sheer force of will she kept it inside, channeling it deeper into her heart and soul. She wasn't sure how she felt towards her mother, but she hated Kerim'El and his father for what they had done to her. More importantly, it further fueled her hatred for her father, for it was he that put Ilia in that position, and Thyss would finally find release in Mon'El's death.

22.

Thyss paced relentlessly back and forth across a ten foot stretch of grass, much to the annoyance of King Kerim, who endeavored to ignore her as he consulted with his generals. Their side of the savannah was perfectly flat, and it was nearly impossible to see anything of the two armies as they thunderously approached each other, whereas Mon'El benefited from an elevated ridgeline. It wasn't even the lack of visibility that caused Thyss' anxious patrolling of that tiny stretch of land. She had to wait for the right time to wade into the battle – it would do no good if she exhausted her strength annihilating her father's peasants – and Thyss hated waiting for anything.

The first screams of the dying screeched as one across the plain when Kerim's troops hurled javelins into the masses of Mon'El's conscripts, and though she could not see, Thyss imagined that they went down by the dozens, perhaps even hundreds. They had no recourse, no way to return the favor as Mon'El would never spend the gold needed to arm his draftees so well. The ground began to shake, as their only defense would then be to charge, to run headlong into Kerim's army, to close the distance as quickly as possible to minimize the damage. Of course, Mon'El's priests could have provided some aid, either by incinerating the missiles or turning them into air or even water, but he would never waste their power so.

Even a half mile away, the first crash of steel as the armies ran headlong into one another threatened to deafen

Thyss, the shattering cacophony blasting her ears for just a moment before it dulled into a near constant low roar. She had fought and killed, but the sounds of thousands of individual duels – impacts of swords on armor, clashes of steel swords being parried, and the cries of the wounded – overlapped in a symphony of death that only full on war could conduct. It was violently terrible and horrifyingly exhilarating, and she longed to be in the thick of it, her palms itching to feel the weight of Feghul's Claw.

She turned as a runner reached King Kerim, bowed, and announced, "Mon'El's army is pushed back." Another arrived only a few moments later and reported, "The enemy reformed the right flank, but still they fall." The king took these reports with a nod and dismissed the runners back to their commanders with a flip of his hand. Additional runners arrived and relayed nothing unexpected.

Kerim locked eyes with Thyss and said quietly, "The Chosen will attack soon."

Thyss nodded curtly and turned to resume her pacing, but it was as if Kerim's statement was either an order given to the opposing army or a prophetic proclamation. Where the air had just been still, if a touch warm, now a cool breeze blew in from the east, and it rose steadily in force, bringing tears to the eyes of those who looked into it. White puffs of cloud that lazed above the savannah blossomed in immensity as they scudded across the sky, joined by more and more until they covered the blue sky overhead and turned to an angry dark gray. Rain fell, gently at first but turning to a heavy, pelting downpour within seconds, and as the two armies fought and died, it was obvious that the storm only attacked one half of the field. Thunder rumbled once, twice, and then turned to a constant, overlapping assault on the ears as bolts of lightning shot down from the heavens to blast Kerim's armored soldiers.

“It is time,” Kerim intoned, and seeing Thyss start forward, he added, “for the Kujari.”

Thyss huffed and stewed in her impatience as Sawraka turned and took a four foot long, ivory tusk wrapped with bands of silver and gold from a waiting servant. The man breathed in deeply, put his lips to the horn, and shot a heavy blast toward the south. Though the wind threatened to carry it away, the penetrating blare drove onward, and it even seemed to rattle the very bones of those nearest by. Another horn, this one less deep but no less powerful, answered in the distance a moment later.

Minutes counted by interminably as men and women died amidst the flashing of scimitars, the streaks of javelins, and blinding bolts of lightning. Thyss ached to lunge to the attack, to charge into the fray and release her own fury on her father’s priests, but every time she shot a look at King Kerim, the man only lifted his palm in a call for patience. Finally, a new thunder joined the tempest and the ground shook with the constant vibration caused by thousands of galloping hooves. The whinnies of horses and war cries of the Kujari joined the clamoring pandemonium of the battle.

A boy serving as a runner, probably barely into his teen years, appeared and panted as he reported, “Majesty, the enemy’s right flank has turned and pulled into his center. It was not a retreat. Are we to pursue?”

“Did not flee,” Kerim repeated in a near whisper as he watched another messenger speed away from the battlefield. “Turn the enemy’s flank. Full attack.”

“He saw the Kujari coming,” Thyss said knowingly, and she tapped a foot as she continuously glanced out toward the battle.

“Hold,” Kerim told her as he awaited the next runner. He wasted no time awaiting the messenger to catch her breath as he asked, “What is it?”

"The enemy's center shifted hard into our army's right flank. We don't know where the troops came from. We are unable to support Prince Kerim'El's attack."

"Mon'El knew," Kerim agreed with Thyss.

"He saw them coming from the clouds. He was ready for it," Thyss almost growled.

She paused for a moment and watched the king as the calculations ran through his mind, as he considered outcomes based on the facts before them. After a few seconds, she sighed loudly, strode to her horse, and vaulted up into the saddle. She urged the animal forward with her heels, intending to ride to the southeastern edge of the battle, but before the horse took more than a few steps, King Kerim appeared next to her with a strong hand on her reins. Her anger flashed, causing her to fume, but his words calmed her ire.

"I would appreciate it," he said, "if you and Sawraka, and half of his complement, would bring back my son."

He released his grip, and she rode over to where the Lowborn general had already joined his commanders. Swiftly, some two thousand strong warriors began to march with Sawraka at their head, leaving behind half to provide security for their king. The thought struck her that these were the best King Kerim had in his army, as they moved with unmatched accuracy and precision. She turned her horse ahead in their path and galloped forward a few hundred feet, only to half turn the steed to gauge the distance from the warriors. They moved more quickly than she expected as they stepped in a perfect rhythm that allowed them far more speed than most of the army accomplished. Still, she fought the urge to charge into the fray, seething at the need to constantly turn and await the oncoming warriors.

As they neared, Thyss spotted the Kujari somewhat removed from the battle and disorganized, their horses galloping about in various directions. Some of the horsemen screamed over the din of combat and the storm, calling their wayward riders back to the mass as it tried to reform. One of the Kujari noted the approach of Thyss, Sawraka, and his troops and took ahold of one of his compatriots. They leaned toward each other conspiratorially as the former shouted something, and then the latter sped his horse toward her. Blood spattered the hooves, legs, and even body of the stallion, but Thyss saw no wounds on it or its rider.

"Where is the prince?" Sawraka shouted as he neared them.

The man pulled his horse sidelong next to the Lowborn general and responded in broken Highborn, "He fell. Our charge crushed many. Bad fire broke us in two. Kerim'El and many separated. We could not reach."

"Is he alive?" Sawraka asked, but the Kujari shrugged. Sawraka said, "We will charge. Have your riders attack on our flank. We must find the prince."

"And the Chosen," Thyss added.

As the man galloped back to his people, Sawraka held a closed fist above his head, and his warriors came to an instant halt. He turned and caught the questioning gaze cast at him by Thyss, and he explained, "We will charge the rest of the distance. You should dismount, Lady Thyss."

She immediately opened her mouth to argue with the Lowborn but thought better of it as she looked across the battlefield. No one was mounted besides the Kujari, and while it would afford her a better view, she considered that it would also make her a target for the enemy, both the troops and the priests. She nodded briefly and climbed down and pointing the horse back the way they had come, she gave it a smack on the rump to send it running away.

She turned and strode over to stand right next to Sawraka, his hand still lifted into the air.

"Are you ready for this?" he all but mumbled the question meant for her alone.

"You have no idea," Thyss replied, and a burning like hunger began to spread through her.

"Then make ready," he said.

Sawraka opened his hand so that his palm faced the battle that raged several hundred feet away and his fingers pointed to the sky as if he dared the lightning above to strike him, and the two thousand fighters behind him drew steel as one. Startled by the resounding ring of so much steel, Thyss hesitated just a moment before pulling Feghul's Claw. She looked at the Lowborn general, her eyes roaming over a not unattractive face that had been set as hard as any stone statue, and then she looked straight ahead. The hand came down in a swift chopping action, as if it were a sword itself, and the entire retinue behind them unleashed an ear splitting, earth shattering cry.

They charged. Some of the warriors, beautiful and deadly examples of strength and athleticism, achieved full speed in a matter of a few steps. Long strides carried them headlong toward the backs of their allies, and many of them outpaced their leader. Thyss, too, was strong and agile, but many of the men under Sawraka's command outpaced and left her behind in moments. This only drove her harder, and as they neared the battle, many of the warriors already engaged moved aside in relief as the fresh reinforcements assailed their enemies.

Steel crashed together, and people screamed in death – mostly their enemies, but some of Sawraka's warriors found themselves suddenly impaled on a chance spear. The charging men and women batted more spears away, severed some completely, and still others skidded off of bronze and steel hauberks. The peasants of Mon'El's army faltered, fell, and ran from this refreshed attack, death and blood pouring across the rain soaked savannah anew. The cry of horses filled the air as the Kujari renewed their assault.

Thyss had no time to observe any of it. She felled two poor men in the first seconds, Feghul's Claw hungrily drinking of their blood as it hacked through their bodies. Three closed on her left flank, while a man wearing leather armor and wielding a scimitar attacked her head on. He was no peasant conscript as he moved with the skill of a seasoned swordsman, and she parried several blows before motioning an open hand to her left. She turned her full attention on her duelist as sudden heat rolled off the wall of flame she'd invoked to protect her from the others, and she smiled viciously when she heard men scream as they were engulfed in it. She struck two quick blows at her foe, sparks flying from the collision of their blades, but while his sword was marred by the strikes, Feghul's Claw showed no knicks or damage at all. She brought the weapon around, and his sword shattered as he parried, splinters of steel showering other combatants as Thyss' sword cleaved him from sternum to cock. She withdrew her sword quickly and struck two more death blows to others who screamed in pain from the steel explosion. A cadre of men with spears charged, and she opened a hand as she leaned toward them and blew them a kiss. Her breath ignited the tiny flame that burned in her open hand, and a spreading stream of fire extended outward and grew to envelop them all. They screamed as hair and clothes burned, as eyes and flesh melted.

Deranged laughter filled the air, overwhelming the sounds of death and battle. As her green hued steel flashed and slaughtered and as her fire magicks inundated and annihilated her enemies, the laughter grew to an unconquerable crescendo. The enemies shied away from her, or even turned and ran full force to escape the deadly ministrations of the battle crazed fire priestess, Thyss came to understand that it was her own voice that was raised in the frenzied, manic emanations. And it carried her to new heights of destruction.

"To me! To me!" shouted a voice from further into the combat, and out of the corner of her eye, Sawraka surged forward with dozens of his armored warriors. They hacked and hewed their way to a group of dismounted Kujari, who fought with their backs to each other in a circle. In their midst stood Kerim'El, dealing as many death blows as any of his protectors. Within moments, the attackers fell under the singing blades of Sawraka's fighters.

As the two men fought side by side, the prince said with good humor, "Your timing is impeccable!"

"Your father sent us to bring you back," Sawraka replied somewhat stoically, "I would hate to fail him."

"Not yet. The battle is not yet won, and the Chosen threaten to rout us."

Backed by several hundred men, Thyss fought her way to one of the priests, slaying those who stood before her with impunity. Most were too terrified to stand and fight, either turning to flee or falling prostrate upon the ground at her passing, but enough challenged her thrust to make it a bloody affair.

An anxiety filled voice called out, "Defend me, or your wives and children will suffer!"

But against Thyss' deadly advance, common men had no chance, and the threat clearly lost any weight as several rows of spearmen suddenly melted away and into the crowd around them, revealing a robed priest. Thyss recognized him from yesterday's parlay, such as it was, and she knew she had seen him around Kaimpur on more than one occasion. His name escaped her, but the robes that shifted as he moved from yellow to orange to red declared his allegiance to Hykan. She grinned a closed mouth, evil smirk for Hykan, Lord of Fire, would never allow this pathetic excuse for a sorcerer to stand up to her. He used the men's fear for their families to force them to fight. He was weak, nothing to her, and as she leisurely approached, the discordant uproar of the battle surrounding them faded to nothing, as if combatants on both sides wished no part of this duel.

Only fifteen feet or so separated the two, and the priest, knowing that death stood before him brandishing that wicked green scimitar, wasted no time going on the attack. He raised his arms overhead, calling out to Hykan, and then brought them down together so that the heels of his palms touched one another. It looked as if he were planning to catch a thrown object, but instead, a torrent of fire rushed from his hands toward Thyss. It meant nothing to her as she continued her deliberate stride. She merely waved her free hand, and the stream of flame redirected somewhere to the priest's right, eliciting the screams of unsuspecting men. The Chosen took a wavering step backward before he steeled his will and brought from the sky a pillar of white hot flame that fully engulfed Thyss. For a moment, she peered at her hands and arms, and she burst out laughing as she noted that her skin neither blackened, nor burned at all. She reveled for just a moment in the encompassing heat that failed to even damage her clothing before lifting her own arms above her head, redirecting the pillar back at its conjuror. The priest huddled and cowered defensively as it struck him, and though his robes burned away, he stood unharmed. However, by the time he realized this, he had only enough time to glimpse the whistling green blade of Feghul's Claw as it severed his head from his neck.

As the defenders continued to merge into their fellows, seeking any escape from Hykan's own siren of death, Thyss gloated in satisfaction as she stood over the dead priest, his blood seeding the battlefield.

After a few moments, she took stock of her surroundings, finding that none of her father's army seemed intent on engaging her. To an onlooker, it appeared as if her mere presence had cut a wide swath through the enemy, like an obstruction amid a river of ants. In saving Kerim'El, Sawraka and his warriors, while aided by the reformed Kujari cavalry also pushed back the enemy, leaving scores if not hundreds of the dead and dying in their wake. The riders had again pulled back to consolidate their forces to charge. A hundred feet away, Sawraka and his prince faced their own Chosen, a man called Nekhet, and Thyss hesitated just a moment before rushing to their aid.

Sawraka, intent to charge the sorcerer, raised his scimitar overhead and shouted, "Death to the Chosen!"

Before he could act further, a blinding flash burst from the clouds overhead, and a mind numbing thunderclap buffeted both armies. The lightning bolt struck the raised tip of Sawraka's sword, and it scorched and transformed the general into a smoking, cracked ruin instantaneously. An explosion flung Kerim'El, as well as about a dozen of his soldiers from where the bolt struck, and Thyss lost sight of the prince as it tossed his body into a formation of his enemies.

Too late to save the dead and blackened Sawraka, Thyss lurched into action. She ran toward Nekhet, paying no heed to Nykeema's symbols upon his dark blue robe and headdress, and she screamed unintelligibly as she went, her ears still ringing from his attack. The priest turned her way, and she almost skidded to a halt, extended her fingers, and blasted hellish streams of flame toward her target, heedless of whether they engulfed friend or foe in their passage. Unsurprised by her attack, Nekhet met it with a frigid onslaught of water produced from thin air. The two elemental forces met on his side of the halfway point between the sorcerers, and scalding steam exploded from their collision. Warriors of both sides cried out shrilly, their skin blistering as they burned. She was unprepared for the strength behind Nekhet's response to her own magick, and it began to gain ground, pushing her elemental flames backward. Perhaps he had withheld his attacks, reserving his strength for when he would need to save his own skin. Or perhaps it was his age and power, for Thyss knew Nekhet to be at least a hundred years old.

As the meeting point of the two elemental forces pushed closer to her, Thyss screamed, "No old man will best me!"

She began to give ground, stepping backward to buy herself precious seconds as she reached deep down within her burning heart for the reserves of strength that rested there. She felt Feghul's Claw bolster her as it sought blood, but this was not enough. She dug in her heels, refusing to fall back further, and she silently called on Hykan.

I need you now, My Lord of Flame. Your fires rage within me, and you are the greatest of all the gods. If I am yours, if I truly am Chosen, give me the power I seek. If it is not so, then go burn!

She opened her eyes to find Nekhet, so sure of his victory, had closed half the distance between them during her brief prayer. Even the conscripts and officers under his command approached slowly, preparing to overwhelm her at the last moment if necessary. The competing elemental streams met only three feet from Thyss, continuing to exude copious amounts of hissing clouds, but she held it there even as her adversary approached. He came to stand only six feet or so away, an enormous leer splitting his aged face.

"Give it up, Thyssallia," he said, raising his voice over the continuous creation of scalding vapor, "you cannot win, and your father does not want you dead!"

Thyss steeled herself and retorted, "I care not what *he* wants!"

The rage – rage at the mention of her father, rage at the priest's use of a name she discarded long ago, and rage at the mere thought of loss to this worm – detonated within her core. Every ounce of her being, every nerve and fibrous muscle, her heart and gut, and her very flesh and soul ignited all at once. She screamed in fury as an infernal blast radiated from her, its white hot intensity seemingly greater than even the sun as it instantly disintegrated hair, flesh, bone, and even melted bronze and steel. The anguished cries of dozens permeated the air, including that of Nekhet, and when the radiant heat cleared, Thyss stood in the center of a circle of scorched devastation ten yards across.

And suddenly, Thyss could barely keep her eyes open. She fought heavy eyelids as they threatened to close, and every time they did so, she forced them back open. She began to lose that battle, as all strength fled her limbs, and her legs collapsed under her weight. The sounds of battle blended together, a coalescence of deathly clamor, and Thyss tried to climb back to her feet, staring at the blackened ground from her hands and knees. She could manage no more, and as she fell on her stomach to let rest claim her, she no longer heard the cries of Prince Kerim'El calling for help. The sounds of the Kujari faded away, despite the terrified screams of the horses as boulders erupted from rumbling ground to block their path. She contended with exhausted lassitude just one more time, managing to pry her eyelids open for half a second, but she couldn't find the willpower to care about the dozens of men that cautiously approached armed with spears and swords.

23.

The rough hands that gripped and dragged Thyss by her upper arms across the battlefield released their pressure, all but throwing her to the ground as the death throes of men sounded in the distance amidst the clangs of steel and crackles of elemental energies. She was beaten and battered. No wounds had been dealt to her, at least nothing that wouldn't heal on its own without medicinal or magical help, but she knew bruises would mark her body in the coming days, if she were allowed to live that long. Thyss had fought and slayed, ending two of her father's priests as well as countless other foes, but defeating Nekhet had drained her too much. When they took her, strength returned, though briefly, and she slew many before the newfound well ran dry. She fought until they fell upon her, beating her down into submission, though avoiding any permanent damage by order of her father, no doubt. She lay with her right cheek on the hard, trampled grass, her breathing labored and deep as if it took all of her strength to do only that. She could almost be asleep, so utterly exhausted was she, and she thought she even dozed here and there for a moment.

Thyss struggled to open her left eye at the sliding hiss of steel nearby. It had already begun to swell from a fist she'd taken from an unseen enemy, and she wondered if she would even be able to open it at all the next day. Feghul's Claw, its curved, razor sharp blade reflecting the blinding sunlight into her eye, impaled the ground only a few feet away from where she laid as one of her father's personal guards backed away from it. A mournful, winding note filled her heart, and Thyss reached a weak, yearning hand toward the weapon. A sandaled foot kicked into view and connected with her wrist, knocking her hand up and away from her sword, and Thyss rolled slightly with the momentum to flip onto her back.

Mon'El of Kaimpur stood before her, light blue robes fluttering and swirling in the winds that swept the battlefield. She fought to keep her eyes open as they threatened to close and usher her to sleep every time she took in a breath, and each time she forced them back open, two Mon'Els had to reform into one. He stood expressionless, his golden face turned down toward her, but there was a hint of something in his silvery gaze. Was it pity? Sorrow? Thyss couldn't be sure, but she felt new anger begin to warm her body, limbs, and muscles.

"My daughter," Mon'El intoned in hushed serenity as he raised his eyes and looked across the legions of dead and dying, "why has it come to this? Did any of this truly have to happen? I know I have some blame in it. In hindsight, I could have just waged war on Kerim, killed him and his son, and taken his lands. You might have even joined me in battle, but I thought... well, I thought that perhaps a peaceful marriage of our two kingdoms, his and mine, had more merit. Perhaps I was wrong to expect my fiery willed daughter to go along with my wishes for her, but I never thought it would bring you to stand against me. Ah, perfect."

Mon'El turned away from his daughter, and for a brief moment, she begged Hykan for strength, for just enough to regain her feet, free Feghul's Claw from its place in the ground, and liberate her father's head from his neck. It had begun to build from the moment she saw him, but if she tried anything, her movements would still be slow and clumsy. She would accomplish nothing before one of his bodyguards kicked her legs out from under her or knocked her senseless with an iron fist.

As she watched, Thyss saw two steel thewed Lowborns all but carrying a golden skinned man wearing a leather jerkin and leggings, both rent in several places, and blood oozed from wounds that would not heal on their own. His soft boots dragged in the dirt, and his head drooped forward so she couldn't see his face, long dark hair hanging so far that it almost touched the ground. At a nod from Mon'El, they released their captive, and Kerim'El caught himself, managing to land on outstretched palms rather than fall face first onto the ground as Thyss had. As he looked toward her, his golden skin shone ashen from loss of blood or exertion, probably both, and he coughed several times, blood speckled phlegm landing in the dirt before him.

"A brave man, this prince," Mon'El announced. "He fought with daring and skill. How many did he kill, Guribda? Fifty?"

Thyss' eyes shot over to the mixed blood man she hadn't noticed before as he replied, "By my count almost a hundred, Majesty."

"Impressive," Mon'El said as he nodded, and Thyss' heart threatened to leap into her throat when he yanked Feghul's Claw from the ground, "but not enough. In the end, your Kujari are scattered by my Chosen, sent back to their nomadic paths. How many of their chiefs fell, and how long will it be before they dare to unify under one king again?

"It does not matter. My battle is with your father, not those savages. Look, Prince Kerim'El, across the field and know that your cause is lost. Your father's lands will soon be mine. Do you have anything to say?"

Thyss stared at Kerim'El, waiting for him to find strength or do anything that could motivate her to action, but as she searched his face, she found only loss and despair. Thyss cast her gaze across the blood soaked savannah and saw the bodies of thousands strewn across it, the grasses trampled into the dirt and turned red. The vultures already circled high, and some aggressive few had already landed to begin their feast hundreds of yards from where the battle still raged. It seemed that Kerim's army had finally broken, the last remnants of Sawraka's company surrounding the king and they themselves surrounded by thousands of Mon'Els conscripts. These fought not for king and country but for fear of the king and his priests, and they inexorably moved in on King Kerim's final retinue. Within minutes, it would all be over.

Kerim'El struggled into an upright position, blood running more freely from numerous wounds across his torso, and he spat, "When you bed her, your wife will call my name for years to come."

Mon'El sighed and shook his head slowly, sorrowfully, and in an ungainly maneuver that showed his inexperience with steel, he brought Thyss' sword around in a flash and severed the prince's neck. Blood spurted up out of the stump as the head caromed forward and away to the left, and the body fell forward lifelessly to pour red across the ground. Having almost lost his balance with the blow, Mon'El recovered his dignity and tossed the sword to the ground just scant feet from Thyss. Her eyes shot to the weapon for just a second before she forced herself to train them on her father, and her heart pounded against her breastbone.

"I still think it beneath our station, but I must admit that was thrilling, killing a man with a sword," he said, and as he peered into the distance, Mon'El stepped forward past the body, ignoring how his sandals squished into the blood as it tried to soak into the earth. “Very good. King Kerim has fallen, and it looks like the rest of his soldiers are surrendering. Hopefully, some of his generals survived. They may be useful in bringing order to our new lands. Perhaps now that it’s all over, my daughter, you will accept my forgiveness and return home.”

At these words, the blazing rage returned to Thyss, and it boiled over no differently than a stew pot left over a raging fire for too long. It brought new strength, new willingness to act, and for a short second, she wished that she had that newfound vigor before her father had killed the prince. But she had no real care for Kerim’El, and it took her father’s brazen gift of forgiveness, as if she were the one who acted wrongly, for her to find that energy. Even after everything, he still did not understand *why* she hated him, *why* she sought to take revenge or, more importantly, for whom. He thought so little of those he slaughtered in Calumbu that it hadn’t even occurred to him that her heart burned to avenge them, the Lowborns who had built a kingdom of cooperation and peace amidst a world of power and war. He couldn’t fathom that it was *he* who should beg *her* for mercy, but even as she would spit on him were he to grovel thus before her, he was incapable of such an action.

She felt her anger infusing every muscle, every sinew and tendon, and Hykan fed her fury as he had before.

Thyss leapt to her feet, retrieving her sword from where it lay, and struck at her father from behind. As her sword flashed in its deadly arc, a huge, dark form jumped between her and her prey – one of Mon’El’s dark skinned and hulking guards. The man shouted a warning of some sort as he brought his own scimitar up just quickly enough to deflect the blow, but Thyss’ steel hewed right through his, slashing wickedly through a massive bicep. He screamed in agony as blood drained from the useless muscles, and Thyss brought her sword back in a reverse swing that severed his right leg at the knee. As he fell to the ground, a third strike removed his head.

By that time, Mon'El had danced out of danger some fifteen feet away, and five of his guards moved to surround Thyss in a circle of death. She was prepared to kill every last one of them, and she held Feghul's Claw ready in both hands as she stood on the balls of her feet, its cool hilt reassuring against the callouses of her palms.

"Stop," Mon'El's voice thundered on the wind, and the guards looked over their shoulders questioningly. He held one hand aloft before him, and then he motioned off to the side. His guards lowered their swords before backpedaling away from Thyss' terrifying blade, and once they were well back, the king said, "you wish to fight me?"

"If you are brave enough to face your daughter," Thyss sneered. To the guards she said, "One of you, give him a sword."

"No, my daughter," Mon'El said darkly, tipping his face forward just enough that shadows played across his features even as foreboding clouds filled the sky to be split by thunder and lightning, "you face me as you were meant to, as Chosen."

24.

For the second time in as many hours, Thyss lay on her side on the hard ground, exhausted and defeated. Every magick she'd thrown at her father, he simply dismissed or deflected with a wave. More than once he challenged her, and each time the contest ended with Thyss being flung a dozen feet or more. She continued to rise, continued to fight to her feet, though more slowly each time, and yet she could never break through his defenses. He was too powerful, or perhaps she was too weak, but either way, Thyss couldn't even come close to her father. Certainly not close enough to let the battle end with a slashing of steel.

He would have never let it happen, and now he stood over her crumpled form with her own sword held lazily in one hand as he peered down at her. Mon'El's eyes were, as they always had been, unreadable to her, his feelings obfuscated behind a wall of emotionlessness. It was cold and impenetrable, and she knew now more than ever that Kingpriest Mon'El of Kaimpur had never loved anything or anyone except his own power.

And despite her hatred of him and everything he had done, she pitied the now childless wretch who would one day die alone.

"It is done then," Mon'El intoned softly, "and what am I to do with you? Am I to kill you, kill my only child?"

"You are not my father," Thyss wheezed, barely finding the strength to do even that.

"I suppose not," he agreed, "and I suppose I dare not let you live. As long as you do, you will hate me."

"Then kill me," she spat feebly.

"Your mother would never forgive me," Mon'El shook his head, almost sadly.

This fed Thyss a small amount of strength, just enough to say, "And where is mother? Why is she not here to celebrate with you?"

"It matters not," Mon'El said.

"It does matter. You gave her to *them*, didn't you?"

"She did," Mon'El faltered, "what the kingdom needed her to do."

Thyss sensed weakness, and she attacked, "She did what *you wanted* her to do, and she hates you for it."

"Silence!" Mon'El thundered, his voice carried on a sudden, rising gale.

The clouds overhead darkened again, thunder clashing amongst them. He loomed over her then, seemingly growing taller amongst the storm, and he raised her sword above her prone form. A terrible moment of stasis struck as he stood there, contemplating the death stroke, and for just a moment, Thyss thought she found a chink in the armor of Mon'El of Kaimpur. She smiled weakly, willing to accept that small victory, but the wind eased into a gentle breeze. As quickly as they grew angry, the clouds again softened and dispersed into wisps of white, and Mon'El turned and motioned for several of his personal guards.

"Bind her well. Gag her so she may not speak and blindfold her so she cannot see. Take her by horse to the southern border. There you can release her. Return her sword and give her food and water," he commanded as he handed Feghul's Claw to a dark skinned warrior. He turned back to Thyss and said, "If she ever returns to any of my lands, and she should know that one day my lands will be all of Dulkur, she will meet her end by my hand."

As she looked up into Mon'El's face, Thyss saw nothing but naked honesty, and he hid nothing from her, for there was nothing to hide. She wanted to go on hating him, but as his guards carried her south, bound and blindfolded, she found it impossible to find the energy. One day, Mon'El would fall to some enemy's magicks or blades, and when he did, no one would mourn his death. And that knowledge, the understanding that no one anywhere in Dulkur loved the man she once called her father, came to be enough.

EPILOGUE
MANY, MANY YEARS LATER

Thyss tossed and turned listlessly in her bed. It wasn't for lack of comfort, for the mattress was by far the plushest the inn on the northern coast of Tigol had to offer. Neither was the bedding the culprit, as she had per pick from a wide selection of satins and silks to accommodate whatever she desired. The pillows were soft and overstuffed with down. The entire suite of rooms with its space, heated marble bath, and comfortable divans offered an elevated level of luxury, even to her. Naran owned the inn; as one of the Seven Lords, he owned much in Tigol, and thanks to the man who was once the love of her life, Naran owned much in the West as well. The huge Shet would never hear of Thyss being offered anything but the best in any establishment he owned, and he would offer it as long as she would have it. Once or twice, her thoughts lingered on how he had long ago offered her more than that, and while she enjoyed the discomfort it gave Lord Dahken Cor Pelson, she never had any intention of taking him up on it. Nor did Naran anymore, likely out of silent respect.

Her mind returned to the previous evening, her failure to find solace in a man's arms. A year passed before her mind even considered such a thing, and then she missed it immensely – the feel of a body against hers, the strength of arms wrapped about her or perhaps struggling with them, the warmth of a lover. In the last six months, she had tried three times and each time, including last night, she failed to find what her body desired. Something about it didn't feel right, and each time she pushed her would be lover out of bed, out of her suite, and into the hall beyond, sometimes in rather compromising stages of undress. It wasn't that they weren't quality specimens, as they all seemed fit enough to keep up with her expectations, and it certainly wasn't for lack of experience on their part. This last man seemed to be extremely proficient. But it simply wasn't what she wanted, what she needed.

Even though it was. She kicked off an offending bedsheet that had threatened to wrap around her left leg like a boa after her last toss and flipped with a loud sigh onto her right side, forcing her eyes to stay shut against the soft, silvery moonlight that shined through silken drapes. As she lay, shifting every few seconds in a vain attempt to get comfortable, her mind drifted not into sleep but into memory. Memory of the only man who ever truly calmed the beating of her heart even as he made it race faster. He was an oddity to her the very first time she met him, with skin the gray pallor of a corpse, and a burning hatred for a Loszian sorcerer. He fascinated her, so much so that she dared to conquer him, though not in battle, that first night. Even after many nights she never did so, but she enjoyed the trying. She found something in him she'd never had before.

She never understood what he'd found in her. Perhaps it was the danger she represented – the chaos and entropy of fire personified, the sheer force of will that made her beloved of Hykan. The truth that she could almost grasp before it slipped through her fingers was that they were two sides of the same coin. One of them spent his years always resisting the destiny that others wrought for him in search of his own, while the other spent her years with no set path but always seeking one.

She knew she must forget Cor Pelson. He was gone, literally condemned to live out his days in the chair of the Chronicler, his only company fallen gods imprisoned in their Vaults. He had chosen it, as it was the only way to defeat the greatest foe either of them had ever known, but also to be certain that their world would always be protected from those hailing from the stars. She still didn't understand the latter part completely, and Thyss wasn't sure she ever would.

With an annoyed sigh, and barely resisting the urge to set the entire bed aflame with a flip of her hand, Thyss climbed out of bed and strolled nude over to one of her suite's windows. With a sweeping motion of her arms, she spread the silk curtains and looked down onto the grand avenues and squares of the city several stories below. Few were out this late, the streets lit only by the moon and the occasional protected torch, but there were a few. One such hooded traveler stopped for a moment, angling his face upward to behold her. She cared not; let him look. Men always looked, and once she took pleasure in their roaming eyes. Now, she couldn't care less.

Movement caught her eye from a balcony across the way. The balcony belonged to a wealthy apartment, perhaps a well to do local merchant or maybe even a minor warlord under the command of Naran, and the balcony was encircled by fine linen shrouds to keep away prying eyes, despite a slight billowing in the night's breeze. The apartment was lit somewhere beyond that balcony by orange light which cast the shadows of two figures onto the linen curtains. The act was plain, but it was the rhythm and the movements that showed it not to be so simple as just fucking. Thyss tried not to watch, but she found she could not pull her eyes away. A deep melancholy washed over her, and she wrapped her arms about her against an imagined cold, for solace against the loneliness. Though, she found none.

A knock sounded three times from her suite door in the next room, breaking her from her thoughts a bit, but she ignored it. She watched the shadows holding each other in the night for just a moment longer before letting the silk fall back into place over the window. She could still barely see through a sliver where they didn't meet, and the knock came again, firmer this time. Thyss turned to face the arched passthrough between her rooms, looking in the direction from where the knock came. She called out, "Go away," but the offending knocker either didn't hear or didn't care, and the sound came again, this third time insistent with more volume and a faster tempo.

"Fucking man-whore," she whispered venomously, for she had no idea whom else it could be. The inn's servants knew better than to approach her so directly or so late at night, so it had to be the prostitute she'd hired last night, no doubt returning to make another attempt. She strode forward, stopping long enough to retrieve and shrug into a silk robe that hardly hid anything in its scantness, as she stormed into the next room and toward the door. The knock sounded again when she was just a few steps from it, and she slammed the bolts clear as she swung the door open, saying, "I will burn you alive where you stand, you -"

And then all of Thyss' words died in her throat. She simply stopped, unable to issue a sound as she held her breath beholding the man who stood outside her door. He was dressed plainly enough – a basic, short sleeved tunic, worn breeches, and soft boots of all black. He had the deep brown, straight hair common to Westerners, along with prominent chin, jawline, and cheekbones that most Westerners found strong and attractive. But it was his color that most people, whether from the West, Losz, Tigol, Dulkur, or anywhere in the world would have taken as a bad omen at least. His skin – face, neck, and the exposed parts of his arms – were all a sickly gray, a color associated with flesh as it lay in the grave to rot, though it was completely without blemish.

Gone was the bizarre black armor that the two of them had recovered from an ancient undead Dahken in lost catacombs under Losz. The stylized hauberk of a muscled torso, the plate legguards held together by black chainmail, and the so bizarre, visorless helm that looked like the head of a giant beetle were nowhere to be seen. He stood there unarmed, carrying neither Soulmourn nor Ebonwing, his companions before Thyss had ever met him – the single edged longsword with its skull-headed pommel and the bleached skull fetish with its black batwings.

This could not be. She had finally fallen asleep, a fitful sleep that forced her to dream of that which she'd lost, that which she wanted most in life, as dreams were wont to do. She wanted it to end, to wake alone in the soft bed, so that perhaps she could throw herself from the window to end the suffering that after a year and a half she still clung to. But she could do no such thing. All Thyss could do was stand and stare, ignorant that her robe hung open at the front, revealing both her nakedness and also the scars of a recent past.

"Hello, Thyss," Cor Pelson said simply, his voice exactly as she remembered it, and she began to tremble with the sudden understanding that he somehow stood before her.

Numbly, she dropped her hand from the door and backed away unable to blink, or perhaps afraid to lest the illusion be gone when she again opened her eyes. She whispered, "But I left you. Down, in that place."

"No. I left you," he whispered, tears building in his eyes as he stepped through her doorway, and as he closed the door behind him, Thyss melted against him.

Some hours later, after the tears, the lovemaking, and yet more tears, Thyss asked a simple question by way of one word as they merely lay together, "How?"

He was silent for a long moment before he answered somewhat haltingly, "It's hard to explain. Do you remember how Dahken Rael came to us that day in Aquis, and how I told you he'd been killed by a priest of Garod months before? He was brought back by Dahk, and it has to do with something Dahk told me long ago. Everything in the world is made of all the same stuff. I just… made myself another body. I think it is something the gods called 'cloning' in their language. Do you remember the Chronicler, a man named Paul Chen? When we released him, he died, but a woman who loved him used this magic to bring him back."

She edged away; her flesh no longer pressed against his as cool air flooded between them. "You mean this isn't the real you?"

He reached out and caressed her arm slightly, and his touch lightly brushed down her golden skin until his fingers intertwined with hers. "I promise you this is as real as ever I was," he assured her.

"But are you still down there?" she asked softly, seeming to accept his answer as she nuzzled back up against his chest.

"I am, and if I close my eyes and concentrate," Cor said, doing just that as he spoke, "I can see that room and all of those things the gods call 'computers' around me. I can see a small, dirty child in Tigol searching back alleys for food, and a dark skinned warrior facing a rhinoceros with a spear and scimitar. Keth argues with a priest in Aquis, trying to convince the man that the Dahken are to be trusted after… what happened, and a Northwoman cries out during labor. And I see even now, one of the great vessels that passes between the stars hovers high above Rumedia, its captain likely trying to decide if he dares to land, as I have told them all not to.

"But all this I see and can act on, if I so desire, so long as I stay connected to that chair, and I must. It is my duty to this world, a destiny that I have chosen, but I also have a duty to you. I never lost sight of that, but I had no choice in what had to be done."

Thyss interjected before he continued his ruminations, "You do not have to explain it to me. As unaccepting as I appeared to be at the time, even I knew this."

From where she laid her head against him, she felt Cor's body shudder for just a moment, as if a great burden had suddenly been lifted from his very soul. She caressed the muscles of his abdomen as she set her chin up on his chest to look into his eyes. A track of a lone tear wound down the right side of his face having fled from the far corner of his right eye.

"How long can you stay with me?" Thyss asked, her voice almost breathlessly faint.

"As long as you'll have me. As long as we both live. The chair keeps me alive, and I can keep this body alive as long as I need to. One day, my love, you will grow old and die, and when you do, I will build you the greatest of funeral pyres. The entire world will know of it, and even Hykan will know he lost the greatest mistress of fire that ever lived. And I will lay down on that funeral pyre with you."

As she pushed herself up to lay atop him, their lips touched with heavy, longing pressure, and no truer words had ever been spoken or heard in her life. All the years spent wandering, all the years of fighting, slaying, and resisting those who would control her, led to strong words she once spoke to the Dahken so long ago outside a Loszian stronghold.

I go where I will and do as I will when I will. I create enemies only to slaughter them and bathe in their blood, should I so desire. I shall challenge the tallest, strongest peak with my blade and force it to submit to me. I bow to no kings, no queens, and challenge even the stars themselves to shine brighter than I. I shall force the chaos of entropy upon the world and laugh as those who would rule struggle vainly to contain it. I live for my own desires, here and now, for as long as I live, and no one shall take that from me, lest they take my life!

A sense of peace came over her as she remembered the speech some twenty years ago – the day she knew she had broken Dahken Cor Pelson and bent him to her will. And yet, it wasn’t true, for she spent the next twenty years being his partner in adventure, battle, love, death, and sorrow. She did not rule him, nor he her, and oh, the things they had seen and done. Their lives could end here, now, and she would accept it.

As they made love again, Thyss felt the cool serenity of Nykeema, the water goddess, wash over her and extinguish the fires of Hykan that burned in her soul, and for a moment, she could even feel the disdain of her patron god as he no longer had any grip upon her destiny. She thanked him for the power he granted her so many years ago and the strength it had infused into her, but she didn't need her old gods anymore. The one and only thing she ever needed, the person for which she had sought her entire life, lay with her in her arms, and that was enough.

THE END.

AUTHOR'S AFTERWORD

I have long loved ambiguous endings and generally find the standard Hollywood Happy Ending to be unfulfilling in many, many stories. Maybe that is why I have so often gravitated towards horror in movies and books, because quite often there is no happy ending to be had. Whether we're talking about a slasher movie, cosmic horror stories the likes of which were popularized by the at once great and problematic H. P. Lovecraft, or the great sci-fi monster movies of the '80s, protagonists very rarely have the opportunity to win in a meaningful way. It is usually all they can do to just survive, which is often the way life itself works. For every victory, every challenge overcome, there exists an equation that determines whether or not it is a happy ending. And as the losses escalate in an attempt to reach the opposite side of the equals sign, the happy ending tends to be diluted to the point that it is lost, and we are left with merely the opportunity to carry on.

All that being said, I have always had a sense of sorrow for what I did to Thyss and Lord Dahken Cor Pelson, to say nothing of their friends Menak, Rederick, and Mora. As I am wont to do, I visited extremely harsh events upon those characters, and while the latter three rested easier in the victory of the former two, that victory was wrought at enormous cost to Cor and Thyss. Neither could ever be happy, but only survive, the cost of the left side of the equation being too great to enjoy the victory of the right side. Maybe now, they too can find solace.

Who is Martin Parece?

I'd really rather you not ask me questions like this! Well, are you asking who I am or "Who am I?", because the latter is a completely different question that forces one to look deep into the heart and mind. It is the question humankind has been asking since there was humankind.

Who I am, on the other hand, is just some guy who loves to read and tell stories. As I look back, I have always been a storyteller, from my first short stories to my first faltering attempts at playing Dungeon Master. I still love TTRPGs, all sorts of fiction, heavy metal, and horror movies. In fact, this last will be readily apparent should you read my anthology Tendrils in the Dark. A lot of shout outs, homages and influences there...

I returned to my creative endeavors around 2009 as my business of seven years began to burn down around me during the recession. I suppose adversity causes growth, and though I shelved my projects for a few years, I returned to them with the publication of Blood and Steel in 2011. Regardless, people seemed to enjoy the world of Rumedia, and I returned to it with five more novels.

In the end, I'm just a guy who loves to tell stories, read other persons' stories and head bang in the car. I have so much more to come, and I hope you'll join me on the journey!

Turn the page for an excerpt from

The Oathbreaker's Daughter

The Dragonknight Trilogy
Book 1

Available Now!

Every time the swords struck each other, the ringing of steel carried on the subtle wind currents of the warm summer day. Training for one to two hours per day, three days a week for the last two years had wrought tough, lean sinews in Jenna's arms and legs. While other girls her age mooned and obsessed over boys, many of whom noticed certain differences between the genders, Jenna crossed swords with the one armed teacher of the village's children. She was the only one among them Brasalla took the time to mentor in swordsmanship and, to a lesser extent because she left it to Jenna's mother, archery, and Jenna swelled with silent pride even as the other girls jeered at her. Two years of training to help her gain strength and then learn the basic forms of fencing had finally led to sparring with real swords, though with dull edges and blunted points. Brasalla had several of these weapons in her cottage, as well as a number of wooden practice swords and other such weapons, so as to avoid any real wound besides bruises and damaged pride. The one armed woman had taught Jenna so much, and yet every time a new lesson was unveiled, Jenna found herself bested once again. She had never once defeated the former Protectress, despite the woman having but one arm, or even landed a single point. But still she fought, knowing that one day…

Brasalla attacked with a downward stroke meant to slash down and across Jenna's body starting at her right shoulder, and Jenna knew her opportunity when it presented itself. Bringing her own sword around, she easily parried the blade to her left, and scraping steel on steel, thrust her blade forward in such a way that it would skewer her opponent, if not for the spherical mound of steel that made the weapon's point. But her sword met nothing, and in her hurry to take advantage of Brasalla's careless attack, Jenna stood suddenly off balance as her arms extended well forward. Brasalla's weight came to bear on her parried blade, forcing the point of Jenna's sword down to the ground as she could contest neither the woman's weight nor strength, to say nothing of leverage.

"You over extended your thrust, little dear. You're dead, I'm afraid."

"I know. Damn it all," Jenna swore angrily.

With a disapproving glare, Brasalla eased her weight and lifted her sword from Jenna's, allowing the girl to recover her blade, and she said, "If I were your mother I'd likely tell you to watch your language."

"Then, it's a good thing you're not, huh?" Jenna shot back, but the tone held more playfulness than challenge.

"I suppose."

"Just once, I want to kill you. Just once," Jenna complained.

Brasalla chided, "Don't do that."

"What?"

"Whine," Brasalla explained. "It's unbecoming of you. You're strong and brave, and you're growing into a beautiful woman. Such bellyaching is unacceptable, especially among the Protectresses."

Jenna's eyes narrowed, and she immediately returned, "I don't want to be a Protectress."

"Is there something wrong with being a Protectress? Something wrong with being a trusted defender of Abrea and our way of life?"

"No," Jenna replied quickly, noting her teacher's suddenly solemn tone and emotionless face. She chose her next words carefully so as not to give further offense, "It's just not what I want to do."

"You cannot do what you want to do, Little Dear," Brasalla gently reminded the girl, and it was now Jenna's turn to grow silent. "Anyway, do you know what your mistake was?"

Jenna sighed quickly, puffing a snort of air out of her nostrils in annoyance as she clenched her draw and turned her head from side to side, looking at nothing. After a moment, she answered, "I assumed."

"Assumed what?" Brasalla asked with slightly raised eyebrows.

"I assumed that you, a trained warrior, someone who has killed people far more skilled than me, made a basic mistake."

Brasalla prodded, "And?"

"And I tried to capitalize on it."

"As you well should've, but that wasn't the fatal mistake."

"No?" Jenna asked, looking up at her mentor, and her face betrayed a mix of impatience at the drawing out of the lesson and aggravation at her own ineptitude.

"You did the right thing, but you're right in that you assumed. Never assume your enemy has made a mistake, but be ready to take advantage of it if they did."

The impatience turned to more annoyance as Jenna worked to unravel the riddle in her mind. "How does that work?"

"Even the best trained warriors make mistakes," Brasalla explained calmly, indicating her missing arm with a pointed look, "and you must take advantage when they do. You parried my poor attack perfectly, but you were so certain of victory that you telegraphed your thrust badly."

"What does that mean?"

"I knew the attack was coming because I was testing you, but most trained warriors would have seen it coming, too. You pulled your sword arm back just a few inches to give more force to your thrust."

Jenna breathed in a slight hiss of air between her teeth as understanding dawned on her. "So," she reasoned, "by doing that, you saw the attack coming and had more time to react to avoid it."

"Exactly! We're fighting with swords, not clubs or staves or some other weapon that we have to bash each other's brains in with. Your father's sword came from Vulgesch. It is so strong, can hold such an edge that it can easily punch through most armor, except maybe Vulgesch plate. Fight with grace, finesse, dexterity, not force."

"I…" Jenna began, but she suddenly wasn't sure what she wanted to say, so she nodded and replied softly, "I understand."

"Maybe a little, but I think you'll understand more in time. There's one more thing I'd like you to consider, just keep it in mind. As a woman and not particularly tall, people, especially men, will underestimate you. Take advantage of that. Lure them in, and do something they don't expect. Remember what I told you before – fair fights are for suckers."

Jenna nodded idly at this, her eyes downcast as she mulled it over. Without warning, she shot her left foot out, hooking her soft leather boot right behind Brasalla's right knee while giving the woman a sudden push with both hands. Caught completely unaware, Brasalla's legs bent as she tumbled backward and landed hard on her back, only the thick grass behind her cottage slightly cushioning her impact. Even so, she felt the wind painfully knocked from her lungs as she struck the ground.

"You mean like that?" Jenna asked with a wide, proud grin. She pointed her practice sword at her mentor and said one word, "Yield."

"You little shit," Brasalla spouted angrily as she struggled up to one elbow, and then she noticed the tip of the sword, blunted with a sphere of steel as it hovered only a half foot away from her. Laughter took the woman for a moment, and she tipped her head backward, answering,

"Yeah, something like that. Here, Little Dear, help an old woman up."

Turn the page for an excerpt from

<u>Wolves of War</u>

A John Hartman Novel

Coming October 2024!

Darkness filled the ancient woodland, permeating everything around Hartman just as much as the frigid air chilled him to the bone. Nothing about his slow, quiet trek through the forest felt pleasant, and a sense of foreboding hung heavily in the air, tempting him to abandon his mission and start hoofing it back to France. It wasn't the first time he longed to be back with the regular Army, taking it to the Jerries in a straight fight, but this was different. John just couldn't shake the pervasive dread he felt as he ventured deeper into the German wood.

He shouldn't be alone out here. It was one thing to undertake a solo operation, a task he had accomplished many times in the past. But this time, he was supposed to have a guide with him who knew the woods better than he, but his contact failed to show up at the designated rendezvous. Maybe the he had gotten held up by German soldiers, or maybe he had to hunker down somewhere. After a while, John decided he couldn't wait any longer, steeled himself and went on with the operation.

For the fourth or fifth time, John wished he'd procured a heavy coat to keep the damp cold at bay. He found a tiny break in the eldritch canopy, through which shined a beam of pale light from the full moon overhead. He stood in this welcome dispeller of darkness long enough to unfold his map and become certain of his bearings. He had only a few miles left to traverse until he broke from the forest into the open where he would have little protection from watchful German eyes, and yet, he would breathe more easily once free from this place.

A shiver ran through Hartman, and he thought, *Damn, it's cold!* He began to fold the map back into itself, but his hands seemed to slow with each progressive crease. Surely, they were cold, but it wasn't the near freezing night air that made them react so. He slipped the map into a jacket pocket, and his motion slowed to a complete halt.

He stood perfectly still, and the hair on his neck and arms would have stood on end were it not for his appropriated German uniform.

Narrow set, disembodied red eyes materialized out of the gloom some distance in front of him, seeming to glow with an inner, baleful light. They hovered perhaps a foot off of the ground, but Hartman couldn't for the darkness be sure if they were five feet ahead of him or twenty five. He knew only that he stood transfixed by that hellish glare, apparently frozen to inaction while they regarded him. He needed to act, draw a pistol and shoot at those eyes, ready a knife, something, but his limbs wouldn't obey his brain's commands. The entire encounter felt eerily familiar. He had been in some freezing German wood at some point before and had seen those eyes there and then as well, but this was also different. Hartman was alone, and the darkness and cold were all pervasive, not simply offensive to the senses. And there was only one set of eyes, though he remembered, on that other occasion that other attackers had come at him from the sides.

Hartman broke his paralysis just in time to see a silver and black streak from the right as it caromed off of the back of his legs. The energy from the blow knocked him off balance, and it was only his superb athleticism that kept him from tumbling to the forest floor. Just as he regained his footing, another rush of dark motion attacked from the other direction, but this one drew blood. A fierce snapping of unseen jaws severed tendons in his left leg, causing Hartman to collapse, and as he clutched the wounded limb, warm, steaming blood coated his hands.

Either out of a preternatural sense or pure luck, he managed to get his left forearm up just as a huge wolf of silver and black lunged at him. A mouth of wicked, yellowed teeth opened wide in anticipation, and Hartman wedged his arm as far into the mouth as he could. Like a dog whose chewing bone had gone too far backward, the wolf chomped its jaws trying to dislodge him. The power of those jaws wrought tremendous pain, and Hartman felt the teeth puncture the skin of his arm even through the layers of his jacket and sleeve. But it also bought him precious moments. His free hand reached for his knife, but before he could find it, another beast charged from his right. This canine minion of Hell he caught by the neck, and it took all of his might just to hold the thing at bay as it snapped at his face, rancid carrion breath caressing his face. If he could somehow manage to get his legs underneath the creature in front of him, perhaps he could launch the beast just far enough to access his knife or gun. Then, he could turn this fight around.

This glimmer of hope flickered in his mind only to be extinguished in an instant as a third monstrous wolf stood less than a foot away to his left, mouth agape and tongue hanging low out of its mouth. It panted softly, but seemingly out of anticipation rather than exhaustion, and Hartman knew he couldn't hold this one off; he was simply out of arms. It lunged toward his face, and all he could see was teeth and then darkness as the wolf's jaws clamped around his face.

Hartman bolted upright, his clothes and the bedsheets of the hospital bed soaked in sweat. As his heart and breathing gradually slowed, his head cleared so that he could regain his bearings. Two nurses moved around the room, drawing back curtains to allow in the first rays of the autumn sun, which told Hartman it was around seven in the morning. There were only six men in the score of beds in the room, and of them all, he was the only one unwounded. He was vaguely aware of a rifle toting guard that stood in a gray uniform next to the room's entrance.

One of the nurses glared his direction as he watched them, and as she made her way across the room to his bedside, he reached down and rubbed at his ankle, which was shackled to the metal frame of the bed. She stood to his right in her uniform - a dress of narrow, vertical white and blue stripes under an apron of white. Her collar, also white, contrasted against the dress, and was pinned closed severely by an emblem of the Third Reich. A black German eagle clutched a red cross in its talons, though the cross had been extended and resembled an inverted Christian cross.

"Gut morning. Nachtmares?" she asked in a hodge-podge of English and German. She wasn't pretty in the least, but she hadn't been unfriendly to him despite their nations' adversarial nature.

"*Es ist nichts*," Hartman replied in perfect German, "*Danke*."

"Nothing? It's nothing you say? You come into my country, my Fatherland, and kill my sons and brothers, and it is nothing?" she asked, her English becoming clearer though accented. Her eyes began to glow with an unholy red light as she continued, "You come here to fight a war that doesn't belong to you. You kill thousands of good men and deprive the Fatherland what we are owed by right. You do not know what you face, what this Old World can unleash upon you!"

She seemed to grow as she spoke, her uniform tearing at the seams as her bones popped and elongated. By the end of her tirade, her words were nearly unintelligible as her human mouth reformed to that of a wolf's toothy maw under bright red, demonic eyes. Hair, fur of silver and black had sprouted across every inch of her, and razor sharp claws extended from each of her fingers. The room grew dark, as if her very presence alone blotted out the light of the rising sun.

John shouted in alarm and leapt out of the bed as if a great spring had been compressed underneath him, except the shackle around his ankle prevented him from going too far. His back slammed hard onto the cold floor, and he would've cracked the back of his skull as well were it not for his flailing arms somehow breaking his fall. His leg remained suspended in the air, attached as it was to the bedframe, with the hospital bed acting as the only barrier between Hartman and the monstrosity.

"Captain Hartman?" a worried voice said in his ear, and cool hands cradled his sweaty face. "Captain Hartman, wake up."

John Hartman blinked his eyes and shook his head once to dispel and clear away the fading image. He indeed lay on a cool floor, but it was that of the Army field hospital in France. His left leg was propped up on his bed, his ankle wrapped up in bedsheets so twisted to be as strong as thick rope. The room was dimly lit, except for the warmth of a soft glow emanating from the hallway beyond the door. Somewhere in the next room, he heard a muffled announcer's voice calling a baseball game. It sounded like the World Series that just ended two days ago with the St. Louis Cardinals beating the St. Louis Browns.

"Captain Hartman are you all right?" the brown haired night nurse asked.

"I'm fine," he replied with a hardened face as she helped him stand and get back into bed.

"You know, I could find something to help you sleep," she offered, likely referring to whiskey or some other such spirits; being an officer had its privileges.

"No, thank you very much," he replied as he laid his head backward to stare wide awake at the ceiling. "I've slept enough."

Made in the USA
Middletown, DE
28 July 2024

58025806R00159